Murder Across the Board

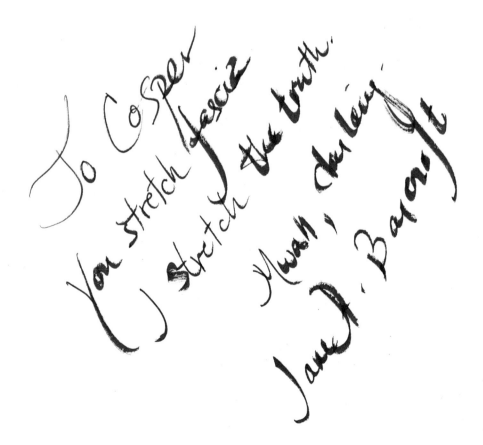

To Cosper
You stretch [...]
[...] stretch the truth.
Mwah, darling,
Janet J. Barcott

MURDER ACROSS THE BOARD

An Arlington County Mystery

Jane Barcroft

iUniverse, Inc.

New York Lincoln Shanghai

Murder Across the Board

An Arlington County Mystery

iUniverse books may be ordered through booksellers or by contacting:

iUniverse
2021 Pine Lake Road, Suite 100
Lincoln, NE 68512
www.iuniverse.com
1-800-Authors (1-800-288-4677)

ISBN-13: 978-0-595-36852-5 (pbk)
ISBN-13: 978-0-595-81264-6 (ebk)
ISBN-10: 0-595-36852-2 (pbk)
ISBN-10: 0-595-81264-3 (ebk)

Printed in the United States of America

To all of the die-hards who, right, wrong, or crazy, give up their second Saturdays to ensure that a dialogue continues between the government of Arlington County and its citizens. In the words of Mercedes de la Roja, "Nothing changes when people do not care, and they cannot care if they do not know."

In the clearing stands a boxer
And a fighter by his trade,
And he carries the reminder
Of every glove that laid
Him down or cut him till he cried out
In his anger and his shame,
"I am leaving, I am leaving—"
But the fighter still remains.
—Simon and Garfunkel, 1970

Disclaimer

What follows is a work of utter fiction, yea, arrant spoofery. Paige Smith's Arlington is the county that would exist if Arlington's civic life were far more exhilarating, and a great many of its citizens a great deal wickeder, than is the case in real life. No superficial characteristics perceived as resembling those of persons living or dead should be construed to indicate an actual portrayal of any such person. To the author's knowledge, no one within the Arlington County Government nor the region's loyal citizen opposition has ever been credibly accused of graft, destruction of evidence, adultery, domestic violence, coercion, subversion of police procedure, aggravated assault, kidnapping, brandishing of firearms, robbery, or ceremonial magic.

The area's press corps likewise boasts many eccentric and colorful characters, but the author in no way implies actual knowledge of any of their personal histories.

P R O L O G U E

▼

Angelo Pastorelli, Logan Airport, August, 2004

There are rules about how cops do things, and pretty predictable ways they behave, so when I saw the older officer slam down the trunk of the Lexus and boogie, trying not to make noises that he couldn't help, I knew it was bad even while I was laughing. Stiffs are a part of police work—EMS too, and I've done both—and you don't get used to them, exactly, but you learn to stop reacting. Then again, it was August. The breeze was blowing my way from the water, but there wasn't much of it. I decided just to be glad about the wind direction.

Older Cop pulled out his radio. I wasn't close enough to hear what he said and wasn't going to get noticed by trying to hear, but I didn't really need to. Pretty soon this place would be crawling, with the ME, extra cops, medics and yellow tape everywhere. Parking at Logan sucks already. People would be direly pissed. It was time for me to move on; I'd seen enough, anyway. I'd be able to sort out the details with a few conversations, maybe only one if Uncle Beppo was in a good mood.

I headed into the airport. If I managed it right I could get to the North End for some calamari and have time to phone Mom before my return flight. I didn't plan on letting her know I was in town. I just wanted to get a feel for whether the news had gotten back to Malden before I got home. The car would trace back quickly, they'd track down next of kin, and Mom would be the first to hear about it. It would take her a while to figure it out, but she'd hear about it. With luck I'd be back at Reagan so fast I'd be able to walk into the recess meeting that night as if I'd just come from work. My answering machine would be lit up like Times Square when I actually got home, but by then I'd have figured out what to say to people.

CHAPTER ONE
EARLY RISERS

Paige Smith, April, 2004

People think I show up early for County Board meetings because I have some kind of obsessive-compulsive fixation about whether they start on schedule. I put that in the paper because it's a shtick, but really, I get there early because I don't sleep. This was not always the case, but it looks likely to be for the rest of my life. People also think I am married to my work, maybe even some sort of *virgo intacta* journalistic monk, but I can tell you that it is a shabby substitute for Meg, who when she left to take the job in Chicago did not have to add that not only my paper but I bored her half to death.

All right, local journalism is not exciting. Maybe I'm not either. When I was trying to be realistic, I would tell myself that someone as smart as Meg could not be expected to stay in her first job at a little weekly tabloid forever; and that a man nearly twenty years older and an inch or two shorter, a little frugal (all right, cheap), a little pedantic, who could never seem to get his hair cut right, could hardly expect to hold someone so effortlessly beautiful. But I still loved her and I had come to fear that I am a one-woman man. I like the theater and sometimes I take some nice women there, but when I wake up around four most mornings I still feel for Meg's feet under the covers. It's hard to think it only lasted about a year.

I don't get back to sleep after that, so I come into the office if it's a work day, or over to the County building if it's Board Saturday. The regulars, some say the civic wackos, are always there by eight. I guess by now I'm one of them.

Pastorelli, who is only a little over six foot but comes across larger than life, is always there with a briefcase that looks like it ought to have a bomb in it, and usually so is Bob Beach, looking like a prematurely aged young man or a very sprightly old man—actually it's the anti-retroviral drugs, but I'm not sure I'm supposed to know about that. Schulz is around most days, and I try to avoid him. His politics make more sense than any lunatic's I've ever met, as long as you don't have to meet him face to face, but it usually only takes about five minutes for him to start spitting his P's. He's nearer sixty than fifty, but with his intensity and lean build—he'd almost pass for a high-mileage runner—he seems closer to my age. He wears the same pair of cargo shorts April to October. I think.

All three of these guys have something to say at every County Board meeting, and when you consider there are less than 200 thousand people in the County, you wonder how they all find an issue twice a month. But it gives me something to put in the paper other than Lions Club awards ceremonies and neighborhood parades. I tell myself they're obsessed, I'm just paid. Some days I even persuade myself.

Quite often you also get Perry Reardon. He was here this morning with a sheaf of his *Taxpayer's Watchdog* newsletters. I have a soft spot for Perry, not just because he's never met a tax he liked (I've met few myself), but because once in an unguarded moment he confessed to a carnal crush on Betty Bravo, the only woman currently serving on the Board. You have to understand that Perry is the shape of one of those inflatable snowmen that people put on their lawns and about the same size, and Betty could be handily cast as Peter Pan in a local theater production. The visual makes me smile every time I think of it, and few things do that these days.

So there we all were on the bad modular furniture, waiting for it to be closer to eight-thirty so it would make sense to go sit on the even less comfortable wooden pews inside the boardroom. Pastorelli had one of the first two speaker slips; he always does. I remember that as Angie, the building security officer, came in he waved to her and mooched off toward the head in the back of the boardroom, which was the only one in operation up here this morning because something was malfunctioning in the lobby men's room—at least, a crudely lettered sign hung from a sagging strap of colored Scotch tape advising that it was OUT OF ORDER USE FIRST FLOOR. It was like Pastorelli to annex the privilege of using the bathrooms beside the Board offices instead; he usually did it anyway, I think to annoy them.

Paulsen wandered in. He's so young it's hard to realize that he's been serving on the Board ten years; he looks like he should still be clutching his law school diploma for the camera. For some reason, whenever anything goes wrong in boardroom politics, Pinky Paulsen ends up holding the bag—it's as if the universe views him as the natural mark for a snipe hunt. No one thinks he is brilliant, but he manages to be polite through it all, unlike his mentor Friedman, a chunky paterfamilias who periodically indulges weird tirades that at least liven up my editorial page. (I never miss the chance to bust his chops; he just ticks me off, I'm not sure why.) It's nakedly obvious that he hungers for State office, or maybe a gubernatorial appointment, and sooner rather than later, but without a little Paxil it's probably not going to happen.

The other two Board members were already in the recess room back of the dais—Hugh Sprague, who is lithe, gay, bright and, I think, likely to go to Richmond before Friedman does, and Hector de la Roja, Friedman's other protege, who had about learned to speak without a crib. We have plenty of quite dynamic Latinos in the county and some of them are even legal. Why the party ran de la Roja always remained a mystery to me. He could put the *Taxpayer's Watchdog* to sleep by walking into the room. I should play tapes of him when I wake up at four a.m.—sometimes it seemed as if he even affected himself that way.

Anyway, today he was going to have to come up to scratch. Betty had been chairing the meetings since her rotation came around in January, something of a routine election-year ploy since the chairman gets more visibility (at least among those who care enough to notice who their elected representatives are at all). Now she had surprised us by announcing at the last meeting that she was going to step down as chairman, something I don't ever remember anyone doing before, and expected least of all from Betty, who would normally clutch the reins of power until they wore a groove into her flesh. Supposedly she had returned to full-time outside work for the first time since her original election, but I sniffed something else; sooner or later I'd find it. This left Hector as next up.

Toni Messner, the Board secretary, started trying to get the meeting agenda in order on the projection screen inside. A few other die-hards and political hacks were starting to filter in, bantering as they filled out their speaker slips. Outside, on what was promising to be a terrific Spring morning, throughout the County people were starting their lawnmowers and jogging and chivvying the kids into the car for day trips, and for some reason that suddenly escaped me we were all here in neckties with piles of paper, hoping to utter or record something for the slender posterity likely to read it in the fishwrap that I edit or watch it on local cable. I remembered an argument that had once erupted between Pastorelli and Schulz, who, sublimely disregarding his own persistent attendance, had started ranting at the County's die-hard conservative contingent that they were only here because they didn't have a life and needed to get laid.

That made me think of Reardon and his Bravo fixation again and I smiled, turning it into a smile at Pastorelli, who had spotted me on his way back from the head and obviously had something to pass on to me. He makes good copy with his bombastic speeches and whimsical props—Mike Caparici, my cartoonist, loves him—and I depend on him for weird levity; I think some members of the Board do too, except for Betty Bravo, whose face goes rigid every time he whips out his dinosaur puppet and asks it "Can you say 'fiscal restraint'?"

I started to creak up from the squashy sectional, thinking I was too young to feel this stiff even early in the morning. A truck backfired outside, making several people start and, for whatever reason, look at the clock. It was within a hair of eight-thirty. I turned my attention back to Pastorelli who was handing me a sheaf of scripted comment in his usual oversize type. The rest of the crowd was filing in alongside us, except for Schulz, who was out of my sight line, and Reardon whom I would have thought incapable of disappearing from anyone's sight line.

I looked up the aisle. No de la Roja. Nerves probably. I would have my big news item for today: new chairman gavels meeting to order three minutes late. Sigh. I was still thinking that when there was a distinct ruffle on the dais. Betty, who had assumed her chair to the right of center, rose a little in response to some indistinct sound from the recess room behind. I saw Friedman and Sprague pass in and out of sight, and something about the body language looked very wrong to me.

Even after eight years editing a rag that consists mostly of real estate ads, I still have some kind of newsman's instincts. I had snapped away from Pastorelli and out the door into the boardroom lobby before Betty Bravo had quite finished saying "Have you called 911?", and the door shut on Pinky Paulsen saying "Ladies and gentlemen, please stay in your seats." Around the corner, past the elevators, I could hear Angie's radio crackling at what seemed an unnecessarily high volume, and that was what I was tracking.

I rounded the corner and nearly toppled over Perry Reardon. He was being industriously sick into the trash basket of a bulky janitor's cart parked in the short corridor that led past the offices and restrooms and up to the recess chamber. There was a keen smell in the air that had nothing to do with disinfectant, or with what Reardon was doing either, and Angie, half turned away from us, was frantically waving me back as she snapped into the radio, doing a little hop-skip that looked completely grotesque until I realized she was evading a dark trickle that moved across the floor with fascinating deliberation. I pushed past Reardon anyway. The sound of several sets of feet on the lobby stairs told me I only had a few seconds. Oh, I am a cold blooded hound. I had gotten out my cellphone camera and nailed two shots before a crew of paramedics pounded around the corner and into the narrow passage, bodily extruding me and the still retching Reardon, barely bothering to speak directly to us as they boiled us away from the men's room door where Hector de la Roja lay half in and half out of the corridor. It did not look like they were going to be able to do a lot for him.

I did a quick mental review of who was next in line for chair. I definitely had something besides the Lions Club to write about this week. Pinky Paulsen was holding the bag again.

Chapter Two
Lunch in the Plaza

Ed Flanagan had found his bliss, live and on camera. Direct assumption into heaven seemed an outside possibility, and the potential scoop may have been the reason I was sticking around.

It's a tough life being a small town police chief when your small town is a bedroom community in sight of the nation's capital. You come into the job—at least if you are a pluperfect narcissist like Ed Flanagan—expecting a lot more incident and glamor, and you realize sourly after a breaking-in period that your patch consists of numerous routine car thefts, an immigrant community shot through with squabbling gangs that your political handlers want you to pretend don't exist, and the joys of traffic enforcement. When the terrorists hit the Pentagon Flanagan thought he had finally made the cover of *Newsweek*, and hung around the mobile command post at the nearest fire station night after night, hoping to be mobbed by press.

It didn't happen. A year later the Beltway snipers ranged into Virginia and Flanagan was reported to be in a state approaching euphoria. But the closest they got was the far side of the Falls Church line, and Flanagan never even got a quote in the paper. He'd had to go back to primping hopefully for reporters at drunk-driving checkpoints and designing new uniforms for a fed-up corps of thinly spread police officers. He was a big man, with a touch of Irish giant about him that should have made him a photogenic police chief, but something about the smarminess of his personal presence negated the effect. Photographers actually seemed to avoid him when they could.

Now he was over the moon. The *Post, Times* and *Journal* papers were all snapping his picture and the local channels were taping a statement. Yes, the death of Hector de la Roja had been ruled a homicide—hard not to when the deceased has a nine-millimeter perforation in his person. No, they had no one in custody but investigations were ongoing. He wished to commend his officers—he mentioned Angie Macready by name—for securing the scene without incident and maintaining order in a mildly panicked boardroom full of people who had been looking forward to several hours of trying to keep awake, at best. (He didn't mention Pinky Paulsen, whose general demeanor of acknowledging no problem on earth more serious than a botched pizza order had had a lot to do with calming people down. Nor did he dwell on the fact that, though de la Roja could have only been dead a few minutes before he was found—I thought of that "truck backfire" and felt queasy—no entering police officer, and none of those who searched the building and parking garages shortly after, had found a trace of a fleeing perpetrator.

I was probably the most laid-back person in front of the County building at this point. Everyone else had a deadline; I have a Web page that goes up when I have it composed, and if it had been Osama bin Laden that Perry Reardon found wedging open the door to the men's room, the *Spectator* publisher would not have budgeted for a special before next Wednesday's edition. So I was still hanging around the plaza after Flanagan stood down reluctantly from the mikes, and saw Angelo Pastorelli heading over from the direction of the police station like a galleon under full sail. He always leans forward as if into a head wind.

He looked frayed. Angelo has a reputation as the biggest ego in the county and a camera hog to rival Ed Flanagan, but he ruffles more easily than some people might think. I don' t really know what makes him tick; unlike Schulz, he appears sane and unlike Reardon and Beach, he still works full-time. He has other hobbies, if being obsessed with the emergency services is a hobby, but his every remaining minute must be dedicated to serving on committees and harassing the Board. If he didn't bitch about the tax rates I would be half convinced he lived at the County building.

He had a reason to be ruffled—but he was already making it into a standup routine, shaking his head and pacing his delivery. "I'm telling you, Smitty," he said, "I'm rethinking this thing about eating a lot of roughage." I winced, knowing he would fall in love with this opener and use it many times more no matter what the company. Though he had a point. If he hadn't made that pit stop in the men's room just before the Board meeting, he wouldn't have spent the last several hours being interviewed. The last person known to leave the scene where a body's been found can become amazingly popular.

The good thing about this for me is that for a guy who wears glasses like paperweights on a stalk, he picks up an amazing amount of information. And he likes giving it to me, as long as I go through the motions of giving him first peek at my own gleanings. I waited.

"What was Flanagan willing to give up?" he asked.

I checked my notes. "De la Roja was pronounced dead in the ER," I said. "Probably already gone when Reardon found him. He'd been shot a few feet inside the restroom and managed to get partially through the door before collapsing. The fatal trauma was consistent with a nine-millimeter handgun fired point blank..." I suddenly felt myself go a little weak in the knees, maybe because I hadn't had anything since a dusty-tasting breakfast bar around six a.m., maybe because I had answered a lot of questions to set-faced cops myself; maybe because reading this stuff out loud made the whole familiar Courthouse plaza, with its plantings and benches and brass railings—now festooned with yellow tape—into a hostile place that I'd never been before.

"Let's go sit down." I moved in on one of the wrought-iron benches; it helped, too, not to feel that Pastorelli was looming over me. It gets old always having to look up at the person you are interviewing.

"Common as dirt," he said.

"What?"

"A nine. Every asshole who feels like he needs to go around armed gets a nine, like a nine-millimeter Glock, some piece of shit that's going to misfire and shoot off his foot. Every little homie on Potter's Run who wants to be a big hombre gets himself a nine. They get the bullet?"

"Yeah."

He was not as casual as his language suggested. Pastorelli is not someone with a lot of color in him anyhow but in the early afternoon light he looked drained. He likes to think of himself as a friend of the police; still, some people on Flanagan's department probably looked on the chance to bust his chops as an early Christmas present. A lot of them would be happy to send their chief on a long cruise but Pastorelli's luck, he probably got interviewed by one of the sycophants instead.

"So what can you tell me?" I said.

"A little, if we can go and eat something."

There was a deli inside the plaza, between the jewelry store and the newss-stand, and some tables now deserted in the past-lunch hour. "I really didn't see shit," he said. "That's what I had to tell them. I wish I had. Brother Rearend saw way more than me. I said hello to Hector, I took my crap, I came out again. I didn't check who it was in the last stall. I ain't one of these sensitive New Age males."

I pondered that maybe these Board meetings start too early. The traffic in that restroom seemed remarkably brisk—though not brisk enough that anyone ran into the retreating gunman. How the hell could anyone have gotten out of there? It made sense that they'd spent hours on Pastorelli—even though he was the most unlikely murder suspect in Creation. Reardon had spent so much of the morning ralphing, or close to it, that only the grossly reality-immune could cast him as a killer; if he ever accounted for a Board member, I mused, it would be Betty Bravo squashed flat in a moment of passion. Um. Hunger was making me spacy. I concentrated on some kind of wrap I'd ordered without really thinking about it.

"Of course, we have no gangs in Arlington," Pastorelli was saying.

"Hm?" I realized he had continued talking while my mind drifted.

"Gangs. Smitty, the first Latino on the Board gets killed, just before he was about to come out with an initiative against gangs, like the ones that originated in *his native El Salvador*." This was a phrase used so often in de la Roja's campaign that we had started chanting it in the *Spectator* office. "I'd bet on it because I'd been pushing his ass to do it."

"OK, there could be a connection."

"You think?" said Pastorelli with mock doubt.

"Who can tell? We know zip at this point." I could already hear him turning this into a podium-pounder at the next meeting. Angelo, and the beat cops, and I, and anyone in the neighborhood, know you don't want to walk through Pot-ters Run after dark, and that the decorations on businesses along Liberty Pike aren't free-form art. Just don't ask Flanagan, or Betty Bravo, to talk straight about it.

"We know they probably have the gun too, and they probably found it in the trash bucket."

I felt tiredness receding. "How?"

"Stuff I heard in the background. I learn to listen. *'Ballistics didn't get any prints off it, musta been the puke.'* That wasn't someone talking about the door-plate. You just didn't hear it from me." His cellphone beeped. "Hey, Phyllis."

Silence. "Right around the corner with Smitty. At the Wrap Artist. Thanks for coming up." Pastorelli usually walked to board meetings. I guessed that Phyllis Bell, who was a regular on my letters page, was bailing him out of a return walk after his long siege at the station. People used to think they were an item, though she's twenty years older than he is. I finally figured out that Pastorelli just enjoys talking to women old enough to be his mom; Phyllis is only one of them. They bond over police work and a mutual loathing of Ed Flanagan.

She hove into view around the side of the county building a few minutes later. Phyllis is large. She is Southern. She strikes me as the kind of woman who could tell any man in her home town what to do and no matter how outlandish the request, he would say "Yes M'am" and do it.

"Smitty," said Pastorelli rising, "I got some more things on my mind for you, but I gotta get some sleep. Let me call you."

I was chewing, and waved my hand vaguely yes, then nodded at Phyllis.

"Hey, Smitty," she said. "I thought of something on my way up here?"

"Yes?"

"Don't tell anyone this came from me, OK? But when you talk to Flanagan's PIO?"

"Mhm?"

"Ask them about the dead chicken with the pennies on its eyes, OK? Just ask them about that."

That was so weird I stopped chewing my wrap.

"Oh, and Smitty, the gun?" said Angelo. "You know Jim Schulz has more guns than he has saucepans. They still have him in there. Believe me, no one wants to see him out of circulation more than I do, but if he did this, I'm a Democrat." He turned toward the parking lot. I really wanted sleep myself, I really wanted to talk it all over with Meg, and instead I was sitting in the deserted courtyard behind the county building with a mouthful of slimy avocado, watching the two of them move statelily away from me.

I closed my eyes, and perceived a sound of hysterical weeping in the middle distance. My guess was that the widow de la Roja had arrived.

CHAPTER THREE
THE WOMEN OF TROY

I wasn't so sure about Schulz myself, and I was even less sure when he called the newspaper office that evening—I was there because I had no place else to be, I admit it—and began spitting P's down the phone line before I'd quite gotten my interview questions lined up.

"You print that I'm suing Flanagan, and that bastard Paulsen with his goddam dog flunkeys, and that this will NOT affect my run for Congress, in fact the unlawful detention of citizens is going to become fucking campaign issue number ONE," he said in a out-of-breath voice that suggested this tirade had been going on some time before he dialed my number. A tired female voice in the background, too distant for me to make out words, made me suspect his wife had been the initial audience.

"They hold that putz Pastorelli to make it look good, but this was about trying to hang it on me," Schulz ranted. "They've just been waiting for something to hang on me. Do you know Flanagan's fucking PD has me on a list? All my firearms are legal, right? Licensed, right? I don't carry them, they're in my house, I have to watch out for the fucking little gang bangers and whoever Pindick Paulsen sends down here at night with their mutts, don't try to tell me he doesn't, they crap all over my lawn but I'm the one on a list. It's not safe, in case you didn't know. It's not safe around here."

With him on the loose I could believe it. "The PIO told me you weren't charged with anything," I said carefully.

"You're damn right I wasn't charged. They couldn't find anything. They wanted to like hell, they kept trying to trip me up, but they can't make anything stick. You watch though. The bozo who grilled me is going to get demoted because he couldn't hang anything on me. I prophesy that to you right now, Paige Smith. They want me out of circulation and they'll kick the ass of the guy who failed them so the next one will know to try harder. Write that down."

I had nothing else to do, so I wrote it down.

"This is about trying to kill two birds with one stone. I don't know who actually did it, who the hell could know but they're behind it. I mean, never mind all that de mortuus nil nisi bonehead, you know? What was Hector? He was a suit. They wanted him to be a suit. Then Betty had to back out for some reason, do we know why that was? Would that woman ever give up control of a load of laundry? I say he had something on her and he saw the chance to do things his way. Their wind-up Hispanic that they put up to appease the other Hispanics showed a sign of life and they had to wax him. You write that down."

I didn't this time. I wasn't going to get a decent interview until his meds kicked in, if he was taking them, and being told what to write down does not make my day. The long-suffering female voice in the background drew closer and receded, and he made sputtering noises at it with the phone half covered. I looked up. It was getting close to eight. I really had to stop pretending I had anything to do here and go home.

"They ever find who fired that gun, it'll be one of the same sonsabitches that Paulsen sends around at night to snoop on me with their sonsabitches."

Did I mention Schulz doesn't like dogs?

Fate saved me. The other line rang and I put him on hold. It turned out to be a wrong number, because since the Spectator offices moved we've had a few numbers that are one digit away from the Pizza Hut, but it got me free. I told him I had a double deep dish with pepperoni and olives to deal with and hung up. I don't think he listens to a word anyone else says, so it didn't matter.

By nine the next morning I was pretty sure the sobbing woman at the Courthouse hadn't been Senora de la Roja. She looked strained but dry-eyed; the prostrate one was the dead man's sister, who it turned out had been flying in from New York to celebrate her brother's new station in life—someone had lined up a salsa party at Cecilia's on the Pike—only to have her flight delayed and arrive at the courthouse to find nothing waiting for her but mobs of police and really, really bad news.

Our Lady Queen of Heaven is distinctly the liberal church in the county, and the movers and shakers of the ruling party—a surprising number of them Catholic anyway—make a point of being seen there. Relucantly, the conservative crowd has started showing up too. I recognized a slightly dissipated-looking Mark Lewis—a half-term board member who'd gained a Board seat for the Republican minority during a by-election and lost to de la Roja during the November rematch. Bravo and Friedman were regulars anyway, and Hugh, who being gay normally hangs out with the Unitarians, was in a pew close to the front with his partner. Paulsen hadn't shown up. I fantasized he was down at Schulz's with a team of Huskies.

I'd had a brief chance to talk to the widow and to Mercedes de la Roja before mass was scheduled to start. Observances for the murdered man would be later in the week but it was clear that today's service would dominated by his death, so I had made sure to be there and bring a shutterbug. As tactfully as I could, I asked the two women if they would share some reminiscences of Hector with me for a memorial article. Mrs. Hector was composed and said they would meet me after Mass; Mercedes uttered a muted wail.

I had chosen a place in the rear, as press people tend to do. So when Shelley Selby—my best photographer, whom I wished would get married and give up his maiden name, or embrace his ethnic identity or something so I could address him without stammering—slipped in he found me immediately. "Something kind of peculiar," he said.

"What?" We were getting down to, as I suspect the priests think of it, curtain time.

"Hector's wife. I was here early, just wanted a few shots of people as they drove up if I could get them, you know?" He arranged his camera equipment and limbs in the pew with some ado; he is not unusually tall, except perhaps compared to me, but manages to look gangly anyway. "She got here early too I guess, I spotted her coming out of one of their little phone booths in the back. She must of had something she really needed to confess."

Shelley is African Methodist. I was starting to explain to him that a priest was a priest, and the whole business of confessing before Communion, but at that moment the congregation rose and the clergy and altar boys began to file in. I was one of those kids once, and in case you were wondering, I never had any priests come on to me, but somewhere along the line it started making less sense without leaving my system completely. I mean, during the Credo my voice was reciting along with everyone else's, but I was both thinking about Meg's feet and feeling vaguely guilty about it. I guess to a newspaperman, nothing much is sacred except press time.

The priest's homily was brief and kind: it was, after all, as touchy-feely as a Roman church gets. He chose to embroider on the Beatitudes: "Blessed are those that mourn." He reminded the congregation that among them were those in the shock of mourning and loss, and asked for their prayers that their bereaved sisters be lifted up as the Virgin was lifted from her sorrow, etc. As poor Hector was not going to roll aside the door of his tomb—or, I thought with a wince, of the Arlington Hospital morgue—I suspected it would take a while. I just hoped I wouldn't do too much damage with my interview. I am a boring journalist because I have no ruthless instincts.

I waited outside until the commiserators, the fellow mourners and embracers, had run their course, and a plainish Anglo woman—I recognized Friedman's wife, now—was walking the de la Roja women to their car. She gave me a hostile glance as I approached.

"No, I told him we could talk," said Mrs. de la Roja with almost no accent. She was devastatingly calm; I suspected a very good prescription. Her sister in law had subsided into mere sniffling. "Hector should be remembered. He had so much to give." She could have been talking about someone on her church committee.

In the end we went back inside. The verger or sacristan or whatever you call people these days let us use a small room downstairs adorned with twelve-step mottoes. Yes, Hector had indeed shined shoes in his native El Salvador; the family had emigrated to New York; distant family ties had brought him to this area where he had met her, Elisa, and when she would not hear of leaving college or of living in New York he had found work here. He had started out with the regional planning commission, running the copier, progressed to become the Hispanic liaison for our Permanent Local Congressman, Brian Murphy, and now...

Immigrant rags to riches, and very little I didn't know. There was nothing in it, nothing that could set a man up to be killed. In fact, nothing could have been duller than Hector de la Roja's government career. My own life seemed dazzling next to it.

"One other thing," I said. "Toni Messner, the secretary, said that Hector hadn't given her any printout copy of his new chairman's statement. You know that the chairman always states his direction, his goals for the county, at the start of the first meeting where he presides? She said that he told her he was going to speak extempore, but I've been covering the Board for ten years and I know nobody ever does that. Did he talk with you at all about what he was going to say?" I didn't add that I doubted Hector could welcome you to his house without a cheat card; the man just was not a speaker.

"He was working a lot at the computer. He did not talk to me about it."

"If there is anything that he had typed up or saved...? I'd like the piece to have something about his vision."

"I will look. I can send it to you if there is anything."

"If it's hard copy, call me and I'll send a courier." I didn't say that this meant bribing one of our two interns with comps to the concerts I didn't want to go to.

The three women took their leave. As Selby rose I said "Favor?"

"Sure."

I flipped out my cell phone. "Something I haven't told the cops yet," I said. "Can you get a really good image off one of these cheesy little cameras?"

"If there's anything to see at all. What is it?"

"Scene of the crime."

Selby whistled. "You weren't kidding me you were right on top of it."

"I almost got woopsed on by a four-hundred-pound tax activist."

"Why'd you keep this under wraps?" he said, tossing the phone and catching it.

"Bad vibes?" I said. "I don't know. I don't really trust Flanagan's police department. They'd rather leave a crime unsolved than have to admit some things in public. If there's anything there that doesn't match with the official statements...?"

"You got it," he said. "I'll call you when I get something. But won't you need your phone?"

"Matinee today," I said. I write most of the theater reviews *and* the editorials, though not, as some have accused me, the letters page as well.

We passed out of the church. The wind carried voices to us.

I glanced over to the far end of the gravelled lot. The rear door of a large sedan was standing open, and Friedman's wife was at the wheel with the engine running, but Mrs. de la Roja and Mercedes had not yet gotten in. They were facing off, and their voices were not raised far, but the tension in them carried. Neither of them was one bit happy with the other.

I looked at Selby. His brows arched.

"*Definitely* I'll call you when I get this done," he said.

The play was a local university production of *The Trojan Women*. Bad choice. Halfway through, the women lament the death of Hector, and the play ends in utter despair.

CHAPTER FOUR
THE SHOESHINE BOY

I was in at the usual early hour the next morning, whiffing the disinfectant that still lingered from the night cleaning crew and putting the touches on my memorial piece. I usually put minor stuff straight on the Web page myself, but I was glad that our whizkid—Sean, an intern from NoVa with about twelve piercings and a Brady Bunch, sunny disposition—was around to backstop me for a leader. He codes advanced HTML and can make a Web page walk and talk, whereas I tend to make them lurch and hiccup.

All four surviving Board members had sent me handsome, fond reminiscences of their late associate, bland texts under which shock and disorientation ran like a cold-water current. Mark Lewis had sent a recollection of something especially gentlemanly Hector had said to him when he conceded last fall's election, e-mailed at about two in the morning. Mrs. de la Roja had not surfaced—if Hector had had a vision, the Spectator readers would not be privileged to learn what it was. But his former employer, Congressman Murphy, dispatched an encomium (probably written by staff, if I knew Murphy) suggesting he would have been the first Latino president had it not been for the twin inconveniences of being a naturalized citizen, and dead. Et cetera. I wove it all into the right size bundle of copy and called Sean over to troubleshoot the inevitable screwups that tended to leave ampersands and square brackets visible in my lead pieces.

It had gotten past eight then and I figured I could make a few phone calls. Phyllis Bell is always up early; too early for me, apparently. "We're glad you called," said her voice on the answering machine. Phyllis has been a widow for years. "Leave a message. If you need to come by, Fang will be here to entertain you."

I've never met Fang. I have this vision of large, Southern Phyllis seated on her porch swing with something half dog, half dinosaur at her feet, chewing on the severed leg of the last person unlucky enough to try something on her.

"Phyllis," I said. "Paige Smith here? You said something Saturday about a chicken with pennies on its eyes. Would you mind telling me what that was about before I go asking questions at the PD? I'm too old for surprises." I put the phone down. Sean was looking up at me from the computer screen.

"That's Santeria, boss," he said. I swear he does not yet shave. "Who told you about that?"

"Someone I talked to right after this all happened," I said. "What do you know about it?"

"Not much," he said. "My girlfriend's roommate, though, she's from this Cuban family. They do shit like that back in Miami. Chickens, who knows what else. It's like this voodoo stuff all mixed up with saints and black magic."

"Yeah, I've heard about it."

"Pennies on the eyes is something I remember Dolores talking about. I don't know what it means."

"Well, someone must have found something like that around here."

"I'd ask at the Botanica."

"The what?"

"It's a Santeria shop on the Pike. You've seen it. Down there by the bike place."

I tried to keep a straight face. I had indeed seen the sign *Botanica.* I thought it was a plant shop.

"They sell candles, all the voodoo junk, who knows what. Dolores would go there when she was hacked at her boyfriend. Something must have worked because he always showed up with gifts."

I looked around me to make sure no one had come in to hear the community college intern explaining things to the editor. Look: I was born in a little town in Pennsylvania. The closest we got to black magic was girls pulling the petals off daisies and counting to see what the first letter of their husband's name was going to be.

"OK, this is ready," he said. "You want bold headers?"

"Yeah."

He looked at me a little more keenly. "You OK, boss?"

This was a funny question to be asked by a twenty-year-old, especially when I thought of the first weeks after Meg left, when I had had trouble remembering what I was doing from minute to minute and still managed to keep it from showing. "I'm fine, why?"

"You look sort of not fine."

Well, it was April."Allergies," I said.

*   *   *   *

I had a breakfast meeting with a local transportation group to cover at eight-thirty and a dentist's appointment at eleven. Coming out onto the Pike at noon, I decided to have a look at the Botanica shop for myself. If nothing else, it would make me look more savvy when I talked to Phyllis. I fed the meter and walked past the framer's, the bike shop, the optician's, then lingered looking in the window of *Botanica.* Candle glasses ornamented with the flaming heart of Jesus jostled garish painted statuettes of unidentifiable female saints and books with titles I couldn't translate. I had a feeling of butterflies, quashed it. I walked into the shop, and almost collided with a very not Hispanic vision: Dvorah Steadman, standing in the nearest aisle of the shop and contemplating a chunky ornament that might have furnished some magical ceremony, if I could only glean what it was.

"Smitty! What are you doing in *here?*" Dvorah, who seems to turn up at political functions across the county without adhering to any particular group, is the final heat death of any human male's equilibrium. It should not work on anyone, but it does. She was wearing a short leather skirt and boots that laced up to just above her knees. The rest of the outfit was cut skimpily enough to advertise some sparse freckles well below her collarbones. Her lipstick was glossy, and vivid.

I once saw Dvorah at the Civic Federation, deciding her vote for each item on the legislative agenda by testing the swing of a crystal pendant over the printed program. I suppose I should have expected to find her in a Santeria shop.

"Newspaper work," I said, trying to achieve a soft tone of voice and producing a croak. She had on just enough expensive-smelling perfume to make you wonder what it was.

"Oh my gosh, are you doing a *story* on *Botanica?*" She reached, actually took hold of my necktie and gave it a flirtatious little tug. "Oh, this is the most *amazing* place. I come in here all the time."

"Uh, actually, I was going to ask them some questions about this stuff. I...maybe you would know?" I compared the thought of interviewing Dvorah with that of questioning the rather dumpy Hispanic lady who was chattering briskly on the telephone behind the back counter. "There seems to be some kind of ritual angle on a story I'm following up…" She had about eight bangles on the wrist of the hand that was still drawing a line on my necktie, and a belt buckle bigger than a beer coaster. "An animal sacrifice thing?"

"Ohh, I bet I could tell you but—you know what, not in here. Look, you don't want to come in here and just start asking Micaela questions like that. She'll think you're the cops. People already tried to shut her down once, it's so unfair. She's really nice. But she won't want to tell you all that stuff."

"Can I…?" I gestured toward the street.

"Not right now? I have some things to get and someone's picking me up…Look, why don't you come see me at my place? Are you in a hurry for this?"

"Um, not really, no story this minute." The laced-up boots had stack heels, the only reason she was looking me straight in the eye. "Can you call me?" I fumbled in my shirt pocket—I had to reach past her hand on the necktie and into my sweater vest to do it—and pulled out a card. *Arlington SPECTATOR, Paige Smith, Editor.* She took it between blood-colored salon nails and tucked it into her purse.

"This isn't about de la Roja, is it?" she asked suddenly in a huskier whisper. "The poor man."

"Um, not exactly, I just finished writing about him…"

"I need to get this." She picked up the ornament, which I could now see had a barbaric but strangely benign female figure embossed on it, and moved toward the back where the proprietress was now closing her phone call. "Micaela! I need two of the black candles."

She must have seen the expression that crossed my face as the little, slightly mustached woman looked under the counter. "Oh, you must think I'm doing something Satanic! Black is for releasing. I have to get some awful *vibes* out of my house. My ex's *wife* was in there dropping off the kids. She left this awful *yuck* hanging in the atmosphere. What a *bitch.*" She peeled some bills out of the small string bag and laid them on the counter. "Micaela, this is my friend Smitty." Friend? I am sure I simpered absurdly. "He's on the newspaper. He's *not* a *cop.* He just finished writing a story about poor Hector. You should fix him up with something so *lots* more people will read his little paper. I'll be right out!" She had caught a sound behind us and turned to wave at someone stepping in off the walk.

She patted my sweater vest again as she collected her change. "But you just come talk to me about that other thing. That's best. I'll call and leave my number. Coming!" She double-timed briskly to the front door and grabbed the arm of the man waiting there. I squinted as a heliograph from a passing car almost blinded me, then saw—Mark Lewis? Unmistakably. He was looking at her very hungrily as they moved off down the sidewalk. She waved. He did not follow her wave.

Huh. The last I saw, Mark had been dating a high-powered, scary-smart woman lawyer. Then again, the last I saw Mark had never seen a woman he didn't like. A voice recalled me.

"You write for the *Journal?*"

I jumped a little, shook my head. "No m'am. The *Spectator*, the Arlington weekly."

"You writing a piece about Senor de la Roja? Poor, poor man. Such a shame. Nice man, his wife nice woman too. You come here so you must talk to her, how she come in here all the time?"

"Uh…yeah?"

"She really, really crazy about him. Love story. She do anything to help him succeed. That why he got so far. She buy candles, do all the right things." The heavy woman sat back on the barstool behind the register, put her chin in both hands and looked at me with a strange, and not unattractive echo of Dvorah's flirtatiousness. "What we do for you? Your little paper need some success?"

I managed a smile. "I think Dvorah was just kidding."

She smiled back. "I think not. You worried about it. Also, you sleep bad." I felt my smile fall off.

She reached into one of four glass-fronted cabinets behind the counter and withdrew a small brown glass dropper bottle. "You take this," she said. "When you get up, not when you go to bed. Keeps your heart close to your body all day so it can find you when you need to sleep, instead of you go looking for it all night." She plunked it down on the counter, then bent to pull three green candles out of a box underneath. "These you burn three nights together, once sun is down. Light one candle and look into flame. Say, my work will prosper. Then put all from your mind and go away and leave burning.'

I envisioned one of these things burning down into a puddle next to my computer terminal.

"Don't worry. This will not call *orishas*. Much too difficult for you, I will not play you that kind of trick. Just easy magic any person can do."

Somehow I found myself paying, taking the brown paper bag with the candles and vial in it. As I turned to leave Micaela said, "Even Elisa, I told her to be careful with the *orishas*. They are very particular."

"Did she…?" What exactly was an *orisha*?

"No, no, I should not talk. Maybe when you come back for your pink candle. Or red one." She winked at me. "Pink for love. Red for very hot love! Go, go home, make your fortune. And sleep better."

I found myself blinking in the sunlight, almost without a transition. In fact I wanted to sleep right now. It always catches up with me in the afternoon. I would go home and check my messages, then write my transportation piece in the evening. God, the excitement of newspaper work was killing me.

Perhaps Meg would say I was less boring if she saw me coming out of a Santeria shop. Where Elisa de la Roja had bought props and dinguses to forward her husband's career…what had the woman said? 'I told her to be careful with the *orishas*.' Maybe she hadn't been careful enough. Something had certainly backfired.

I shook my head and walked toward my car. Next I would be burning these candles myself. But perhaps, if I went back in there, I should remember to say that I had. It seemed like there were questions about Hector that were still waiting to be asked.

*   *   *   *

I didn't sleep, to speak of, and I didn't get much done when I got up and tried to putter around the condo. For a while after Meg left I would keep finding things like her hair pins or lip balm when I was cleaning under the bed or in the bathroom, and it gave me an antipathy to the whole thing. I pay a woman to come in every week or two and be sure new life doesn't form in the corners. The only thing I try to keep in order is the DVD collection and my socks.

When I gave up, ran by Subway and on into the Spectator offices again, it was about seven—still nice out and edging into twilight. The sports reporter was in a corner, phone wedged against one ear and keyboarding with both hands, and Slate, our other intern (her name is Kelly, but she is firmly feminist and wants to be addressed by her last name to avoid patronage) was going over an ad layout. Press day is Tuesday. Since computers there is less sense of urgency about composing a page but I still get edgy until the edition's in bed.

My message machine was blinking. I'd been without the cell phone since passing it to Selby, yesterday morning, and had begun to appreciate not being called every twenty minutes, but I was glad to see it folded on my blotter on top of a sticky note.

Smitty—I tried to get to you in person but no one seemed to know when you'd be back. Hated to call you at home. Couldn't quite reach you on your cell. :) Call me, or I'll leave a message, didn't want to leave stuff just lying here.

Reasonable. I picked up the phone, punched in my retrieval code, and listened to the first message.

"Smitty." Gradual, Southern, amiable, Phyllis. "I guess I was just wantin' to set up a drama with that horse's ass Flanagan. I'm sorry if it treed ya. What happened, one of the moms around here was down by where Potter's Run cuts across the end of Dover Park. Where they call the Rat Beach." This was an area south of the Pike where on warm days actual rats had been seen sunning themselves on the rocks midstream, enjoying a vacation from the storm sewer culverts, though rumors of beach chairs and transistor radios were probably unfounded. "There was a paper bag that looked like blood soaked through part of it, one of the kids found it and the mom looked in. It was a chicken, had its throat cut, couple of pennies kind of gummed onto the sides of its head with some sorta pasty stuff. She called the cops and they took it and told her not to worry bout her kids, which was a brushoff she didn't like so she called me. I ended up calling the District Commander and askin' him what the hell. He tried to say there was no chicken, but when I mentioned the pennies he said he'd call me back. Didn't. It's some kind of ethnic magic stuff, but I couldn't tell you what it meant. I'm in after the Crime Prevention Council meeting."

Rat Beach, Dover Park. Not too far from the de la Roja house, but not too far from a lot of places—Pinky Paulsen's, as well, and Grover Friedman's. And, of course, the homes of several thousand Latinos who were more likely targets of a spell or curse from one of their own. I tapped a finger on the blotter and keyed to the next message.

"Smith? There's something else you need to hear about." It was Schulz; I held the phone away from my ear. "Those goddam dogs were here again last night. Three in the morning. Every fucking night, three in the morning. The cops won't stake me out. They just try to say I'm lying. I'm telling you, come down here and spend the night or you won't see it. This is a story. The fucking Board is trying to run me out and I'm NOT going, and Murphy is going to hear from me tomorrow night too. He's in it with them. I guarantee you"—then it cut off, quick as that. it didn't sound like a bad connection—more like a deliberate hangup, Schulz cutting himself off in midsentence.

Worked for me. I keyed ahead again.

"Heyyyy! Smitty!" It was Dvorah, talking to me as if I was her best friend from high school instead of someone whose longest conversation with her had been earlier today. "Listen, I don't want to *press,* but if you want to talk, I'm around tomorrow? I have to go to this stupid Republican dinner tonight but you can call me in the morning. The kids are gone till dinner, my roommate's taking them to a movie so I can have my girls group. *Love* to see ya." She left a number, which I wrote down; a distinct improvement on Schulz.

The next call was Selby. I returned it and found him in, mouth full but wholly available.

"They kind of sucked, but I used Paintshop and boosted the resolution," he said. "I'm still not sure what I'm seeing, except that the cops would shit if they knew you took these. You can see it's Hector and you can see he's pretty dead. There's some stuff on the floor around him, did you see what it was?"

"No. I just snapped the shots before the cops got there. Angie had her back turned but not for long."

"Well, I was hoping you could come have a look. Some of it looks like papers, but I can't tell about the rest. I kind of didn't want to leave em on the desk."

"How late you up?"

"You know me. Jazz station doesn't get good till after midnight." Selby's living room is insulated with jazz albums—CDs, tape, vinyl—and has almost no furnishings other than the sound system. Along with photography, it seems to be his whole life.

"OK, I'll probably get by about ten. Stuff to do here." As was inevitable after not-sleeping all afternoon. I rang off and felt a presence at my shoulder, looked up. It was Slate, holding a floppy disk.

"I wouldn't have forgotten," she said a little nervously. "A lady came by with this. She asked me to give it straight to you. Told me not to just leave it out."

I took it. It was labeled in a neat hand in gel pen: *Remarks for Saturday.*

I had a feeling I knew what it was. "Thanks, Slate," I said. For a stipulating feminist, she is wispy and a little shy. She stood there for a while before stepping back toward her desk and collecting her things; I heard the door snick shut behind her a moment later, and realized I was the last man standing tonight, again.

I slid the disk into my floppy drive and double-clicked.

Half an hour later I was staring out the window at the now dark parking lot, wondering who would be the right person to call. I needed to hear someone say "Good Lord" as many times as I'd said it in the past few minutes. But except for Meg—who would say "small-town diddlysquat" and hang up, if I could find her—I couldn't think of a soul.

＊   ＊   ＊   ＊

You have to understand some things about the county. Arlington's an anti-matter universe when compared to the rest of Virginia or, these days, the nation—meaning that it is comfortably in the grip of one party. Actually, they don't even have to grip. They just keep getting elected. What most people think of this depends on their political leanings; myself, I don't like arrogance, and people who get everything their own way year after year become arrogant without even realizing it. It goes by degrees; Pinky Paulsen really isn't cut out that way, and always seems to be apologizing a little for it, while Betty Bravo is fond of saying that anyone who doesn't agree with her needs to be "educated." It makes me think of re-education camps. Caparici pictured her once on the editorial page dressed as a schoolmarm with the more recognizable members of the Republican Committee, including Pastorelli, Beach, and Lewis, chained to parochial-school benches; I swear I had nightmares about that one. As for my editorials, Friedman has been heard to say more than once "Smith stuck it to us again." I prefer to think of myself as fair but strict.

The county's political machine runs pretty smoothly, as machines tend to do. The administrative gears are perhaps less well oiled. Most days, the county manager, and the staff answerable to him, run things and make the decisions. (These days it's Ron Carroll, a decent enough sort who spends the whole weekend of the County Fair greeting citizens without ever pausing—in Ryan's phrase—to eat, sleep, drink or pee.) The Board sets policy, but they're often happy to take direction from whoever's feet are on the ground. Sometimes that works and sometimes it's not so hot, as when there's a turf war between a couple of departments. And every citizen committee involved with housing, parks, schools and so on can name one staff member that takes calls and does zilch, or maybe is too dimwitted to do more than zilch. (Welcome to government.) Since the Board directs by vote, but has to work through the manager, the wheels grind slowly and often to a halt. The Board Chairman sets priorities at the beginning of his term, and usually tries to assume the posture of having a "vision"—Friedman's last vision was of an uninterrupted tree canopy, Arlington as Mirkwood, and the board spent hours deliberating on ways to make various trees sacred. You get the idea. Same stuff, different day, year in and year out.

Real estate around here is sky-high—that accounts for a big part of my advertising revenue—so "affordable housing" is a mantra that comes up every election and every budget cycle. But for some reason, nothing much ever changes in that department. Developers are supposed to include modest-priced units in everything they build, but deals get cut and hands get shaken, and all the cheap housing stays in old garden apartments built fifty years ago, where most of the county's immigrants live in a sort of imposed ghetto. Most of them are five minutes' walk from Potter's Run. And I'd say the majority of the citizens, whatever they say, are happy to keep them there.

Then there is the gang thing. As Pastorelli had said, we have (ahem) no gangs. This is a well known fact, except to the unlucky stiffs who due to anything from idiocy to necessity walk along Potter's Run Drive late at night. They can expect to meet the enterprising youth responsible for the jagged spray-painted tags that decorate half the businesses along Liberty Pike. Wallets, teeth and a fair amount of skin have been left in this vicinity at different times, and if someone is suffering from turf insecurity, you get an occasional rash of police reports reading "Assault by Mob" as if mobs of four or six teenage Hispanic guys just form every now and then and beat up one of their own for no particular reason.

For years, no one has rocked the boat on these issues—it would mean, if you are cynical (sometimes I am) admitting the county had ever done something wrong to begin with. Well, Hector—had Schulz just this weekend called him the Board's "wind-up Latino"?—had apparently planned to damn near capsize the boat, to the extent his position made it possible.

The first point of the speech outlined on the disk was housing reform. It was near to Socialist. Two or three nonprofit contractors had handled the county's "affordable" units for years, and were generally judged to have a comfy racket; Hector was calling for a staff audit of their books going back five years, and a nationwide competitive bidding search for rival contractors as potential replacements. The requirements he proposed for developers were stern and non-negotiable: no buyouts, no tax deals, just build the low-priced units into every new development or don't do business here. The disk contained documents from the citizen commission on housing that detailed deferred repairs, slacking management companies, cozy developer relationships and plain chutzpah in use of county funds. An hour after those remarks went up on my website—had they been made—phones would have been ringing from here to Fairfax.

The second half dealt with the gangs. For years the police department has echoed the government's insistence that those boys on Potter's Run are just being boys (the occasional body in a parking lot has been met with deafening silence). Hector planned on requesting that Flanagan's department cooperate with the gang units that were operating in every other municipality in the area, and not only cooperate, but take direction from officers who had been grappling for years with groups like Puno Salvadoro, the Ligados Locos and Nueva Pearsall. Flanagan would just as soon walk through the Metro corridor at midday in a dress—trust me on that. This is a man who tried to direct the sniper investigation when not one shot had been fired in his county. He wouldn't want to do it—and he wouldn't want to be put on the spot of having to publicly decline de la Roja's request.

Back on Saturday morning—*nil nisi* aside, as Schulz would have said—I would have told you that Hector de la Roja was a nice, mild, ineffectual and, perhaps, stupid man. Now it looked as if he had had the heretical inclinations to define clearly what was going on and the *cojones* to pop the lid off in a way that would force answers. The list of people who would have wanted these remarks unheard was growing in my mind by the minute.

I looked at the blinking cursor at the bottom of the screen again, and hit Save. I didn't know how I was going to use this yet. But I knew I wasn't handing it to Pinky Paulsen, or to Chief Flanagan.

The light on my phone distracted me. I realized I hadn't played through all the messages and keyed up the last one. It was a breathless woman's voice—one I half recognized but couldn't place.

"Hello? Hello, who's there?" You get these—people who can't believe there isn't a live person listening stubbornly on the other side of a machine. "Hello—??" Forlorn, and annoyingly pathetic. I was about to punch the button when a barking male voice burst onto the tape. There was a clatter, the receiver falling: *"Just mind your own business and stop fucking with me!!!"* A scrabble, and then a ringing clack as the receiver went down.

That had been Schulz' voice, I'd bet on it.

Little I could prove. Less I could do. Except mail women's shelter brochures to her anonymously, I suppose. I wondered what Kelly Slate's feminist solution would be.

There was no way I could put my mind to committee news now. I pulled the floppy out of the drive and headed for the door; stepped outside, turned to make sure the door had latched, and that was when a movement just outside my field of vision turned into the dropped-dishes shiver of glass as the light over the entry shattered and left me in blackness. I can't say anything hurt at first. I was aware that whatever hit me hit the back of my head but the blow seemed to come from all directions at once, forcing my body toward the pavement as if half a house had dropped on me.

It seemed there was a long time when nothing at all registered on my senses, and then I was in a wind tunnel. Every move I made smashed me up against something. I think I managed to make half a noise, and after that I can remember feeling the specific and detailed texture of asphalt against my cheek. My glasses had disappeared. I tried feebly to push away what felt like a foot or fist jamming into my ribs, only to find nothing there; pain had printed the original blow on me indelibly. I inhaled, got a gust of coppery blood far back in my nose, hacked, and made a sound I hated to think had come from my throat. Someone rolled me over, someone fumbled at my pockets. A harsh whisper sounded near me; I couldn't tell whether it was man or woman, what language. I coughed again and my ribs bloomed with pain.

After that I can't remember much. They say it's a survival mechanism, Nature makes it that way. When the cycling strobes pushed my eyes open again I thought I was home in bed and wondered who had called the fire department. Then it was black and silent again, for what seemed a very long time.

CHAPTER FIVE
THE GYPSY

They let me out around dawn, once I could convince them I had serviceable glasses at my office and that Selby was my employee. I have never been happier that he stays home weekday evenings listening to jazz.

"Smitty," he said once we got into his car—he flicking his fingers over space-ship controls on the dash, me wincing and settling into the passenger seat in slow motion, bruised ribs strapped, one hand bandaged, a list of "call your doctor immediately" concussion symptoms sticking out of my shirt pocket. My vest, a smutched and bloody mess, was in a plastic hospital sack along with a bottle of painkillers. "Smitty, you're better off outa there because anyone is better off outa there who can walk, but you look like shit. You want to come back to my place?"

I shook my head—or started to. Bad idea. "Drop me at the office," I said. "I never did plug in the piece on the tri-state transportation commission."

He stared at me. "You are nucking futs," he said. "Someone just used you for a soccer game and you're going in to write bird cage liner about the Metro?"

"Thanks for the praise." I winced.

"You know what I mean. The paper'll make it without one more piece to keep people thinking you have your finger on the pulse of the mighty engines of local government. You got a black eye. You just missed getting your nose broke. Boss, you got a friggen *concussion*."

"A maybe one. I don't feel that bad." For what I could recall happening to me, I didn't. "Also, I want to see what's happened at the office. They said there was no sign of entry, but who's to know? And I need my old glasses." I twinged as I remembered Meg playing keep-away with them, saying she wouldn't give them back until I promised to get a pair that didn't make me look like a math professor from the 1950's.

"We'll go open up in a while," he said after a brief silence. "But first you *are* coming back to my place. If you can't face my gourmet toast, I have Slim-Fast. If you can't face that, I have Maxwell House."

I dropped my head back against the seat.

"Trump card: I got those pictures."

"You win," I said shortly.

*   *   *   *

The cop who interviewed me—a short, unsmiling woman I remembered from a piece on drug busts on the Pike—had spread out the inventoried contents of my pockets as they had been when the ambulance brought me in. "Wallet but no cash, looks like all your cards. That's normal, punks are figuring out that their dealers won't take your Visa. Anything else missing from it?"

My driver's license was still there, my Costco card, my blood donor card. "Nothing, I think."

"OK. Here's a set of keys—did you carry more than one?"

"No. There should be the business office key, my condo key, key to the Toyota. One for the Spectator PO Box." I'd quit carrying the key to the outside door when we got a combination keypad; it was one less thing to worry about losing. I was glad now.

"That's how many there are." She laid the chain aside with a clink. "There's a comb, nail clipper, about half a buck in change, Visine. You had some business cards and three pens in the shirt pocket. Cell phone. Was there anything else?"

I started to say no and then remembered the floppy disk with Hector's speech on it. "You didn't find—"I stopped. I looked at her peaked hat sitting on the table beside her, part of Flanagan's "look" for the police department, and decided to say something else. "Some folded notes," I said. "Nothing really important. For an article about rapid transit."

"No," she said looking at me guardedly, as if she knew I had held something back.

"They might be on my desk. Everything's a little blurry."

"It will be," she said with the fatality of someone who knows from experience. "OK, if you sign for this stuff here it saves the hospital people a trip." I did, and she handed it back to me. "Lucky you had this," she said as she passed me the cell phone. "And good thing you could keep it together enough to use it."

"I didn't," I said.

"You don't remember," she said. "Well, it happens."

"No, seriously. There was actually a call?"

"How do you think we got there so fast? When they broke your watch, you must have been shielding your face, it stopped at 9:50 pm. We had a medic unit on the scene at 10:12. It's in the dispatch."

"I didn't call."

"Well, I don't think the scumbags who did this phoned in for you. Dispatch said there was a call about 9:55, said a male RP reported an attack at the *Spectator* office. Then she lost you, and they had to cross check the address. It came back to this number OK, but this phone is old enough we can't get a position fix. That's what slowed us down a little. We were worried about securing the scene but there wasn't anyone in sight but you."

"I don't remember."

"People don't sometimes. Don't worry about it."

She put her card down in front of me.

"Call me if you do remember anything else though. What they looked like or how they sounded. Or if you think of…anything else they might have taken that we could trace? Only, they could have gotten your car, spent time beating you up instead…this seems kinda personal."

I was saved from reacting to this by Selby's arrival. I never thought I'd be glad to see him when I was dressed in nothing but an overwashed cotton johnny with pictures of fire trucks printed on it, but in this situation I had no inclination to be picky.

✴   ✴   ✴   ✴

"So someone called it in and it wasn't you?" He was pouring water in a drip coffeemaker whose carafe had the mahogany patina of long unwashed use. "Be a first. Muggers call the cops to clean up after em."

"I didn't, and I don't think I could have," I said. "I skinned off most of one hand here. The other one's my stupid hand. Got the phone out of my pocket? Called 911 and then turned it off and put it back in my pocket? In the dark?"

His sober expression agreed this was a stretch. He set down two crackled cups on the table. "You feel up to looking at those pics?"

"If you don't mind me holding them up to my nose."

The coffeemaker snorted and bubbled as if it might be developing asthma. I felt for it. Selby came in and set out two enlarged prints on Kodak printer paper, blown up enough to be grainy but far clearer than anything I'd ever gotten off that little cellphone cam. In the first one, de la Roja was visible from about the chin down, his jacket fallen open to reveal an almost black stain on his shirt front. In an image that reminded me disturbingly of the medical handouts tucked in my own shirt pocket, a folded pad of papers, half blotched with blood, was sticking out of the pocket up to about his collarbone. Probably the text of the speech I had read. I reminded myself to ask if it had been catalogued in evidence.

"You must have stepped back for this," said Selby, laying down the second one. You could see the top of Hector's head in this one, and the trickle of blood creeping from under him. By his head were two elliptical-looking objects…no, discs, foreshortened by the way I'd had to hunker down for the shot. Copper pennies?

Ask them about the dead chicken with the pennies on its eyes.

I told her to be careful with the orishas. They are very particular…

I began shivering for no explicable reason. Aftermath of the whole thing, I supposed. It is horrible to realize that people you have interviewed—and judged, characterized, and filed away in your head—can leave this earth half in and half out of a men's room; that you can be minding your own business and someone can come along and beat you to a pudding without anyone or anything intervening until they have finished.

"Just chill for a while, Boss," said Selby almost tenderly. "We'll go in later and fuck with the fishwrap if that's what you gotta do. I have photos to turn in for the layout but they'll be OK if I get there by eight. Crash."

His voice was already becoming remote.

$$*\qquad*\qquad*\qquad*$$

The lady cop may have been right; memory after an injury like that can do strange things. The next thing that is clear is that we were in the early morning hubbub of the *Spectator* offices, and I was flashing back to the previous spring, Meg and I greeting each other in the newsroom as if we had not been looking for her left shoe under my dresser, or sharing a single cup of coffee under the blankets, an hour or two before.

I had found the old glasses in my desk drawer, and was wincing as I settled them on my bruised nose. Sean was saying "Man, that *sucks*" over and over, and Ryan Tabor, who covers the boardroom when I'm away, was typing assiduously so as to get the story of my mugging into this week's edition. I wasn't sure how I felt about this, but it was better than the publisher of the rival paper, whose publication had to tersely report his arrest for indecent exposure a few years back. I figured I retained some comparative dignity.

The transportation committee notes were on my desk. Selby whisked them away and presented them to Ryan, who nodded as if to say he would slap them into shape too.

I looked down at the blotter. There was a number there, and I remembered after a moment's blankness whose it was. I tore off the corner with the number carefully, and put it in my shirt pocket.

"The funeral's tomorrow," Ryan was saying. "And I'm covering Perpetual Congressman Murphy at the Civic Federation tonight. It'll amount to kicking off his campaign but maybe someone will ask a decent question. Is there anything you wanted to spot his answers on?"

"On the record, no. But if any women get in a fight in the lobby, get their names." Murphy had the veined nose and big shoulders of an Irish pugilist, which he had been once, and walked like Lurch the butler, but had somehow managed to occasion a hair-pulling fight between two rival girlfriends whose age didn't quite add up to his own, just in the past year. How he did it I don't know; the power thing, I guess.

"Ha ha. OK, I think we have this all ready to go. Come look."

I slid into his computer chair and read his terse account of my attack. It suggested nothing more than an ordinary mugging—I had answered his questions with that in mind—and gave little away. "Looks good," I said. "Is Sophie in?"

"Not till ten. She was doing the kiddie theater last night."

"Tell her I want her on the funeral." Sophie Grint usually does the warm fuzzy stories, the children's Classique drama troupe and the school features where Mrs. Muchnick's class sponsors an orphan in Bosnia. The empathy oozing off her makes her a natural for funerals; I have seen her shedding more tears than the bereaved, but she does her homework, too. She also speaks decent Spanish, which is more than I can do. I have always suspected that Ryan can't stand her, but he nodded.

"You got it."

I rose, felt myself sway a little. "I'm going home then," I said. "Any problems before press time, call me up." I knew they wouldn't.

*   *   *   *

The early sun in my eyes started my head pounding. Before I was in the door of my unit I dry-swallowed one of the Darvocets. Probably it would knock me out, but I had a couple calls to make.

Both got machines. Was there a time when people picked up their own phones? "Hello, this is Elisa de la Roja. Please leave a message and we'll call you back." The terseness was explained when her voice came on again a split second later: "Ola, esta Elisa de la Roja…" I suspected the tape was new. I left a message that I needed to talk to her about Hector's speech, with all my numbers and my e-mail. I wanted it to see the light of day, attested, and I didn't want his colleagues or Flanagan's police department tipped off that I had it.

The second was a nicer call to make. "Heyyyyy! We're not here, but please leave a message for Dvorah, Batia, Joaav or Jeremy. We won't be gone long." I told her I was away from the office today, but not why, and left the cell number for her to tell me if I could talk to her when her women's group or whatever it was ended.

As I moved toward the sofa—the bed seemed too far, suddenly—my eyes fell on the paper bag from the Botanica, which I had emptied out on the coffee table but not tossed. In the watery early-morning light the green candles looked a little crude and cheesy. The vial was beside them. I opened it and sniffed it. It wasn't bad actually, with a faint pong of cinnamon and something a little bitter and green. To hell with it. I was tired of night running into day and neither offering me any rest. I squirted the full dropper into a swallow of water remaining in a glass I must have left there nights before, chugged it—nothing terrible happened right away—and stretched out on the sofa, tossing a DVD jewel box out from under the small of my back. The world dropped me out of its hand. I slept.

I was sweating when I woke up, greasily. A sad-faced Selby, dream-vivid, had been confronting me in the door of the *Spectator* men's room, saying "You shouldn't have made Meg step down. We all knew what you were doing. Stay in here or you'll die before you can give your speech." I knew that if I clambered up the doorframe and over him I could get out, and was still straining with my arms, climbing, for several seconds after the room started to come back into focus. I almost slid off the couch, caught myself and winced at the stiff bite in my side.

Bandages or no bandages, I had to shower. I was toweling when I heard the beep that says my cellphone has gotten a message. "Hi, it's Dvorah? Smitty, come on by at three or so if that's OK? We'll be finishing up then. The kids won't be back till six so we can talk about this stuff. It's twelve-twenty South Quince Street? Near the firehouse? Just come on over." I clapped the phone closed, it was one of the newer ones that folds like a clamshell, and looking at my fingers on it thought *prints.*

If someone else used it, there would have been prints.

Why didn't the cops even try to dust for them?

I wondered if any were left and if I had spoiled them. I had not made that call.

I deliberated, then walked damply to the kitchen and put the phone in a sandwich bag. On consideration I peeled several more bags out of the box and packaged everything that had been in my pockets, including my wallet, handling everything by the edges. I folded some spare cash around my driver's license and buttoned it into the hip pocket. It would do until I figured out how to see if prints could be lifted without asking anyone in Flanagan's PD to do it. I don't think blows on the head make you paranoid. It was just starting to come naturally.

*   *   *   *

South Quince Street is only a few blocks above Potter's Run Drive in the twelve-hundred block, and signs up and down the street advised me that if I wanted to park there after seven at night I'd need a zone sticker; overflow from those hive-dense apartments ripples out into the neighborhood when the two or three extra people that aren't supposed to be in each unit all come home. This time of day the curb was pretty empty.

The Darvocet was wearing off but I didn't want to take another one; the pain seemed to be coming back before the buzz left. It made the steps down a slope into a truncated front yard look daunting; I could already feel the jolting in my head.

A glossy, dancer-agile black cat pranced through a small knot of concrete lawn ornaments and regarded me challengingly from the porch, then skipped down as the barred storm door pushed open from the inside. Female voice-over-voice goodbyes and an exaggerated *mmm*-kissy noise preceded three women out onto the short walk, a small woman in what was almost office dress and two taller, one of whom reminded me of a rock-climbing grandmother I'd once featured, one looking as if she could stop a truck by standing in its way, and would like to. Dvorah followed them out. "I'll have the books next week! Cyrus, get out of the way, you little *shit.*" This appeared to be the cat. "Smitty, come iiin. Byeeee!" She had clearly never met a vowel she didn't like. I slid gingerly down the steps, clinging to the rail, nodded to the women—they looked at me guardedly, with murmured hellos—and stepped up on the crumbling cement stoop.

"Oh my gahhd, what *happened* to you? You look *awful!* Come in. We were just finishing up. Are you hurt? What happened?"

"Someone invited himself to the cash in my wallet," I said. "Last night. It looks worse than it is."

"Would you like some pot? It helps me."

"Uh….no."

"Well let me get you some tea."

The kitchen, visible beyond the little, cluttered front room, looked as if the pots and pans from every cooking show on television had been sent there to die. Another large, mottled gray cat was crunching at a dish in front of the breakfast bar. I heard water running and the click of a stove ignition; lowered myself onto a sectional couch that went around the front corner of the room, spanning two windows. A flicking tail below the curtain half drawn back from the side window betrayed the presence of a third cat. Mismatched chairs had been pulled up to make a complete circle around the small coffee table. Another table at the end of the couch held dazzling, chunky crystals that must have cost in the hundreds of dollars, a small menorah, one of the candle glasses from the Botanica, and a recent-looking hardened pool of red wax.

Dvorah sat down across from me and tucked her legs; today she was wearing shorter boots, and a plaid skirt that suggested Catholic school over a black bodysuit. "So what's going on?"

I told her, stepping around the details of where I learned it. "That would probably be someone calling Oshun" she said. "Think Venus? She's for love but money too. It was right down here in the park?"

"Where Potter's Run cuts across near the trail. Right by the water, I'm told."

"Ahhhhh." She reached up to a bookshelf behind her. "I think that means…" She riffled pages. "I don't really do Santeria, but I like Oshun. I like Venus under any name. She's one of the Santeria gods. They got them all mixed up with saints, I think to stick it to the Catholics. I hate that animal sacrificing stuff though. Where IS it?" She tossed the book on the table, rose to range through the bookcase for another one, paused to go in the kitchen and pour water in a teapot, then returned to the shelf. "If you want something, you petition the god in charge—there are special spells for each kind of thing. I saw this one somewhere. You do it by the water, Oshun likes clear running water. Ick, I can't see her coming to *Potters Run.*"

She pulled down a paperback. "Here we go. It was in here." She shuffled a moment. "*If you want a better job or to improve your work, take a diamond chip. Five chips would be best as it is her sacred number. Sacrifice a chicken and let the blood drip over the diamond chip while you* moyuba *Oshun.* Hm, hum…*While she likes gold, her favorite metal is copper…She should be propitiated on a Saturday or on the fifth of the month. Petition Oshun at the river's edge if you do not have the materials for her altar.*" She passed the book to me. "Sound anything like it?"

I thought of Micaela, saying "She do anything to help him succeed." I suspected it had not stopped at green candles. Could I reconcile poised, groomed Elisa de la Roja, an award-winning social worker, with dead chickens at midnight by an abode of rats?…

"Something's really bothering you," said Dvorah. "It's just coming off you in waves. Is there anything I can do to help?"

"Thanks, no, I'm OK…"

She pushed the mug of tea across the table at me. "Would you like me to read for you?"

For a disoriented moment I could only think of bedtime stories. Then I saw she had taken a silk-wrapped packet from the bookshelf, and was lighting two or three sticks of what turned out mercifully to be fairly mild incense. The phone on the end of the bookshelf burbled as she worried the knot out of the silk. She looked at the Caller ID.

"Oh, he's such a *pest.*" She picked it up. "Heyy. Hey, I told you, I have the group this afternoon…no, I *can't* come over. I told you last night. Tomorrow? I have to go, I'm reading for someone." She hung up. "Oh, he drives me *crazy!!!* Okay, here, I'm going to pick a card for you…"

It was an unfamiliar Tarot deck, not that I'm very familiar with any of that kind of thing. I am a rational man, I like to think, no longer an altar boy or anything descended from one, but something about watching her shuffle made me feel defensive. The gray cat came in to observe.

"This is you." She put down a card showing a monklike man with a lantern. "You're trying to find truth. Of course, you're a *news* man. Now crossing you…." she laid another card athwart it. "That's funny, I've never seen the Lovers as a cross card. All right. Behind you three of Swords." She looked up at me with surprising concern. "Did something happen really sad? Or is that just from being *beat* on by those horrible little gangbangers?" She laid another card down. Crisscrossing wooden wands made up most of the picture. "Oh, there's going to be some kind of violent fight—but it won't expose the truth you're looking for. It's a fake fight or at least the real rivalry isn't on the surface." She laid down two more cards, which both showed human figures. "Queen of Cups reversed, a very, very ruthless woman who has laid the ground for what's going on…and an extremely angry man that you're going to encounter, maybe again and again." She slapped down four more in an ascendng row. A juggling figure intrigued her so much she picked up the card and looked at it. "If we were closer to the County Fair I'd say this was about your fair issue. You always like doing the fair issue, don't you?" (True; it was one issue where all we had to do was report that people were having fun.) "But I think this is about deception and game playing. Those are the circumstances you're in. Here's your house—" she touched the next card. "Or where you live in some higher sense. Four of swords." The image pictured was a sculptural tomb: *The grave's a fine and private place, but none I think do there embrace,* I thought unwillingly. She must have seen my expression. "Oh, you're not going to *diiie!* That's where you *already* are. Just out of the world a little. Now here's what you're looking for." The card was a severe figure holding another sword aloft, between twin pillars. "Everyone getting their just deserts. Don't we all wish." She picked up the last one. "And here's what you get. Knight of swords. I think a kind of crazy-brave person is going to help you out, or maybe you'll do something kind of crazy-brave yourself. That isn't bad." She looked up. "Let me get a picture, OK?" She swept into one of the rooms off the hallway, came back with a small digital camera and perched up on the chair over the table. "I'm sooo bad at this. Let's see." She began to snap, look critically in the digital window, and snap again until I was about to tell her not to bother. "I'll send you the best one and you can meditate on it. It's good to meditate on your reading. But you know, you should be really careful of this woman. I don't know who she is, but I bet you do."

I bet I do, I thought.

"And if you know who the Knight is? Make sure he knows you need him. The cards are honest but you help yourself if you make an effort with what they tell you." She opened up the scarf, put the unused cards in its center and was about to sweep up the reading; I leaned forward to get a closer look, jumped as I forgot and leaned my bruised cheek against my hand.

"Are you *sure* I can't help with something?" she said. "Here—sit back. I'll turn it around." She reversed the table mat the cards lay on, pushing it across the table for me to contemplate. In my slightly goofballed state, stiffness holding me against the comfortable couch, I was as happy to peruse a New Age card reading as do anything.

"Let me get you something for that," she said. "I think this will work better than the stupid drugs. Did the cops give you a hard time? I used to have to call them all the time before I got rid of my ex. They yelled at *me*. Like it was *my* fault I got hit. I *hate* cops." She was rummaging in the kitchen again, came out with a bowl of water steaming from the tea kettle and a reasonably clean-looking towel. It was my day for mysterious little vials; this one was full of a murky and herbal-looking solution, and an astringent huff filled the air as she poured from it into the bowl. "Just sit back. This is what I use for Bee and Joey to take the boo-boo out." I must have had a look on my face, because she stopped in midstep and said "Look, I'm a *Jewish mom*, I can't *help* it." That made me laugh—when had I done that?—and I rested my head against the cushion as she arranged the hot cloth against my thick-feeling cheek, then lifted my damaged hand to hold against it.

"That is better," I said after a while.

"See? That's why I've been doing this stuff all my life." She dipped the cloth again and tucked it behind my head, where I had been smacked by what the ER doctors suspected was a leaded sap. Her other hand was resting on my forehead, and stayed there until the towel began to cool.

"You've got a lot going on and this is just the surface part, isn't it?" she said.

"Um…that's newspaper work," I replied, feeling I was having to call across a great distance.

"You're sure I can't help with the other stuff? I won't talk to anyone. I mean I *talk* but I know what to keep quiet about. I'm a Minerval Order in the OTO." She eased the towel out from behind my head, touched the puffed cheek gingerly. It did feel less tender. "You know what I think, I should kiss it better." She was kneeling on the cushion next to me, and I went nearly rigid, arresting a gasp as my ribs twinged, to feel her cup my unhurt cheek in one hand and press her lips softly against the other. The faint but not unpleasant greasy smell of lipstick reached me; my glasses, the ill-fitting black-rimmed spare pair, nudged into my nose. She pulled them off.

"I think you little guys with these birth-control glasses are just ticking away like tiny time bombs," she chuckled. Her lips touched both my eyelids in turn. I became aware I was opening and closing my mouth like a grouper in a fishtank, no words making themselves available for the occasion. Her cheek slid down along mine and she stopped the grouper movement by kissing me in earnest, something that made me feel as if I had suddenly achieved weightlessness. I pressed a palm into the cushion to be sure I was not starting to float. She drew back and ran her fingers down to rest on my collarbone.

"And those little woolly argyle *vests*. That is absolutely what Mom dressed you in to go to junior high school, isn't it?" She undid the buttons, slid the vest back across my shirtfront and felt the tape strapping my ribs. "Oww, you didn't even *tell* me about this!" The perfectly matched, parlor nails flicked open shirt buttons and traced the edges of the layered tape. "Oh, that must hurt something awful." Her lips started at the top of the tape and began to work along its edges. I rested the unhurt hand on her head, half wondering if I should push her away, but she trapped my hand with her own instead. She only let go when she got to a point where the bandage ducked under my slacks; she was clearly determined to work all the way around the damage. I tried to lift up to make it easier for her; she slid to her knees on the floor and pushed me back against the couch softly with one finger.

"You just relax," she said. "I'll handle everything."

And she did, for quite some time. I made a few feeble protests at first, involving the kids coming home and the half-shaded window, but found my fingers once more laced tight in those of the hand that wasn't busy, wondering what she would say once she started talking again. The view out the window was full of clouds and flowers, and except for the black cat, who jumped up on the outside sill quite late in the proceedings, I don't really think anyone could have seen in.

*   *   *   *

I was halfway home before I noticed my ribs actually had stopped hurting. My head was clear, too, and my hand on the wheel flexed painlessly. I thumbed my cheek experimentally; it felt about like your shin might a week after cracking it, no worse. "Magic can be very simple," she had said, her eyes sparkling, showing me out. Medical science reeled. So did I, and I waited through two cycles of a light before someone drove up honking behind me and nearly pushed me through the intersection. I indulged in deep breaths the rest of the way home.

CHAPTER SIX
THE BOXER

"I still don't think this is a good idea," said Ryan Tabor, pulling out of the traffic horseshoe in front of my condo. "You were going to stay home. *That* was the good idea."

"How wrong can it go?" I said. "If I pass out, we're right at the hospital. It's *better* than being home by myself. Besides, I feel fine." I did, and it was spooky. I felt almost artificially bright and brittle and apprehensive at the same time. Underneath our conversation, my mind was racing, and I didn't want to watch the movement too closely. Trying to pay attention to an evening at the Civic Federation would ground me if nothing else did.

"Okay, okay. At least you let me drive." This was a concession. Ryan's car was a walking and talking midden of archaeological stature; I had once with my own eyes seen a paper on the back floorboard dated 1993, sticking out from under the passenger seat. I didn't look too closely at what he tossed into the back to make room for me in said seat. Well, there was cat hair on my clothes already, I thought fatalistically.

The usual suspects were accumulating in the hospital auditorium—another one of those comfy little developer gifts that Arlington periodically absorbs. The hospital also hosts Lamaze classes on Tuesday nights, so occasionally a spectacularly gravid woman would cut through the crowd, often with a husband, carrying blankets, in tow. One of them jostled me and I backed into Perry Reardon.

"Hey, Smitty," he said, handing me a *Taxpayer Watchdog* as if I hadn't last seen him throwing up into a wastebin next to a dead body.

"I'm—uh—glad to see you made it," I said, looking over the cartoon-laced list of budget peccadilloes.

"Gotta carry on, Smitty. Gotta carry on." But I could tell his usual bonhomie, which characteristically involved nuggets of lurid and usually unfounded gossip, had departed him for the moment. He leaned to right and left as we talked, passing issues of the newsletter to Federation delegates and a few annoyed pregnant women. "I read your story. Good job. I heard the Board liked it too."

Sharp tones carried across the lobby to me. Schulz was standing in the inner doorway to the auditorium; I thought of the last call on my tape last night and felt cold. He was having a fervid but not quite audible set-to with Pastorelli, who seemed, not for the first time, to be counseling him to keep cool. As I watched Schulz waved his hands in a gesture that was more than dismissive, Pastorelli answered with an echoing gesture of total futility and walked back out into the lobby. "Brother Perry. Smitty." He looked down closely at me through his bottle-bottom glasses. "You been dukin'?"

"Walked into a door," I said thinly. At the moment, it looked no worse than that; bruises and swelling that should have taken the rest of the week to go down were resolved to one dark mouse on my cheekbone and a scrape half hidden by my glasses.

"We're trying to get some questions to throw at Murphy," he said. "It's narrowing the list down that sucks. Are you doing the piece or is Ryan?"

"Mutual project," I said. "He's doing the copy but I just wanted to keep my hand in." I deliberated. "You were going to tell me something else the other day."

"Yeah, uh—do you want to go in?"

I took the plunge. "Can you talk now?"

He paused, shrugged. "I don't have anything to present till later and I've heard Murphy run his gums. What?"

I withdrew into a corner that held a few empty chairs and a baleful-looking plant. "The black magic thing that Phyllis was talking about," I said carefully. "I found out a little more about it. And...well, I didn't walk into a door. Someone mugged me last night."

He took in whistling air through his front teeth.

"The same someone *might* have then called the police to come get me," I continued. "And *might* have known I was working on more than was in my lead piece about Hector. Because I was missing something when I got out of the ER. They don't know it's on my computer already. I hope."

He went dead serious and quiet—something that rarely happens with Pastorelli, who is either indulging the bogus brand of fat-boy humor that makes Caparici's eyes mist up when his name is mentioned, or pounding the podium with exaggerated bombast. But I had judged the right nerve to touch—for a man who loved to see his name and even his caricature in the paper, he loved a secret more.

"Or it might have *been* the cops," I said carefully. His eyes narrowed. It is a risk to say anything bad about the police to Angelo Pastorelli, except in certain narrow contexts. "Because there are some things involved that Ed Flanagan would hate to have to deal with in public. Angelo. You were in Boston when he had a department up there. What kind of outfit was it?"

Angelo glanced toward the auditorium, then back to me with a very sober face.

"It was a department that wasn't above a little ass-kickin'." he said. "But punks. Pimps. Not reporters."

"Bent cops?"

"We busted one for violating his wife's restraining order dressed as an Avon lady. I guess that's pretty bent."

People were filing into the auditorium; while we were talking Congressman Murphy had come in, and his tall, looming, wide-shouldered figure half-filled the entrance as he talked to Dan Kravitz, the Civic Federation President, who looks about twelve and has about a twelve-year-old's leadership presence. Ryan caught up to them as they were about to move down toward the podium, notebook out; Murphy nodded to Kravitz, turned to answer Ryan's questions. Probably because of him, they had a full house tonight. As Ryan stepped back, nodding thanks, Murphy glanced past him into the lobby, and our eyes met for a moment. I registered a look of what was almost surprise, and not happy surprise; ever since his last couple of personal scandals—I think the hair-pulling women were in a way his worst embarrassment—Murphy has tended to look like a deer in the headlights in public at the best of times, and around the press it gets worse. Seeing nearly the whole senior staff of the *Spectator* in one place clearly made him nervous. Well, good.

I turned back to Pastorelli. "I need to find out something and it's police work that I can't turn over to the police," I said. "It's a long shot. Probably a dead end. But I really want something fingerprinted."

A surprisingly wide smile spread over Pastorelli's face. "Ahhh," he said. "I know who can help you. It just so happens....but you'll have to wait a while."

He didn't elaborate. I could hear Kravitz turning over the podium to Murphy; we paused to listen as he greeted the Federation delegates, thanked them for inviting him to this meeting, and said that he wanted to preface tonight's remarks by honoring the memory...De la Roja had been Murphy's staffer for years, so that was to be expected. Before long he had segued into patting himself and his staff on the back for the great things they had done for the Congressional district this past year.

"Let's go listen to Moron Murphy for a while, okay?" Pastorelli said. "Then it will be my pleasure."

I followed him into the auditorium. We made as if I had been getting a statement from him, notebook and all; probably a bad move, because seeing that notebook out brings a certain kind of citizen like honey draws flies. I spent the next ten minutes being told about the failure of traffic calming in one of the Metro neighborhoods by a small woman with an indeterminate accent who had perfect the art of speaking without breathing, so that I finally had to duck into the men's room to escape.

"Mr. Schulz," Kravitz was saying as I came out, in a flustered student-council president's voice. "Mr. Schulz, I'm going to have to ask you to sit down. We agreed that any delegate could ask Congressman Murphy one question. You are over time, Mr. Schulz..." I sidled into the back near where Pastorelli was standing, glancing around defensively for the traffic calming lady. Kravitz was losing the fight as Schulz shouted "This is a campaign appearance! It's biased! Where is the equal time for rival candidates? Where is the Republican candidate?" (Good question; they hadn't yet found one.)

"Mr. Schulz!!!" Kravitz tried to shout, his voice cracking instead like a tense choirboy's. Hectic little spots were rising in his downy cheeks. Before he could succumb to complete frustration, one of the Caerleon Park delegates, a former Navy pilot who I judged wasn't scared of much, approached Schulz and began speaking softly to him. Schulz was about to sit down, but the pilot walked him up the opposite aisle and out into the lobby, talking quickly, I think just to prevent Schulz answering and keep him engaged more than to say anything. I looked at Pastorelli whose eyes had rolled to heaven.

"One of these days he really is going to shoot up the boardroom," he said.

Murphy finished praising himself for his annual women's conference, his newsletter and his Congressman's Roundtable on local cable. You would think he had never been investigated for taking drug company money on the eve of Medicare legislation, accepting sweetheart loans, or roughing up (at different times) his wife, a constituent, a ten-year-old kid, and one of his colleagues on the House floor. You would think, too, that the Republicans could run an opossum and kick the man out of office, but as Mark Lewis, then the party chairman, once said to me, "Smitty, I'd put someone *out* there if I could find anyone to the left of Oliver Cromwell." At this point, Schulz was his most viable opponent, which was scary.

There was a brief break, after which, Kravitz reminded us, there would be a question and answer period with Board member Hugh Sprague on water safety, then voting on the Metro corridor development initiative (Federation votes are non-binding but put citizen sentiment on record) and the Caerleon Park traffic calming project. Ah, the stuff of my paper, the pulse of civic life, the reason Meg was in Chicago…I felt the no longer painful spot on my cheek and bit my lip.

"You all right?" Pastorelli next to me, looking at his watch.

"Yeah. Goose over my grave." I looked out into the lobby. Schulz was getting animated again with the Caerleon Park president; with his wavy, thick silver hair, wrists popping out of buttoned cuffs, khaki shorts and sandals, long legs knobbed with bone and roped with narrow muscle, he looked like one of those kids' games where you assemble parts of different figures to get a laugh. As we stepped through the doorway, he went shrill again; he was turning an ugly purple-gray color. "*Fuck* you! *Fuck* your bipartisanship!! Haven't you figured out it's a big fucking machine??" Kravitz was hurrying up the aisle, saying in his schoolboy voice, "Jim, that's *it*. I'm going to have to ask you to leave the building." "I might as well, no one listens to me," snapped Schulz. He turned and started to push his way through the bodies in the lobby. It was only bum luck, I guess, that he rounded the obtuse corner by the restrooms and collided with Murphy. His clipboard and papers went everywhere.

"I'm sorry," began Murphy diplomatically, though he didn't look a bit regretful. Schulz dropped to one knee to scrabble for his effects. "Yeah, I bet!" he said. "Just like you're sorry you put up your little machine buddies around here to intimidate the opposition! You think knocking one of them off wasn't a public service? Everyone knows you're corrupt, everyone knows you're a thug—" Though this last was too close to the truth for comfort, Murphy did the only thing I would have wanted him to do, which was turn away as if Schulz was nothing more articulate than a barking dog. Just at that moment Reardon crossed my path. A second later there was a fleshy *smack* and the bomblike noise of the lobby coffee urn capsizing off the literature table.

Screams, hubbub and a discordantly appetizing smell of hot java. I tried to push Reardon aside, which was about like trying to push a minivan, and dodged under his arm instead. Schulz was picking himself up off the floor by the urn, blood streaming from between the fingers clapped over his nose. Hugh Sprague was pulling on Murphy's arm, not very successfully; the fists that had once boxed Golden Gloves were both clenched, the meaty knuckles thick and tufted with white hair.

Pastorelli at my elbow was calling 911 before Schulz was fully on his feet. I wanted to tell Schulz to stop it right there, he was hopelessly outclassed, but he shouted, spraying blood onto neighboring suit jackets and agendas, "That's right! Show them the fist in the glove! The only way you've stayed in office is intimidation and—" He was thrusting a pointing finger into Murphy's face as he spoke, and at the third thrust Murphy caught his forearm and yanked him sideways off his feet, like someone starting a lawnmower. This time the Navy pilot and Lenny Gore from Aurora Heights, who is an ex-Marine like Murphy himself, both got a solid grip on Murphy's elbows and frog-marched him backwards away from where Schulz had landed hard on both bare knees. No one went to him until, muttering "Oh, shit," under his breath, Pastorelli reluctantly stepped over and lifted him into a chair.

Hugh Sprague, pale but poised, moved to stand in the sightline between Murphy and Schulz. "He went for me," Murphy was saying thickly. "You're a witness. He went for me." "I think you'd better just sit down, Brian," said Hugh.

Cremora from a broken jar was now mingling with the coffee on the floor, making a fragrant mucilage. A roll of paper towels had landed just at the edge of the puddle, and when the medic crew, closely followed by police, came in the hospital lobby, Schulz was holding a moist wad of them over his face while Pastorelli, who had worked ambulance in Boston (he never tired of talking about it), probed his knees for damage. People were streaming out of the lobby so thickly that Phyllis Bell had to push to get in. She caught Pastorelli's eye.

"Well hell," she said. "Looks like I missed all the excitement."

"Oh no, Phyl," said Pastorelli, leaving Schulz to the medics. "I think it's just beginning." He looked at me. "You wanna stay here and watch them handcuff a Congressman before we go to work on your little problem? Or you wanna leave that to Ryan?"

"Uh, I think this is something I ought to stay for."

"Good," he said, rubbing his hands together. "I been hoping to watch this for years. Pass the popcorn."

*   *   *   *

A breeze and a little rain had come up half an hour later. We'd been chivvied out of the lobby but no one said we couldn't stand in the parking lot. The rear door of the nearest cruiser had just slammed, drowning out what Phyllis was saying.

"I said," she repeated when I raised my hand to my ear, "that I always expected to see that but I never thought Jim Schulz would be the one to get it done."

"Murphy in the bracelets. My, my, my," crooned Pastorelli. I have rarely seen a happier man.

"I guess we're not going to vote on traffic calming?" said Phyllis rather drily.

"Better than that," said Pastorelli. "Smitty here is going to lose his buddy Ryan, and we're going to take him back to your place and see if your friend Marlaine is on duty."

There was a brief silence. "Oh, I see. I don't think we're going to get to bed anytime soon then, are we?" Phyllis said.

"Nope," said Pastorelli." "But it's getting to be worth it."

✳   ✳   ✳   ✳

I left Ryan interviewing Hugh Sprague. He looked relieved that I had found another ride; he clearly intended to be around here a while.

"I parked down the bottom," said Phyllis. "You keep sayin' walk more. This about does it for me." She moves deliberately, almost in slow motion, but comfortably, as if she comes from a world where things are not as urgent.

A few car doors were still slamming; some were closing behind people coming to the hospital late—relatives in the ER, perhaps, or late visiting hours. A little generic compact slid into a space below us; a woman got out. For a brief moment her face turned up into the streetlight. I felt my heart jump out of my chest.

"Meggie?" I called uncertainly. She glanced curiously in our direction. I realized these glasses were old, and the drizzle and flickering sodium-vapor light nearest the car made her image swim. I had read Meg into her, still glassy with vague guilt and confusion, and the incontrovertible absence of pain in my head and the presence of a lightness in my body that should have had nothing to do with anyone but Meg. Her face turned back toward the fairground lights of the two cop cruisers remaining by the auditorium entrance; after a moment she got back in and ramped the tiny engine.

"Citizens of the Great White North End of the county finally faced with street violence," said Pastorelli. "Maybe we'll get some action on gangs now. Starting with the Democrats."

I slid into the back seat of Phyllis' car. It was only half as cluttered as Ryan Tabor's, and comfortably larger.

*   *   *   *

Phyllis' front room was a frightening extravaganza of commemorative ceramics, needlepoint chatchkas, and what I assumed were dog toys scattered over the floor. "Let me go let Fang out in the yard," she said. "I been out all evenin'." She progressed past a formal dining room filled with cartons of file folders and stacks of envelopes, almost covering an antique drop-leaf table and a marble-topped sideboard. I dropped into a recliner diapered with crochet antimacassars. There was little else I could do, as a step in any direction would have collided me with something.

The door slammed. "Now, Marlaine is on shift till midnight," came Phyllis' voice. "So we got time for you to explain why I should bug her. You want sweet tea?"

I don't remember saying yes, but presently she emerged from the kitchen and found a place for a glass amidst the bric-a-brac on the phone table next to me. In the dining room I could hear the faint crackle of a police radio scanner. "I'd better start at the beginning," I said, and did—up to the point, at least, where I'd had my thought about the cell phone. "I could be off the wall, but it seems to me they deliberately missed something there. Either they know damn well the call didn't come from this phone, or they wiped it, if they bothered, or there may be some prints on it that don't belong there. I admit, it's a long shot. I just don't trust Flanagan's department to help me with that little question."

Phyllis, who was in the recliner opposite me, smiled. "Well, now, not *everyone* on that department is an ass-kisser," she said. "You just have to know who to ask." She picked up the phone, waited through a couple of rings. "Marlaine. How you doin' tonight?"

"—"

"Good. Hey, I got a chance for you to play with your toys. You on the usual shift tonight?"

"—"

"Well that's entirely fine. We'll be here." She put the phone back in its cradle. "Once upon a time there was a beat cop who wanted to train as an evidence technician," she said. "Better hours, less exhaustin' social life with little punks. And once upon a time, there was a horse's ass of a chief who yanked some folks out of training because he couldn't keep enough regular cops on the force on account of bein' a horse's ass. Marlaine don't talk. She'll be along directly."

"And she can...?" I was getting a glimmer.

"She got some skills, she likes to keep em current," said Phyllis. "She can dust your little phone there and go sort of, well, extracurricular with the results. I don't ask how she keeps it off the record; everyone's gotta have their secrets. Now tell me a little more about this Botanica crap. Sounds like you got a little more light on it than I do by now."

I described some of my conversation with Dvorah, dancing around the way our encounter had ended, though I thought I saw a twinkle of dry humor in Phyllis' eyes when I described the less relevant parts of our talk as "uh, palm reading and fortunetelling."

"So Hector's wife was a regular at that place, and if Dvorah knows what she's talking about, which she seems to" (I heard Pastorelli snort) "someone's been doing Hispanic success charms, right about the time Betty Bravo had to move aside to let Hector take the chair. I mean, the magic part is hooey" (I wasn't sure how certain I sounded there), "but people who'll do things like that usually aren't squeamish about pushing the limit on the practical side either."

"And here Hector was trying to be such a—what's a beaner Oreo? A Tippy's Taco?" Phyllis made a face at Pastorelli, who shrugged, charmed at his own wit.

"I suppose he couldn't help his family."

"I sure can't. Why should he?" Pastorelli drained his tea glass. "Look at me. GS 13 Department of Justice. Cop. Ambulance Service. I got a little punk cousin breaks legs for the mob, you know how that looks on my security check? Dio Del Ricci could talk shop with any of the gangbangers on the Pike, and here I am trying to protect the citizens. Every time I go home I have to make sure the little bastard is under control, and boy, doesn't he hate my guts for it. You can't pick your family, you just gotta deal with em."

"Directly" was about an hour. We tuned in local cable and watched a short standup newsflash in front of the police station telling the world that the local Congressman had been arrested and charged with assault on a civic activist, tucked in between a report of wires down somewhere in Fairfax and a piece on water testing. The knock on the door made me jump.

"I think Fang wants to come in," said the woman who entered without waiting to be let in. "Want me to go get her?"

"Sure," said Phyllis. I felt some trepidation.

Marlaine was chunky, without pushing the department's fitness limits, and the tackle at her belt made her chunkier. She turned sidewise in a couple of spots to bypass the clutter. I heard the rear door open and a jingle of tags. "Go! Catch!" came her voice. A fluffy soft toy flew into the room. A staccato click of nails on parquet preceded a small white toy poodle, weighing about ten pounds, who hurled herself on the fluffy toy, shook it, declared it killed, and trotted up to Phyllis with it.

Phyllis must have seen my stricken expression. She smiled indulgently and tossed the dog a chewy treat. "Fang would probably lose a fight with Taxasaurus." This was one of Pastorelli's props, a dinosaur puppet that appeared every budget cycle.

"So," said Marlaine with a twinkle. "You going to tell me why this town's melting down? Course, I think we're finally doing some things right and arresting the politicians."

"Long time coming," said Pastorelli. Phyllis leaned forward.

"You know Paige Smith here? Puts out the little *Spectator* paper on Wednesdays."

"I read it. Pleased t' meetcha."

She reached out a thick hand. I shook it.

"Smitty needs a little help and he doesn't trust your boss. You got your face powder with you?"

"Happen I do. Camera's in the car. What you want done?"

"Phone," said Phyllis. Marlaine was already out the door. By the time she returned I had the sandwich bags out.

"Smitty met someone who didn't like him much last night," said Phyllis.

"Yeah, I kinda saw that."

"Funny thing is, once they messed him around a little, someone called it in and he says it wasn't him. Looks like his mighta been the only phone on the scene. Think we can figure out if anyone else's prints are on it? Or any of his other stuff?"

"I can do that," said Marlaine. "Pass her over. Phyllis, for crying out loud, I need some table."

"All *right*." Phyllis rose, rearranged some piles in the dining room to make workspace. Marlaine opened a tin of black, fine powder, and took a sheet of typing paper from a nearby stack to make a work surface. "Probably can't do the outside of the wallet without iodine or something, but we'll try."

"We'll need to print you too," she said as she worked, flicking the powder over the surfaces of my phone, the clear windows of my wallet, the exposed surfaces of credit cards, using a fine brush. "I got the stuff for that. OK." Pastorelli was watching keenly as she began a fussy process of fiddling with squares of some kind of clear adhesive and a sheaf of index cards, humming and occasionally uttering a higher-pitched noise that seemed to be some form of "Eureka."

Finally she began to snap pictures at point-blank distance, taking shots of every card until I was forcibly reminded of Dvorah hunkered over my card reading. A few minutes later, my hands were smudged and she had a final neat card drying under the desklamp. "We'll see what matches up. If I find something that doesn't fit, I can run em. Let's say I have a secret identity."

"Works for me."

She finished cleaning the sooty dust off the phone and tossed it back to me. "OK, now you can mess it up all you want." I flipped it open and spent a few minutes checking messages, reaching to reclaim my wallet, keyring, the eyedrop bottle as I did so. No Elisa. Sighing, I called Ryan's number.

Amazingly, he answered. "Smitty. You were going home. If you don't trust me, I can't help you, as the joke says."

"I do trust you. There's a thing or two I need from you, but what's going on?"

"Well, I trailed em to the station. It's a free country. I could always be going to the late show at the multiplex."

"Uh huh. Did they book him?"

"Misdemeanor assault. That's a first, isn't it?" Murphy's history of fisticuffs has been disastrous, but he'd never been arrested yet, even the time he shook his wife so hard by the shoulders that police scuttlebutt said you could see where each finger had been. "They set bail pretty low. First offense, ha ha, and where's he going to go? But it made a statement. Anyway they booked Schulz too. Disorderly conduct. Own recognizance. I guess because he never laid a finger on the Right Honorable."

I sucked in air through my teeth. This was going to be one of my most enjoyable Murphy editorials since the election when I had suggested that people hold their noses to vote for him; it only hurt that tomorrow's edition had already gone to bed, well before I would.

"And *then* someone kind of screwed the pooch and let Schulz cross Murphy's path before his cab got there. I tell you, Smitty, that boy does not *learn*. I guess it didn't help it's starting to rain Snickers bars. Here's Schulz, I have no idea where he was going or who he was waiting for, I couldn't stay on both of 'em, sees Murphy pass under a light, yells 'How does it feel to get rained on just like one of the commoners?' Murphy's not as slow a learner, he looks once and looks away, Schulz keeps yelling, 'One of these days you'll find out, they'll all find out'—I think I'm getting this right—*lady, make up your mind, they only have three colors"* [I assumed this involved a traffic light Ryan was negotiating]— "he says, 'You'll find out some people can get what you have without buying it, you don't know the half of what I know about you.' The cab or excuse me limo pulled up at that point. I'd say that was one thing Schulz wasn't going to get without buying it."

Sounded like vintage Schulz, and not the kind of thing our readers thank us for—people pick up our paper to read high school football scores and be reassured their streets are being maintained. I was nodding. I had to remember the important part.

"Ryan. I don't know if I'll make it in before the funeral. If you're in before I am?"

"Yeah?"

"Boot up at my desk and download my e-mail. If anything comes in from Mrs. Hector de la Roja, anything that *looks* like it's from her, read it and call my cell. I'll be in when I can. I need to hear from her. Then get to a document file called REMARKSFORSAT and print it out and put it somewhere safe, all right?"

"You got it. Now go pack it in, Smitty, for chrissakes."

"I'd have done it this morning if someone hadn't hit me on the head."

"Go. To. Bed." Ryan rang off. I looked up. Marlaine was gone. Pastorelli was on Phyllis' land line, giving the address for a cab.

"Me and Fang are going to call it a night," said Phyllis. "Angelo'll drop you home."

"I'll expense it," I said.

The back seat of the cab smelled like a cheap hotel room that was trying and failing to be clean. Pastorelli gave his address, which turned out to be about three blocks short of mine. The streets were glossy with rain, and empty, a few cars crawling along Liberty Pike. As we waited at an unnecessary light, nothing approaching from any direction, Pastorelli said "I was going to tell you something Saturday, once I got it straight in my head. Don't know if it means anything now. It was Brother Rearend I got it from. You know he has this thing for Bravo. Don't *ask* me, I don't know what anyone sees in Bravo."

"Him especially," I said, since Bravo hardly ever met a tax hike she wouldn't ask to lunch.

"You know he's retired Federal, maybe if you're big as two people they retire you in half the time? Stays up all night surfing the Net and putting together the *Watchdog*. One night last month, it was after that last late recess meeting, he gets hungry at two a.m., goes down to Bill and Evie's the other end of the Pike. He's on his way in when he sees Bravo sitting in one of the booths. He'd know her anywhere, he says."

I thought of my Meg-fantasy earlier that night and wasn't sure. "That's a pretty long shot. *Betty Bravo* in Bill and Evie's?" The original diner was older than the Pentagon, and some people said that the cooking fat was too. I would as much expect to find Betty Bravo, born in a Gucci suit, eating in Bill and Evie's as I would look for her in line at the Bodega Blanca.

"She was with a guy, and that got him all twisted up. You know, one thing if your dream woman is home with her husband at two a.m., different thing if she's splitting a baconburger with some guy in a greasy spoon on the Pike. He said the first thing he thought was Mark Lewis but I told him no, Brother Perry, there's some things even Mark won't touch. I thought he was going to quit speaking to me then but you know, people got to tell their story. He says it was de la Roja. So he didn't go in."

I could think of nothing to say. The cab pulled up in a canyon between two high-rises. I reached into my pocket, waved Pastorelli aside.

"*Spectator*'ll pay for this one. I may want to call you for a witness sometime. Ryan says I'm cheap."

"Cheap is good," said Pastorelli. "But aren't you down off Courthouse?"

"I'll walk."

"You'll get frickin wet."

"I'll manage." Somehow, getting rained on sounded good.

"Anyway," said Pastorelli. I realized his story wasn't over.

"Yeah?"

"She went away mad. I mean they weren't arguing, but you could tell she wasn't happy. I was just saving the story, never waste intel. But I thought I better tell you, for what it's worth."

The cab whished off through the gathering rain, wipers clocking. "When I wake up, maybe it'll mean something."

"Gnight."

By the time I got back to my condo walking didn't seem as brilliant an idea. I undressed in the kitchen, where the floor was linoleum and it didn't matter that I was standing in a puddle by the time I was done. Handily, my towel was still hanging over a chair where I'd tossed it aside to bag the cell phone, about a hundred years ago. That made me think to eye the answering machine as I wound it around me. Still nothing. I picked up the receiver and tried my office voice mail one more time. No Elisa de la Roja. But now I could think of a whole other reason why she might be hanging around the Botanica, at least where her husband was concerned.

Sleep was dreamless. I didn't wake up until a neighbor's clock radio started playing at quarter to seven. I was going to make it in to the office well ahead of Hector's funeral, for which, in garishly poor taste, the sun was shining.

CHAPTER SEVEN
ALL FLESH IS GRASS

Selby met me in the gravel lot. The light hadn't been repaired yet. He caught me looking at it as we went in.

"You never did see who jumped you?"

"Glasses came off first thing. I don't even know how many there were." I looked up the aisle between desks to my station in the back—we are not grand enough for me to have my own office, but a bulletin-board partition keeps out the distractions on two sides. Someone was moving there; after a trepidation I saw it was Ryan.

"Good news and bad news," he said as I approached. "Yes, you got some e-mail from *elisaroja@earthlink.net*. Bad news part, when I clicked on it the system locked up. I tried to reboot and now that's all the damn thing'll do, reboot. Virus in it, I guess."

"Shit," breathed Selby.

"I shut it down. I don't think it got into the rest of the network. Sean'll be in this afternoon, he should be able to figure it out."

"You think this is an accident?" said Selby after Ryan went back to his desk with the notepad from last night. Another story to dance around; local congressman beats daylights out of local nut. That would look superb next to the Soroptimist Awards and the Wayland-Woodley neighborhood stream cleanup day.

"You think Elisa's a secret computer criminal?" I said. "Shel, I'm the one who got hit on the head."

"You think Elisa's the only one who can send you e-mail from Elisa? Last week my brother's kid got into his account and sent the whole family suggestions for his birthday present."

"I don't think they had kids."

Selby shrugged. "Well, call her."

I did. I shouldn't have been surprised to get the machine again. This was the day her husband was being buried, after all. I said as much to Selby.

"Someone doesn't want the stuff that was on that disk to get out, boss. We don't know who. It ain't rocket science to figure you'd save it to your hard drive. Just watch your *back*, okay?"

I didn't know how to watch my back. I thought about Marlaine's uniformed bulk as she dusted for prints.

"Should have just hired her to follow me around," I said.

Selby looked curiously at me and said nothing.

A little more rain had blown up by the time we got to the church. It felt almost as if we had traveled a closed loop back to Sunday, except that everyone was much more formally dressed and flowers, some tied with the colors of El Salvador, were everywhere. The Friedmans were still flanking Mercedes and Elisa de la Roja—Hector had always been Friedman's particular protege, and Grover looked as if he might not have slept since Saturday, his usually genial, mustached face (Selby said it belonged on a spaghetti can) colorless and tired. The rest of the Board had formed up on either side of them. Hugh, the tallest, looked oddly displaced, without his partner today. Betty Bravo was wearing an iron grey dress, as if to say that even convention could not force her to fade to absolute black.

Mark Lewis, as the most recent past Board member, seemed to have gotten an honorary place in the row. The lady lawyer was with him today; he looked rumpled as if he had gotten up late, and dressed in a hurry. Murphy loomed off in a pew to the right, forward of the Board but at the same time almost furtive. I judged it had been less than twelve hours from the booking officer to the church door.

Selby looked over the rest of the crowd. "Wonder what would happen if I yelled *'Imigracion!!'?*" he said.

"Shel." I winced.

"Us niggaz get an extra annual allowance of remarks like that." If you mention, for instance, rap a pained look will pass over Selby's face, but now and then he throws me that kind of curve. I knew it was nerves.

There was a not-so-subtle police presence in the church, to include Flanagan in full uniform in the pew behind the Board, alongside the County Manager, fire chief, and Toni Messner. Less identifiable members of the department were standing in the back in plainclothes, almost casually, as if they had simply come in late and didn't want to push to the front, but I could spot a bulge where one of them needed to consult his tailor. I recognized the woman who had interviewed me at the hospital.

A little click of heels announced Sophie, who had a small tape recorder strapped over her shoulder in a tiny handbag. "Paige," she said. "I heard about the other night. Are you—"

I cut her off before she could whip up any more empathy. "Nothing serious," I stage-whispered. "Sophie, I need you to get a word with the family. Just ask Mrs. de la Roja to talk to me if you can grab her before the cortege leaves? Tell her it's about what she sent me. She'll understand."

Sophie nodded. The music shifted, and I won't bore you with where my mind wandered while the service progressed.

Dispersal after the ceremony was muted. The family and de la Roja's closest colleagues were proceeding to the cemetery; that made a sizable procession, and the rest of us were left in a faint limbo as it formed up out of the parking lot. I used the time to interview people who had either worked with the dead man, or could have expected to.

"Spider" Walters was affable if a bit unnerving to look at, the head of one of the two main housing contractors. He was skinny and had an unctuous funeral-director's manner that put him right at home in the surroundings. "We were very much looking forward to working with Hector," he said. "A very impressive advocate for his community. Sad, sad, sad. I can't think who could have done something that desperate. No one disliked him. It'll turn out to have been someone who wasn't all there."

"He certainly wasn't there when the cops arrived," I said drily.

"Oh, you press people. I suppose you get hardened."

"Sometimes. Mr. Walters, had Mr. de la Roja talked to you about any plans to overhaul the low-income housing system in the county? A couple of people have suggested to me that he had some very ambitious plans. I'm sure you would have been the first person he consulted."

"Nothing that I knew of in that line, nothing at all. In fact our discussions all centered on how well the current agencies were working with what they had. I do think he had hopes of attracting more funds for some of the present projects. There was some talk of a developer buying Hadley Terrace, for instance, but with a decent allocation, the county could purchase it outright to avoid displacing hundreds of tenants."

Hadley Terrace was what one cop I interviewed at a crime scene called "job security." One of the September 11 terrorists had actually been living there for a while on county grant money; a couple of renters had been booted out, after great raising of dust, for running extortionate hot-flops where illegal immigrants bunked around the clock, according to the shifts they worked.

"I see," I said.

"Put in on record that we think of Hector as our friend and a grievous loss."

I scratched on my pad as if to make it official. Walters withdrew. I looked out into the drizzle and found myself standing next to Chief Flanagan.

"Mr. Smith," he said. My paper has not been terribly kind to him, and I half expected him to ignore me.

"Chief." I was looking for Sophie, and for Selby who had gone off to shoot the floral tributes.

"You're looking well. I had heard there was an unfortunate incident."

"Not as bad as you might have heard," I said carefully. "I lost some cash and a little skin but nothing else."

He seemed to be sizing me up. "Yes, I see. Well, with this very high-profile situation going on, let me apologize in advance if you have any difficulty maintaining contact with the officer in charge of the case. Please let me know if anything is a problem."

You could almost see him lift an inch out of his shoes with the words "high-profile situation." I realized now he was gazing out over the damp parking lot towards the local cable truck that had parked at the end of the row and a small clutch of photographers—the Post, Times and a Spanish-language weekly—who were capturing the cortege. I spotted Selby.

"Let's step outside," said the chief. You could see he was laying a straight course for the little cluster of cameras. "I'd like to personally speak to the escort officers."

"Can I interview you later…."

"Absolutely—call my press offic…"

"…for a piece on the gang situation in the Potters Run area? You could say it's gotten personal now."

He looked at the gravel, arranged his face in a small smile that belonged on a Halloween mask of a politician.

"I don't think you necessarily need to immediately think of gangs," he said. "We have really seen very little evidence of organization in the County."

Selby came chugging up at that moment and Flanagan escaped towards the motorcycle cops bringing up the rear of the line, and not coincidentally towards the newsmen photographing them.

"We going to the cemetery?" he said.

I shook my head. The family had requested no press at the interment. Motorcycles blatted and squirted gravel in several directions, including some at Sophie, who jumped, almost turned her ankle and clipped across the lot to us.

"Paige, I did try," she said. "In Spanish. I said I was sorry beyond words for their loss, and so was my boss, and he had called several times and hoped he wasn't bothering the Senora but at her convenience…well, it was like the minute I started speaking, Friedman and his wife practically body blocked me. 'These ladies aren't up to talking to reporters,' he said. But I'd just *seen* them with Friedman, talking to the Post guy."

"Did they say anything?"

"Not a word. But the young one, the sister, she kind of lit up when she heard me speak Spanish. I don't think she speaks any English. Poor kid."

We split up, Sophie to her car and Selby and I to his.

"You find out anything?" he said, pulling out of the lot.

"Yeah. De la Roja adored Arlington Residence Gateway, and we don't have gangs in the county."

He snorted, turning up the wipers. "Bets?"

"And he was going to see if he could throw more money at Hadley Terrace."

"I *personally* heard him say he hated that place. Talking to your buddy the dinosaur man, when they cut the ribbon on that senior place in Cherrywood."

The office was churning in a midday hum that felt more normal than anything had since Saturday. Sean was seated at my desk, muttering "Shit!" under his breath as the computer began to go through the restart cycle, probably not the first or fifteenth time since he'd started working.

"This is a *bugger*," he said when he saw me approaching. "It's not strictly speaking a virus. It's a worm, which means it activates when you open the message. It's some rip-off of Blaster that isn't in the Symantec database yet, but I can't track the executable file and it's tricky-tricky-tricky. People write the filename to sound a lot like something that belongs in Windows and I'm having to check everything against the files that *should* be in the OS. I get a little less than sixty seconds to get into the directory every time it reboots. I've got class tonight and all tomorrow, if I can't get it working by this evening I'll come in early Friday, OK?"

I nodded, stepped closer to him. I was beginning to look over my shoulder in my own office.

"Do me something more," I said. "If you get it working—the minute you get it working—access a file called REMARKSFORSAT.doc. Get it on disk, get it printed, get it stored someplace where it's not going to go away. And don't tell anyone even in this office that you're doing it."

He looked at me, near-white lashes making his spiked hair look darker. He had about three rings in the ear on this side and no discernible beard. His expression was grave.

"This is about you getting beat up, Mr. Smith, isn't it?" He had caught my soft tone.

I looked at him another long moment. "Yeah."

"Someone wanted that file to go away."

"I think so."

"Cooooool," he breathed. "This is like Watergate." He went back to flicking a highlight down a complex outline list of directory components.

I deliberated, reached into my desk drawer, withdrew one of the few spare keysets to the outside and newsroom doors. "If you feel like some midnight oil…"

His exhilaration was almost painful to behold. With exaggerated stealth he palmed the keys from me and slid them into his jean pocket. "Covert ops," he said. "I get it."

"Just keep it under your hat."

I moved to Ryan's desk, he having gone out, to write copy for the funeral coverage. Sophie clicked in a few minutes later and handed me her few pages of interviews.

My phone rang. I pushed away from the computer, jumped past Sean, grabbed it; I could only think of getting a call back from Elisa.

It was Schulz. My lucky day. "Paige Smith, is that you, you lying little prat?"

I almost slammed the phone down, then sighed. "Jim, why don't you start with hello?"

"Screw hello. Screw you too. What did my wife want with you the other night?"

He was shouting so loudly that his voice carried to Sean, whose brows lifted. Clearly he did not see me as someone who got embroiled in arguments involving other people's wives. I didn't either. Then I remembered the hesitant call, the one ending with Schulz's voice and a slammed receiver.

"I haven't spoken to her," I said evenly. Schulz had always been obsessional, but there was a new note in his voice. Well, I could understand, just a little.

"Well, she's gone. I know she was calling you. I hit Redial and it got your main number. Either she's trying to dish something to you or she's snooping on my calls." I refrained from commenting on this sublime double standard. "I say the cabal got to her. They're still trying to spike my campaign and they've turned her against me. I want to know what she told you."

"She didn't tell me anything, Jim. No messages. Nothing."

"Well, you're the press. It's your job to investigate when there's a conspiracy. I say if this isn't one there's no such thing. I report it and I get no damn help, just more *harassment* from Flanagan's goons trying to frame me. *You* can find out where she is. And I better be the first person you tell."

I laid the receiver back in its cradle a long minute later. Sophie looked up at me.

"Schulz' wife left him," I said. "It's a government plot."

"Well, it's about time," said Sophie. I looked at her curiously.

"He's my neighbor, didn't I ever tell you? We all think he mistreats her. Maybe not physically. But maybe so. I've never seen such a scared-looking woman."

I mused on this. It was hard to imagine living with Schulz.

"I'm for any plot that gets her out of that house," said Sophie. "And I hope she went somewhere and left no forwarding address."

"Probably on Slate's sofa," said Sean, sighing again as the computer restarted once more. Slate volunteered at the women's safe house, and had taken home an overflow applicant more than once.

The phone rang again. "Tell him I went out to cover something," I said. "The Lee-Jackson junior high track meet. The Caerleon Park farmer's market. Anything."

Sean lifted the receiver. "Yes. Yes, he's here," he said. He saw my expression pleading with him, covered the receiver and said with a grin: "Chick."

It was actually Phyllis Bell. "You're hirin' em younger and younger," she said. I reflected that her voice did sound quite young, for a woman whose general presence partook of Mammy Yokum.

"That's our intern. Technically he's not hired."

"Well, hire him. He's polite." She said a few blurred words not meant for me. "You OK to talk, Smitty?"

I looked around the newsroom. Sophie had returned to her desk and was working up something on the computer.

"Shoot."

"I got Marlaine here. She's got something for you."

A rustle. "Well, after studyin on the pictures I'd say I got three prints that ain't yours," came Marlaine's accent, not unlike Phyllis' own but raspier. "One on the inside screen of that little phone, kind of rough but I boosted it up, nother one off your wallet, off one of the little flippy window thingies on the inside, and one off that Blockbuster card where it stuck out." I felt a mild pang; Meg had borrowed that card almost permanently, and left it on the dresser, along with a spare key to my car, the last time she had been in my condo.

I forced my attention back to Marlaine. "Complete thumb, others are fingers, hard to tell which," she was saying. "So *someone's* been pokin in your pants, you should pardon me, that wasn't you. Shall I go ahead and run em?"

"Run?"

"See if they're in a database. Thumb and a couple partials, we could get a match. Take me a little while since this isn't official."

I looked out toward the door where I'd been knocked to the gravel. "Do it," I said. "I'll owe you. You figure out what."

"Ah, I owe Phyllis a few."

"Then let me owe you for something else."

"Ahmmmm. What were you thinking?"

"Can you check what's in an evidence locker?"

"Last I looked I could. It says here."

"The de la Roja scene. I need to know if something's in there."

"Tell me."

"A sheaf of papers about three or four sheets thick, folded over three times, probably badly bloodstained. Also, two copper pennies, country of issue not certain."

There was a silence. "You sure got some details."

"I was there, or didn't Phyllis tell you?"

"These things were supposed to be on him?"

"They were on him. I have pictures."

A long exhalation. "Sweeeeet."

"You don't know that."

"I don't know diddly. OK, I'll check."

Phyllis came back on. "Marlaine's on shift tonight but she can chase this tomorrow," she said. "Little issue getting computer time. Listen, I sent you a little leaflet about the Santeria stuff. Something I got at a training a few years back. Knew I had it around here somewhere—I popped it in the mail this morning, so you should get it tomorrow.....You gonna run that letter about the sheriff's department?"

I had to think. "Next week," I said. "I'm still getting comments from the article."

"OK, you call if you have questions."

I had infinite questions but none that I thought Phyllis could answer. One was how I was going to spend this evening. I thumbed through my inbox, came up with an invitation to the Century Committee dinner with the three local state delegates as guest speakers, and two tickets to Autograph Theater's production of *Anything Goes.*

I ended up taking Sophie. She was married, which made it safe, but her husband had pulled CQ at Fort Morris that night, which made me a hero of sorts. I dropped her off at eleven, and had a review in the bag by midnight. But there were no messages from Elisa.

CHAPTER EIGHT
SHATTERING SOUNDS

By Thursday things seemed to be entering normal, if you didn't count the still dark screen of my monitor bearing a Post-it note from Sean, who had had to leave for class at six on Wednesday, frustrated but undefeated (so he insisted). We were still close to the beginning of a new issue cycle, when the never-breakneck print deadline for Tuesday seems fairly remote, and Ryan and I scratch through the possible stories and share them out. I spent a pleasant hour deciding which letters to the editor were worth page space, referencing the editorial page on the recent edition to make sure I wasn't getting too many repeaters. The cartoon on the facing page was, for once, sober and poignant instead of curdled and cynical: Caparici had drawn the boardroom dais, the center chair draped in a Salvadoran flag side by side with one bearing Arlington's civic emblem, and a single rose lying on the seat. He had drawn Hector more than once as a Mortimer Snerd character sitting on the lap of Grover Friedman, but Mike knew when to quit.

Toni Messner called late in the morning to confirm that the Board business from Saturday had been rescheduled to the coming weekend. "Agenda's mostly the same, I'll have it on the website Friday," she said. "Oh, did the stuff Hilde took over work out OK?"

"Come again?"

"My assistant, Hilde. She said she was walking something over to you about poor Hector. I suppose one of the Board members wanted it sent. I'd really have to ask her, I've had so much doing."

"I don't think I got anything."

"She'll be in tomorrow, call her on 221. Leave today, she has a sonogram."

That sounded about right for the Arlington Notes page. Assistant Secretary of County Board has Sonogram. I was becoming homesick for our dull, trivial news.

I had decided to go to the tree planting at Courthouse Plaza while Ryan took on the daunting assignment of Student Helpers Day at Fairmont Senior Center. It was Spring, et cetera, but I was more up to listening to Grover Friedman drone than watching forty eleven-year-olds plant pansies under the tutelage of the eld-erly—it had been a week with sufficient excitement. Also, it would take less time, and a sly spring gale had sprung up and begun dodging under jacket hems, ragged gray-edged clouds chasing each other across the sky. I only caught my phone because I came back to the desk for my jacket.

It was Marlaine on what sounded like a cellular connection. "Didn't run em, nope, not yet," she said. "I have to wait for just the right little window of time to use that computer. What Flanagan's organization don't know won't hurt em."

"How do you do this, actually?" I said, a bit worried something might backfire on us.

"Don't worry. If anyone ever tries to trace the request, it comes back to a department in Pahrump, Nevada." I heard her radio crackle. "Anyway. I was short on time so I ain't had a look yet but I called my friend Duwayne who signs things in and out of the evidence locker. Well, don't you know, Mr. Smith, there's no letter there."

"No papers? It was bigger than a letter. A little manuscript."

"Nothing like that, he said. Nothin' signed into evidence or signed out by anyone. Not there. But your pennies are, if they don't have to be pennies."

"Run that by again?"

"Well, two pennies are what we don't have. But two subway tokens are what we do, New York or Boston, he couldn't tell me, I'm going to have to check back on that. Sounds like they got everything but the kitchen sink *except* your letter, they even got the Out of Order sign from the men's can in the lobby. Anyway, Phyllis said you might be interested in anything I heard about the investigation."

"Yes."

"Would I be right to think the name Marlaine Givens won't ever be connected to it?"

"Never."

"Well, ain't much. Duwayne talked to the officer running the search team, and he said after sweeping the courthouse area they picked up only one SP. SP, hell. Just one of the winos hangs around there, we're always havin' to broom em.

Diggin' around in the trash can nearest the garage entrance. They asked had he seen anyone leave that way, foot or car. He said a car but he couldn't remember. They took him over the station and gave him a little coffee trynna sober his ass up and then a little popcorn—"

"Popcorn?" This was a new interrogation technique to me.

"Ah, cop talk. Hassle. Some of the boys hassle winos just for the hell of it, but you ask me, there's a place and time. So once they got hard-ass with him he just clammed up, and since it looked like he'd drunk three forties and upchucked five, they let him go. But you always wonder what he'd of said if they hadn't got in his face."

"Yes. I do."

"I'm gonna keep my eye out for him. White, they said, and about thirty. Doesn't narrow it much, I know. I find out anything more, I'll tell you."

"Thanks, Ms. Givens."

I double-timed to the courthouse; running late now, but by the time I got there it was clear I had not needed to hurry. A little clutch of people had gathered around a large raised bed in the plaza, including the Arlington Beautification Committee, the county arborist, a couple of service groups and some of the boardroom regulars. Perry Reardon was there with a notebook instead of his clutch of *Taxpayer Watchdogs,* grilling the arborist on what funds the county had set aside for commemorative trees. I stood beside them, letting Reardon do some of my work for me. Off to the side some khaki-clad Parks employees and a couple of bored-looking men from Public Works were clustered around a flatbed dolly holding a half-dozen cherry saplings, their burlap-clad rootballs jostling one another. The only thing missing was Grover Friedman, whose chairmanship, turned over to Betty Bravo in January, had been marked by a rabid fervor for tree canopy.

"You can get your neighbor's tree declared historic, you know," came an amused voice behind me.

Mark Lewis, whiffing slightly of cigars, was rocking on his heels watching the assembly with a wry smile. He was closer to fifty than forty but, with his open collar and slightly raddled good looks, gave an impression of hoping no one noticed that.

"We pointed that out when they tried to pass the tree preservation ordinance. You can nominate anything a historic tree. On anyone's property. Or actually you can't, because we raised so much hell they had to send it back to the drawing board. Grover was pissed."

"Quote that?" I said .

"Funny ha ha. Anyway, he's late."

It was fifteen minutes past start time. I looked at the tree dolly, thought of something and edged over to Reardon. He was a good windbreak.

"Perry," I said. "The other morning at the boardroom."

He gazed at me somberly. Perry Reardon's face reminds me of Papa in a Victorian family portrait, down to the lush mustache, and he has considerably more *gravitas* than most hugely fat people.

"You told me you were just heading back to the men's lavatory when you saw de la Roja lying there. There was a janitor's cart in the hall—"

"Good thing there was."

"Uh, yes. I wondered, well, did you ever see a *janitor*?"

"No. Hell, they're probably all goofing off."

There was a small flurry at the far edge of the crowd and a short burp of amplified static from a microphone.

"This business alone. You know how much ornamental cherries cost? You know what they are to take care of? You know how much extra cleanup they'll be paying for when the things start blooming? It's like a snowstorm, and this isn't the Tidal Basin. This is brick. Six trees...."

I tuned him out. Pinky Paulsen was adjusting the mike on the portable podium.

"Good afternoon ladies and gentlemen...Mr. Friedman, who was going to speak to you today, has been unavoidably held up, but he has sent a statement. We'll be starting now, we don't want to hold *you* up..." Wind flapped the notes he was speaking from, and flapped some of his words away too. "...model community for tree preservation and planting...incentives and education to promote the planting of more trees..."

Friedman had been talking nothing but trees the whole year he was chairman; I wondered what could have kept him away today. Paulsen must have said something funny off-mike; scattered laughter rippled over the front of the small crowd. Out of it I heard a voice that lifted me the way the breeze was lifting my hair; I glanced to the side and saw Dvorah Steadman standing a little outside the crowd, a demure distance away from Mark.

I drew a deep breath, looked straight ahead, and held my scratch pad front and center. A little ripple of applause started at the front of the crowd and flushed back towards me. Paulsen reached to one side, accepted a spade from one of the Works employees, handed it in turn to a woman from the Beautification Committee. She stepped awkwardly up on the railroad-tie border of the bed in her high heels, levered up a token spadeful of dirt, then gamely, once more applause started, managed two more before she let Paulsen hand her down. The Works employees jumped up a good deal more nimbly and began widening the spaces that had already been made for the ceremonial rootballs.

Hot drinks were passed around from a catering trolley. I poured some too-strong coffee; I'd already had a couple of cups that morning but the wind was slicing through me. Getting quotes from the Parks people, the committee woman and the arborist took a little time; I found Paulsen at my elbow almost accidentally.

"Shame Grover couldn't make it, he's put so much into this," I said.

"Yes, I don't know what came up. I just happened to be here."

"Last minute thing, then."

"I guess I should start getting used to it." His tone was rueful. "I know Grover's taken this all pretty hard. He practically ran Hector's campaign, you know—even the families got pretty close." I wondered if he was thinking of his own first campaign, when he had been Grover's Golden Boy and stayed that way until the day he nerved himself to come down on the opposite side of an issue. Word from Toni was that they had barely spoken except from necessity for weeks, and anyone could tell that Hector had become the favorite son.

Dvorah interrupted us. "Hiiiii, Pinky. Hi Smitty. Would they mind if we put some growth spells on the trees, do you think?? Cherries are so *delicate*."

I held the notebook tighter. She turned to me and ran a fingernail down the knot of my necktie.

"And I'm going to send *you* those cards. I almost forgot."

She whisked off toward the tree bed, chunky bootheels clopping. Pinky gazed after her. I heard myself uttering a muted noise that was compounded of all the known vowels and several unknown ones.

"Well, I have to get going," said Paulsen without moving or changing his focus. Belatedly he turned back to look me in the face. "Good article you did. Tell Mike we all liked the picture too. Any chance we could buy the original for the boardroom lobby?"

"I'll ask."

He stepped to the podium to collect some odds and ends. Past him, I could see Dvorah at the far end of the tree bed, her arms raised, smiling raptly. I recognized the three women from Tuesday, stationed at the other three quadrants, swaying to a rhythm that I presumed only they could hear. The Works employee who was sweeping up traces of mulch seemed to be studiously ignoring them.

I retreated into the County building. Nerves are not the only awkward consequence of too much coffee.

*   *   *   *

Everyone but the work crew was gone when I came out. I nodded ironically to them—the stagehands who made all the County's public ceremonies possible—and was headed to my car in the far lot when I noticed a figure bent over one of the trash containers in the plaza, rummaging. My heart leapt. Random commuters passing by ignored him, some with a pained look of studied obliviousness. I checked my watch, considered a moment, and moved toward him.

He sensed me beside him and looked up. False alarm. He was black, with a black man's sparse beard coming in half grizzled, a greasy jacket too heavy for the day and a vague rancid smell that I was sure would have been much worse without the crisp breeze.

"Sometimes folks don't finish they lunch. They toss in here, you know? Sometimes I get a good lunch. Some folks don't hardly touch stuff." He shuffled through a little more debris, hit bottom. "Nothin'. Huh. They all probly go somewhere else cause big shots havin a do out here. Sheeit."

He looked at me challengingly. "No freakin lunch."

I sat down on the adjacent bench.

"I might just go and get lunch," I said. "Could pick you up something?"

"Hey man, that be boss. That be real class."

"Just need to know a good place, if you hang out here a lot."

"I here all the time. Here'n over at the bridge."

"You know a young white guy hangs out here too? Works the trash like you do?"

"How young? Man, I don't go lookin for young *guys*."

"No, he's someone the cops talked to a few days ago. About thirty." I tried to think of anything else Marlaine had said. "Likes to drink forties." Whatever those were.

"Oh man, that Hoople. You talkin' bout Hoople. Hoople real crazy guy, he can really pound them forties."

He extended a cracked, two-tone paw.

"My name Scrape. Pleased to meetcha."

I shook the extended hand. It seemed to be the source of his name.

"Hoople, he not been here in awhile. Them beaner boys run him off."

"Beaner boys?"

"Yeah, them taco twisters. He scared of beaner boys, them Little Locos, say they got them that beaner juju. Hoople, he really believe in juju."

I considered telling him that Hoople wasn't the only one. "How long ago was this?"

"Few days, man. I don' *know*. Them beaner boys, they like to come mess with him all the time cause he get so bent about the juju. They laugh, they mess with him and run him off. I don't know when he be back."

I had a name for Marlaine, anyway. "How about you, Scrape? You believe in juju?"

"I b'lieve in lunch. And Colt 45. I believe in that, yes sir."

"I'll see what I can do."

Finding a prefabbed sandwich at the nearest convenience store was a quick task, but I found myself fairly becalmed at the other end of the cooler. I finally had to ask the turbaned individual at the register to find me a Colt 45. He looked at me oddly as he rang it up. Scrape's expression as I handed him the brown sack was genial in contrast. "God bless you, sir," he said. He pulled out the sandwich and twisted the sack around the neck of the oversized bottle, snapping off the cap with the last twist and taking a large pull.

"That the stuff make everything better. Yessirree."

"Uh, maybe…Never mind. You see Hoople, tell him to stick around? If a police lady comes to talk to him, she won't be…like the other cops."

Scrape was in the middle of another long swallow. "I see him, I tell him. God bless you, sir."

I started my car with a vague feeling of having offended the civic deities. Well, if he went to sleep under the cherry trees, Selby would have a wonderful candid. I considered calling him.

*   *   *   *

The mail was in when I got back to the newsroom. The envelope from Phyllis Bell, disappointingly slim, was near the top, but I dealt with everything else first, and churned out a page of notes on the doings of the downstate delegation. I could sense Ryan hovering over my shoulder as I finished; I was still using his terminal for composing and e-mail.

"Sophie is a pervert," he announced to no one in particular. "Anyone who can spend half her time reporting on the young is a pervert. Place me on record with this statement. Next time I get to hug the trees."

I surrendered the chair to him. "I'll come in after dinner and finish," I said. In the back of my mind was Sean's promise to work until my hard drive was freed up.

On my way out it occurred to me to call Selby and tell him I'd gotten some news from Marlaine. "I'll be back in the office tonight," I said to his answering machine. "Call me and I'll fill you in."

My refrigerator held a curled pinochle deck of luncheon meat and some sushi from Whole Foods, which hadn't been good a week ago. It had attained the status of some sort of found art now. In the end I heated up some beef stew and read the Santeria pamphlet while I ate. It wasn't that good for the appetite, but like Scrape, I was hungry.

*   *   *   *

The newsroom was dim when I got back, the high windows leaving a twilight punctuated by safety lights, a bank of fluorescents over Mike's drawing board, and Ryan's computer which he had thoughtfully left on. Later, on Sunday and Monday evenings, keyboards would be puttering and faxes running, but right now the place was quiet enough I could hear the ticking of a cheap clock somewhere. I made a point of latching the outside door; you could still spot a few shards of glass on the wheelchair ramp coming in.

I switched on the banker's lamp over my blotter, set down Phyllis' pamphlet and a can of Fresca I'd brought with me. Most people I know say it tastes like wiper fluid; keeps people from stealing my soda, anyway. I felt oddly disconnected as I adjusted the keyboard height on Ryan's terminal (he tops me by half a foot) and began to frame commentary on the half-million-dollar erosion dike at Potters Run and the county's partnership with SPAN-DC, a homelessness project. (I kicked myself for not soliciting Scrape's input.) Usually this kind of thing came like breathing—you could sort the sound ideas from the sound bites, after ten years of watching the county. Tonight it seemed irrelevant which was which.

I rewarded myself with the soda when I had a piece blocked out, then ran over what Ryan had written. At the other end of the newsroom the HVAC system kicked on and off. I realized I was looking at the screen without taking in anything, thinking instead about the pennies which were subway tokens and the letter the police didn't have in evidence.

No scene-of-crimes cop could be that incompetent. Those papers in Hector's pocket—his speech, or I was no newsman—had been disappeared before they had ever been recorded in evidence, or else the evidence record had been tampered. No one in the department lower than Flanagan would have any reason to do that.

Tokens from New York or Boston. Boston, where Flanagan had been chief in one of the outlying townships—a chief who had left his department with a vote of no confidence hanging over him, one whose cops were apparently bent enough that cops from other departments had to execute warrants on them. And New York, where according to the pamphlet I had been reading, someone with serious aspirations to participate in Santeria—like Elisa de la Roja, perhaps—would likely go to celebrate their *asentado*, their initiation, at the hands of an established Santeria priest. Hector had been naturalized in New York, his sister still lived there; it would be a more obvious choice than Miami, the only other center big enough, according to this summary. I wondered idly if Santeria practice could generate computer viruses.

A phone burbled. I was halfway to ignoring it when I realized it was mine. I almost toppled my chair getting to the desk, dropped the phone, nearly knocked over the soda can, picked the receiver up again. "Hello, Shel?"

"Ah…did I dial right? Mr. Smith?"

The voice was familiar but sounded strained. "Speaking."

"Mr. Smith? It's Marlaine Givens. I'm calling from home…? I ran those prints. I think you need to know about this. I got a hit."

Her rural, comfortable accent had all but dried up. I have heard this kind of change in a number of circumstances and it never means good things. I felt myself preparing as if to run in any direction necessary.

"First of all, if you'll forgive me being personal, can you think of *any* reason why someone who's a little, well, outside the law would have handled your stuff? I'm not gonna judge your personal life, just be honest. Anything might embarrass you'll stop with me."

"No," I said, genuinely puzzled. The worst offense I could impute to anyone who had used my phone in months was speeding to file a story.

"Well, I'm thinking the person who matches these prints couldn't possibly have thumped you like you got thumped. But they did come up in a couple of databases, so maybe it'll help you connect some dots."

I swallowed. "Yes, what—well, *what* came up?"

"Are you near a fax?"

"On my desk." I reeled off the number,

"OK. I think that's quickest. Stand by a moment." She put down the receiver, and I could hear a hum as she fed the fax machine. A few minutes later the terminal on my desk gave a muted ring, and began to churn out a page, bottom edge first, with what looked like a series of datelines. I watched as the dates climbed backward in time, realized I was looking at a rap sheet. The bottom of a photo began to come into view. I was dead long before the printer churned out its entirety. I could feel my hand on the phone, and hear the hum of the machine, but I was dead all right.

"Remember, I didn't do any of this, OK?" came Marlaine's voice. "I just broke a couple-three laws, but it's worth it if anything comes back to bite Ed Flanagan in the butt. You got it?"

"Yes. Yes, I have it. Officer Givens—?" I brought up words that were almost impossible to say, dry as old wood. "Thank you." The fax printer was still humming like a loom, printing the name *Margaret Ellen Stannard* above the picture. "I don't think this has anything to do with Monday night. But I did need to know it. I think."

"Are you OK, Mr. Smith?"

"No," I said.

I hung up the phone. The office echoed, empty, a distant fluorescent tube humming intermittently like a bee trapped behind a windowshade. I tried to will myself back into the world of five minutes ago—held off taking a breath, as if that would prevent my moving any further forward into a life where the information on the smudged curl of fax paper had any meaning. Outside, the sky had moved only a few shades further toward night, while the moment before the phone had rung seemed days in the past. I put my head down in my hands, not caring that I was jamming my glasses into fading but still tender bruises.

I remember next walking between Ryan's desk and the intern's station, looking for something that I could not have identified if a questioner had put thumbscrews to me. Sean's side of the bulletin board above the monitor had a tacked-up printout of a whimsical, adorable girl in black Goth clothes, captioned *Death*. A comic character, I gathered. I leaned up and looked into the cute face as if it could tell me something useful about the ashes and twisted metal that filled my whole world. *Death* looked back at me as if she had an absolutely marvelous secret.

I found myself back at my desk. What to do now was not immediately clear. The time until morning seemed intolerable. What did people do in these situations? I opened the desk drawer. Several interns back, a crusty New York girl whose Golden Age seemed to involve H. L. Mencken and the Algonquin Round-table had brought me a parting gift at the end of the semester. "Every newspaper editor should have one of these in his desk drawer," she said. "I'm gonna have one in mine. Here, even if you never open it." I had meant to break it out for the office every New Year's Eve since and completely forgotten it. I reached back behind the hanging files and pulled out the squat paper sack, still twisted around the bottleneck.

My coffee cup from the morning was still next to the keyboard. I splashed bourbon into the cup, noted that a half inch of coffee scummed with ersatz cream had been standing in the bottom, and swallowed the mess anyway. It wasn't too bad, actually. I picked up the fax again. Maybe if I had a few of those, I could read it all the way through. *Soliciting, 04/04/2000. District of Columbia Police Department. Dismissed. Soliciting, 12/09/2001. District of Columbia Police Department. Continued.* Then the ones that piled the final stone on my heart: *Prostitution. 09/17/03. Loudoun County Sheriff's Department. Possession of Controlled Substances. 03/27/04. Cook County Sheriff's Department...*I poured the coffee cup half full and swallowed hard. What was this making me think of? I began to rummage through the rickety little tinkertoy bookshelf that held Strunk's *Elements of Style,* two dictionaries, a collection of theater reviews from the *New York Times,* a signed script of *Oliver!* from the Shirlington Players production, seven years of *Best Plays.* Stacked on the bottom as ballast were books I had barely opened since college. I had another pull at the cup once I got them onto the desk. It was getting easier. Scrape and Hoople, perhaps, were on to something. The third time I poured I managed to get half of it in the cup and half of it on the blotter, but the amber puddle made a surprisingly pleasant shape. After a short hunt I found some napkins from Chi-Chi's on the desk of Sarah Wellborn, the advertising director, and carefully sponged it up before I began leafing through pages. There was a good bit left in the cup to keep me occupied; I tried to see how long I could spin it out, at one point dipping my finger and tasting as if I were sampling cake batter. Then I suddenly became amazingly tired. My cheek was against the damp spot on the blotter when Selby materialized beside me. I became aware that I had heard the outside door slamming.

"Smitty, you gotta—oh, *Christ.*"

I lifted my head and looked at him. He seemed to tower a long way over me.

"What happened, boss?"

I pushed myself back from the desk. The chair demonstrated a mind of its own, catching me in an unexplainable way with its wheels so that as I finished standing up, it toppled over. The steel wastebasket crashed in turn and rolled gently from side to side for several seconds with a pleasing resonance, like a Tibetan musical bowl. I hummed the pitch.

"Smitty, what the *fuck?????*" Selby picked up the bourbon flask from the blotter. Now half empty, it threw out hypnotic reflections from the green shade of the banker's lamp.

I picked up the nearest book and laid it down on the blotter with a slow and careful flourish. I was going to declaim, but choked on the words instead. "*Caeli, Lesbia nostra, Lesbia illa, illa Lesbia,*" I managed.

"Who's a lesbian?"

Selby, a photographer and music buff, probably had little interest in the odes of Roman poets to their faithless mistresses. Never mind. This still demanded an utterance of classical stature. "This she?" I coughed, smacking my fingers clumsily on the fax sheet. "No, this is Diomed's Cressid; O Cressid, O false Cressid, false! false! false!" I tried to sit back down on the chair before I remembered it had tipped over, stumbled, and grabbed Selby as he jumped forward to catch me.

He held me up for a moment and deposited me on Ryan's swivel chair. I held up a hand, rose. I could walk. I stepped on tilting cotton wool to my desk and pulled the sheets completely off the fax, spread them out on the blotter, slapped my hand on them again to tell him to look. "Let all untruths stand by thy stained name, and they'll seem glorious."

He gazed down at the photo, the list, the aliases. The room became very still.

"Oh, hell, boss." He seemed to be deliberating, then simply added, "I'm sorry."

I bent and with great concentration put my chair upright.

"Boss, I know this isn't a great time. But you gotta clean up. I got a lady here has *got* to talk to you."

I fell into the chair.

"I can't," I said.

"*Fuck* you can't," he said. "Stuff's happening and *you* have to get it together. Tomorrow I will *personally* go on a class-A knee-walking drunk with you if that's what you want, and I think I better because you obviously have no *clue* how to go about it, but right now I need your ass *operational.*"

My head lolled back over the chair back, mostly because I couldn't think of a single reason to hold it up. "I can't," I said again. It seemed the plain truth. The room kept moving around, in a greasy, unwholesome way. "You got no choice," Selby said. "Man, I know this hurts, but you had to figure it out sooner or later."

I felt ice in my gut. "You knew about this?"

"Shit, no! You think we would have let that go without saying anything?"

"We?"

He waved his hand around the newsroom. "Boss, we *all* just thought she was a high-box *bitch* but—" I swung a punch at him at that point. He caught it lazily in his hand, like a favorite uncle catching his nephew's lobbed softball. "But we all put up with it because we all loved working for you. You think the whole thing didn't stick out a mile? You think she wasn't throwing her weight around every time she could, dare anyone to screw with her because she's screwin' the boss? We put up with it because we couldn't change what you thought, and you're a decent guy, and you know how many decent guys there are in the world? About twelve. But now you gotta deal with it."

"Shel—"

"Just come over here." With that he turned the chair in a one-eighty, picked me out of it with more strength than I would have expected, and began walking me across the linoleum. I managed to struggle half free, but he just leaned into me with more force, propelled me through the door of the men's room, and flipped the tap of the utility sink full blast. His grip on the back of my shirt was ruthless; he got my head under the cold water, picked up my glasses as they clattered into the sink, and hung on tight as most of what I'd swallowed in the last half hour came up in a series of caustic heaves. I got my hands under the water, managed to swish and spit a little of it, finally wrenched backwards from the pummeling stream.

"Shel, you're fucking drowning me." I leaned on the edge of the sink, the lipped rim cutting into my ribs, pulling breath in and out through a scalded-feeling throat.

"Well, that's a first."

"I hope so."

"No, I mean you can say *fuck*. We were never sure."

I looked up at him owlishly, water coursing noisily from my hair into the plastic basin.

"Now you want to go meet a lady?"

I was still pretty shaky, and now I was also saturated. Selby opened the janitor's cabinet and found a pile of clean industrial rags.

"Here. Dry off. She's waiting, she ain't goin' nowhere. Clean up."

I moved in front of the mirrors, drying in what felt and probably looked like slow motion. Selby stepped out into the newsroom, but reappeared in time to hand me my glasses when I was through with the comb.

"Looking good. Look, we'll talk about the other thing. But this is heavy. Come on out, she's in the break room. Here, chug some of this so you won't breathe on her and kill her."

He shoved the warm half can of Fresca at me. I examined the state of my stomach, used it for mouthwash instead. The man in the mirror looked a little ill, but not downright alarming. I decided to pilot him around the world and see how long I could keep him running.

The breakroom is shut off from the newsroom by a heavy windowed door that always reminds me of a school classroom. A fan of light spread from under it. At first I thought it was empty; then a figure at the end of the long table, stained by hundreds of drinks and greasy pizza boxes, turned away from the row of framed front pages on the far wall. It was a young woman who looked as if she ought to be very cold but stood with athletic poise, hands clasped behind her back, wearing heathered sweat shorts, a hip pack with a water bottle, and a lipstick-pink running top, the kind that looks like underwear but apparently isn't. She was not tall but her legs seemed long anyway, the olive tone of her skin bringing out the shadows of muscle. Her black-brown hair was pulled back in a ponytail which made her look about eighteen.

"Smitty, excuse me," said Selby with a nod to her, "I mean, Paige Smith, I'd like you to meet Mercedes de la Roja."

"*Ola*," she said without unlinking her hands. And then, "Mr. Smith. I am so glad we are able to find you quickly. I think I need to ask you for some help, and I think perhaps I am able to help you too."

CHAPTER NINE
LA CAMPESINA

"Elisa said, "Just play the game and be safe," explained Mercedes, pulling Selby's warmup jacket around her. He had put soft jazz on the stereo and was microwaving something. "That is not me. That was not my brother either. So after a time he told her less and less. He waited his time, but that is not the same as giving in."

Ice chimed in her glass. I had some too, crushed, with ginger ale in it, which was helping a little.

"I tell her this is the time to tell everyone what Hector wanted. I know his plans, we talked all the time by e-mail. She says, no, it is best to leave all things just as they are now. I am angry, but she will not change her mind.

"We talk all Sunday after church, into afternoon, all in Spanish because I do not trust these people. People are in and out, so much *condolencia*, the big fat man, Friedman, and his wife are with us much of the time and they also have police there. I say, this is too much. They say to Elisa, your husband was murdered, there may be danger for you, you need police. I just feel like it is us they are watching.

"I get alone at the computer finally for a few minutes and I find this disk. I wanted to send to you, but I do not think I have time to power up, get into e-mail, find your address—I know something is wrong and they would try to stop me. Elisa is too frightened and she is pushing me too hard.

"So I am thinking, what to do, and then there comes a big group of the office people from the *condado*. I have met one of them, the secretary, not the Anglo lady but Hilde, she is from Salvador too. I ask her, can she take this to you? You ask for it this morning, I tell her, and Elisa is too upset and I cannot figure out computer, and you need it for paper. She should take, please, not try to send on computer. I think this will solve problem, no one knows, and they think because I cry a lot that morning and speak only Spanish to Elisa that I am just some dumb *chica* who cannot see they are hiding something. Stupid, huh?"

She reached in her hip pack, opened a wallet and passed a card to me. *Grafico Arcoiris,* it said, then *Mercedes de la Roja, Graphic Design and PR—Traduccion English/Espanol.* There was a Manhattan telephone number with fax below it.

"Everything is quiet the rest of the day, but Monday, *desastre.* Hilde does not understand the situation, I had no time to explain to her how Elisa wants to be so safe and quiet, so she calls in afternoon to leave message she has taken you the disk. They are listening to all the messages, to help out Elisa, they say, this Mrs. Friedman is always around helping, helping. The *gordo,* Friedman, he is very upset. They almost shout at Elisa, then Friedman argues with his wife. I hear Elisa saying she did not send it. Finally Friedman says it must be honest action by Hilde, perhaps Hector gave her this disk. They must just get it back. But I think they are starting to look at me. I just cry more, and stay in my room.

"Pretty soon another man shows up, a very big fellow, big as two of this Fried-man. He was at the church but so many people, I cannot remember names. I am listening without it looking like I listen, so I miss some things. The big man stays after Elisa goes to lie down, still talking to those two. Friedman makes a phone call, and I hear him say *You should not do it yourself, you could be seen.* The big man says, *I have just the right person to help me.* So he goes. By now it is time for din-ner, and Mr. and Mrs. Friedman seem to be arguing again. They do not get along well, those two, but she still seems to do everything he says. He leaves, she stays and fixes some food that people have brought. Other family is flying in and we have to go get them later at the airport, the old people, Elisa's mama and *abuela,* the *condado* puts them in hotel. Elisa doesn't get up, so it is just us two. She tries to talk to me in bad Spanish. Then another person shows up, regular clothes but I can tell he is from the police also. Mrs. Friedman shows him back into Hector's little office. He stays an hour or so, and leaves her a card. Later I get a chance to look—he is from the Cyber Crimes Unit. I am sure nothing of what Hector planned is now left on his computer.

"Next day they say I have nothing to wear to a funeral, they will take me shop-ping, it is their gift. Very strange. My church clothes, I think, are good enough, but this council woman, Senora Bravo, she insists on helping. I can tell it is a way of keeping me busy. I said so to Elisa and she says just go along, be quiet this week, your tickets back are on Sunday, it is one week and then I will make sure they bother you no more. I am crying for my brother, still, and she is talking like this; now I feel something is very wrong and start to get afraid. So, I go to buy a dress with this Ms. Bravo and Friedman's wife. They are easy to fool; I hear them talking while I am in the dressing room, you can tell they think I am some maid or cashier somewhere. The Bravo woman is saying, *even now I don't think Elisa wants the world to know she's dancing around naked in a seashell necklace, so she'll stay quiet, and anyway we don't know what he told her.*

"I know what that means, so when I get home I start looking around the house. Sure enough, I find up in a closet a coin wrapped in many colors of thread, in another place a bundle of cinnamon and things like oils and *ocre*. There is a lot of this in New York. I don't ask Elisa. Maybe she only plays with it."

I decided to omit mention of the Botanica for the moment. Or maybe being still was just the better part of valor. The microwave chimed and Selby went to fiddle with it, bringing back a plate that he laid on the barn-wood coffee table in front of Mercedes. After a few more moments' half-audible fidgeting he emerged again with a pair of stem glasses and a half-full bottle of Chardonnay. His taste in glassware was surprisingly expensive.

"You're cut off for tonight, boss," he said, pouring for the two of them. Mercedes smiled, for the first time, and tilted her head back against the couch after sipping.

"I would like to see that fat *cochino* right now," she said, "they will be going crazy looking for me."

"Friedman?" I said. Friedman is not in the Reardon league, but to someone with her jogger's build he probably did register as piggy. Someone had once joked that he weighed 250, and without Hector in his pocket 240. I winced at the memory.

"Si, he was around again later that evening. His wife acts like she does not want to leave, but he says he will sit a little while with Elisa and sends her home. I am tired, when you cry a lot you want to sleep. I wake up late in the evening, it is close to midnight, and Elisa and this man are still out in the living room talking, talking. It is very intense but I can hear little, they are being quiet not to wake me. I hear him say be patient. She goes to bed, and I think he stays on some time because I hear him later on telephone, he is saying *It sounds like he will be out of commission quite a while, no worries there. He was alone at the office so it was easy, we'll just have Ryan this Saturday instead.* I do not know what commission he meant. And then again something about this Ryan, *Ryan was right to do it himself.*"

My back hair crept.

"So I just keep my eyes open. The next day is the funeral. I hear you leaving message while I am dressing, they are in the kitchen waiting for me and Friedman says, *The little weasel must be made of old Army boots. After Monday night he should be in the hospital.* So I know for sure they have sent their bully to beat you." She turned her large dark eyes to me over the rim of the wineglass. "This is what we came to America to leave behind, and now I am very frightened. But I can tell they do not think anything at all is possible to them, they are trying hard to seem friendly to me. Only they will not let me be alone very long at all, unless I go to lie down; later that day when I say I want to run, they send the police woman along to protect me. Some rough parts in this neighborhood, they tell me.

"I am e-mailing back and forth with my office in New York on my palm when they think I am sleeping, but I don't have address for you. They give me no chance to get away and talk to you at the funeral, or to the woman from your paper. I see him—" she nodded at Selby "—taking photographs, but by that time we are all in the car."

Selby refreshed her wine. I closed my eyes tight until the brief sound of pouring stopped. *Ryan was right to do it himself.* Ryan had been the last person on my computer before it crashed.

"Anyway." She rearranged herself on the couch, pulling a throw over the lean legs. "I have about said *diablo,* I will just raise hell when I go back to New York, though I am nervous even about that. But Thursday Elisa says we should go to the grocery. The police woman, a different one, drives us. I am looking up and down the *hortalizas* when who do I see?" Her brows arched; the wine was making her a little more spirited. She pointed at Selby. "*Mira!* He is playing with tomatoes."

"I was *selecting,*" said Selby with some gravity.

"You are playing, whatever. So I come up beside him and play with tomatoes too, and I say, You take pictures for little paper, we talk Sunday, yes? I must see your boss soon. Very important, meet me at church in half hour?"

"I have always wanted a lady to make a mysterious request to me over tomatoes," Selby said.

"He is *caballero,* this man. You should pay him well. He says yes without question, and goes to buy his tomatoes. So! I must get away. Police woman is with Elisa, tasting food, where whole end of the aisle is blocked up with this samples table. This seems like nicer police woman but I am taking no chances. So I look around, here is a cart with boxes of salad oil all ready to put on the shelf, I get my foot under it and push. *Fracasso!!!!* Oil and glass everywhere, god-awful noise. Now everyone is trapped by salad oil. I turn and walk straight out of the store and then I start to run. I know where the church is, I have been there twice; it is why I picked the place."

"I had to drive around a little, myself," said Selby. "That's why you got there first."

"I got there first because I finish your Marine Marathon just last fall, three hours thirty-two minutes," she said. "This year I am trying Boston."

She finished the wine. Selby did not pour another.

"So. I do not know if these people can hurt me or not. This is America. But they want to hide things about my brother, his wife is going along, I think this is wrong. You are trying to tell the truth so I ask you for help. And maybe I can help you; if you have this that my brother wrote, I will speak out and say it is real. I have all his e-mails at home. My office can send them."

I finished chewing some gingery ice. "Can you stay a few days?" I said.

She spread her hands. "If you have place…"

I looked at Selby. For a moment I thought we would be drawing straws and it felt indescribably awkward; then I had the answer. I got out my cellphone. She and Selby went on talking while I called, hit paydirt, gave directions; she was looking at the photo-program manuals on his coffee table and they appeared to be talking shop.

"All set," I said. "Looks like Jim Schulz's wife didn't get first dibs."

Selby looked at me blankly, and I remembered he hadn't been around for that conversation. "I remember my brother mentioning the name of this Schulz," said Mercedes. "He is your local crazy man, eh?"

"Only first among equals," I said. "You would have to see them all in a small space."

"But they are all people who care, and that is good," she said. "Nothing changes when people do not care. And they cannot care if they do not know. So we make them know, which is your work, and so to ask questions, and that is, as my mother used to say, like a novena in the eyes of God." She grinned. "Though she would be *histerico* if she saw where I take that idea sometimes. Also, she told me decent girls do not drink wine with men." She rose from the couch, retired into Selby's bathroom; he cleared plates and scooped up bits of trash from the carpet, trying to look as if he usually kept house better than this.

"I am thinking, though," said Mercedes as she emerged from the bathroom, as if there had been no break in the conversation, "and this is the thing that goes to my heart most. These people try to cover what my brother is doing, they want all to stay as it is and they have found some way to make Elisa silent—I think she does not want the world to know about the little button, the candles and all. But I think and think, and I do not think they are the ones who have killed him."

I looked up, inviting her to continue.

"These women, when I am trying on the dresses," she said. "I hear the Bravo woman say to Mrs. Friedman, *Whoever did this, he solved one problem for us but made ten more.* I could not hear the answer.

"Also, I keep wondering. This *brujeria* I find around Elisa's house. As I say, there is a lot of this in New York. Some try to get me to use it. I think these are charms to tie your man to you. Only, I think this does not make sense; my brother loved her like his life. I—oh, it all makes me tired." She dropped to the couch again and rubbed a knuckle under her eyelids.

I was saved from wondering what to say by headlights angling up the drive. A moment later Selby answered the door, and Slate, looking impossibly young to possess car keys, stepped in.

"Thanks for coming, Slate," I said. "If you can see your way to put up this lady for a couple of nights…? Mercedes, Slate works in my office. Slate, this is Mercedes de la Roja." Slate's eyes widened a little but she said nothing; Mercedes stood, a few inches taller and somehow solider. Slate walked straight over and embraced her.

"Sisterhood is powerful," said Selby in an undertone.

"No problem, Mr. Smith," said Slate. "And no one ever finds out who stays with me. That's what you want, right?"

"Right," I said.

I imagined I could hear the car for a long time after its lights receded.

"They'll be up all night," said Selby. "Slate wants to publish Net comics."

I said nothing, staring out the window. *I have just the right person to help me,* I remembered Mercedes quoting.

"I know what you're thinking, boss," said Selby some distance behind me. "I heard what she said about Ryan this and that. Not *Ryan,* man. She got mixed up on names, I don't know how she soaked up everything she did. Ryan thinks those bozos suck, I've been on enough stories with him. You're twisted up because of the other thing. Let go of it."

I half looked at him, couldn't think of words worth saying, nodded.

"You're starting to think everyone's hiding something. Smitty, it was *just her.* And anyone asks, I have no clue, you got me? All I know's what we could all fig- ure out, and if we hadn't already we would of by now. You been walking around like a ghost since she left. Days we wondered if you were gonna make it to quitting time, talk about Ryan, hell, he's been going behind everything you wrote." My throat swelled and I fought it down. "Shit, even the people who couldn't *stand* her were starting to want her back if it would put you back together."

The lights of late traffic stuttered by on the main road a block away. I thought of the last, perhaps only real quarrel we had had, if it was even a quarrel—I (I admit it) peevishly asking why she was becoming so scarce, she throwing back to me that I was the one who had counseled so much discretion. I had thought I was laying at her feet, for her career, her reputation, my delirious wish to announce on Page One—maybe in banner type—that she had chosen me.

"Anyway, that fax is in your poetry book, book's in my car, no one but me's gonna find out about it. But right now I say you sleep on it, all right? Your car's at the pop stand, that's where I go in the morning, you're here, there's the couch. Slate ain't the only one buys furniture at Ikea. Where else can we shop on what this rag pays? You gotta get some new advertisers."

Memories of school sleepovers, unfamiliar pillows and sheets, lights coming in the window at the wrong angle. The back of the sofa smelt faintly but incontestably of Mercedes' cologne; like a lot of Latin women she laid on cosmetics with a robust hand. Deep in the night I half woke from a dream in which I was being shown my own rap sheet by an accusing Betty Bravo. A car gunned outside, spilling salsa music. The bed at least had no memory of Meg's feet in it. Then it was light, and Selby's fearful coffeemaker was hacking and gargling.

*   *   *   *

"Drop me at my place," I said as we pulled past the bottleneck at the I-395 ramp. It was still barely seven. "I'll get a Blue Top in." My clothes were crawling on me, and my feet itched in reworn socks.

"You just don't want people to think we're an item," said Selby deadpan. "Yeah, you got a point." There was a faint impressionistic stain on my left shirtsleeve where bourbon had transferred ballpoint ink from my blotter. "You want me to just step back to your desk and police up the Wild Turkey empties before anyone gets in?"

I winced. We had not been thinking about that last night.

"All part of the service," he said. "Who's complaining, I get to wine and dine a little firecracker like that? I never been anyone's white knight before."

I glanced at him sidelong. He remained deadpan. "I still can't figure it all," he said. "You can tell she thinks big brother walks on water. I'd of never seen him that way, but I never figured him for a reform chairman, either. And who knows if he was steppin' out on the wife or not. I mean, he wasn't a fireball, but—" Selby shrugged and concentrated on a merge.

"Pastorelli swears Perry Reardon saw him with Betty Bravo in Bill and Evie's in the middle of the night, way after that last recess meeting ended," I said. "I just remembered that."

"OK, now I know you had *way* too much. *Betty Bravo?*"

"Reardon wouldn't say that."

"Yeah, he's on drugs, too. Two people want to fool around and not be seen, they're somewhere foolin' around, not drinking B & E's battery acid. Try this: one of em had something to say to the other at that meeting and they had to take it somewhere—can't take it home, county building's closing up. I wanted to talk about something that no one would overhear *or* understand if they overheard it *or* remember if they understood it, that's the place I'd talk about it." He had a point. Bill and Evie's at two a.m. is populated by citizens only slightly up the food chain from Scrape, arriving directly from the less upscale bars. "But now we got another suspect. Reardon saw 'em together, brooded over it till he went crazy, and finally waxed him." He pulled onto Liberty Pike heading toward my condo, which unfortunately meant crawling several blocks with traffic headed for downtown.

"He *was* first at the scene," I said as Selby turned into my side street.

"Boss. *Get a grip.* Newsflash: I get worried, I get funny. I'm scared for you, I'm a little scared for *me,* I'm scared for Mercedes and I'm scared about what the hell is going *on* in this county. But Hector was done by someone who was absolutely stone cold, and we're talkin' about a *big, pukin fat guy.*" He bent forward and reached under the seat. "And take this before I get busted with it." He handed me the crumpled and torn paper sack wrapped around the half-empty bourbon bottle. "Just pulling your chain earlier. But between you and me?" He braked in the horseshoe in front of my building. "Don't try this kind of thing. You ain't cut out for it."

The front-desk woman looked at me curiously. I could only imagine the picture I presented, rumpled, unshaved, carrying a brown bag in the distinctive shape of a bottle. I took the stairs up to my floor, to avoid encounters in the elevator.

*   *   *   *

Ten minutes of steam and spray abated the unaccustomed feeling that some-one had been inflating small balloons in various parts of my head and using a hairdryer on the inside of my mouth. I peeled the last of the tape off my ribs, which muttered only slightly as I dressed. There were no phone messages other than a cheerful recorded voice telling me that a handyman service was doing work in my area; my e-mail included a message from Pastorelli, copied to all my addresses (he always did that), forwarding a cost estimate that Reardon had for-warded to him after a discussion with staff about the bill for a decorative tree bed in Courthouse Plaza. He liked to keep me informed, did Angelo.

I was still a little punchy, in that state where you pick things up and find your-self tossing them across the room, and the pen that should have gone into my shirt pocket sailed under the dresser. I knelt, spotted a glint, reached and pried out from behind one of the legs a wad of dust in which, like a shiny beetle in a spiderweb, a tiny silver heart charm lay embedded. I remembered the morning Meg's bracelet had broken, and the time we had spent hunting for the damn thing, until it was so late we had to drop the matter and leave so as to both arrive on time without arriving conspicuously together.

I brushed the dust and hair off it, held it in my palm a moment, then closed my fingers around it and walked out through the living room. The sun had wedged itself up above the next high-rise and was outlining a hot square of light on the rug, just inside the sliding glass doors to the balcony. I stepped outside, the sharp morning air seizing on my still damp hair, and snapped my arm out and up as hard as I could, feeling something ping in the back of my shoulder but no sense of anything leaving my hand. I had to turn my palm up to see that it was empty, then caught a phantom flash as the little charm dropped through the shaft of early sunlight.

Sophie's car was in its space, but not Ryan's, which despite Selby's skepticism made me more comfortable. Sarah was talking intensely with some advertiser, looping numbers with her ballpoint and then pattering at a calculator; two or three phones went at once in the back of the newsroom, where I could spot Selby, head together with the layout editor. No sign of Sophie. I was so intent on whether my desk showed any traces of last night that at first I didn't register Sean, puttering at my computer, fingers flying in an impossibly rapid cascade whose last stroke coincided with a grin that made him look about twelve. He heard me about the same time I saw him, swiveled the chair and hopped to his feet, then reached to pop a disk out of the drive. He presented it with a flourish, like the envelope at an awards ceremony, and visibly puffed his chest as I read *REMARKSFORSAT.doc* on the newly inked label.

Ryan's phone jangled, making us both jump. I slid the disk into my shirt pocket, felt a moment's puzzlement as Sean held up his hand like a traffic cop. Then I got the picture and high-fived him. He had to walk me through the rest of the routine, but against all odds, I was grinning.

CHAPTER TEN
PAGE AND KNIGHT

"Finally found a string of code where it didn't belong in what should have been a perfectly good registry key," he said. "Killed it, booted up, bin-GO!, and sucked that little puppy right off onto the floppy before your mail was done downloading." He uttered a quite revolting noise exactly like a straw in the bottom of a milkshake.

"Print it?" I said, glancing over my shoulder.

"Two copies. One's in your top drawer, one's here in my bookbag. But don't worry. I have made *mega*-sure that this thing will never disappear again. I know how, trust me. I see why too. He was gonna make heads roll, wasn't he?"

"Maybe not that dramatic," I said. Sophie was approaching; her heels always announced her well ahead of her arrival. "Tell me later what you did," I muttered. Sean winked at me, patted his bookbag and mooched off to his station. I reminded myself to ask him about whimsical Death and where he'd found her.

Sophie had questions about how much space I wanted to give to what story, whether I'd worked with the principal at one of the schools she was covering, which stories could hang till next edition—Sophie's good, but she likes direction. Ryan slid in, glowered at Sophie and began pummeling copy into his keyboard. I caught myself glancing at my computer screen to see if any sign of Sean's activities remained on it; he had closed whatever program he was working in before leaving, and left up a web page for something called goodgoth.com. I kicked up the county website instead.

Sophie phased from her cross-checking mode into her chatty mode. Usually a subtle signal, like giving my undivided attention to something else, was enough to short-circuit this and send all that energy to work generating copy. I surfed my way, through a groove well worn by habit, to the board meeting agenda.

"Oh," said Sophie, "that's right, they had to reschedule the whole meeting. Are you going?"

"Can't not," I said, though without detailing why; plans were beginning to form in my head. "This one'll have the whole rogue's gallery there, from Beach to Schulz."

"God! That man!" Sophie began to turn away. "You know I swear he's got another woman in there already? My husband saw her carrying stuff in out of her car. One of those *crackpots* who actually carry clipboards for him, I bet." I had heard such people existed, but privately thought that the numerous caustic e-mails I periodically received from members of a group called Concerned Fairmont Citizens were all Schulz.

"You want to start writing the gossip column, Sophie?" said Ryan without looking up from his screen. "You'd be good at it."

Sophie flushed. "If someone *peed* in *your* Cheerios, Ryan Tabor," she said, startling us both, "don't take it out on *me.*" She clicked off in a rhythm of controlled fury. Somewhere out of sight, someone (probably Sarah) snorted, and I caught a muffled sound of palms striking slowly together in applause.

Even the back of Ryan's head telegraphed a glare. "Ryan," I said, "why don't you take the day off?"

"Hey, Smitty, I didn't—"

I dropped my voice. "I don't mean because of that. You covered for me all Tuesday, you worked late Tuesday night, you wrangled the kids yesterday. I may need you in the morning. Take a day. You have it coming."

He tried a rueful expression and managed grudgingly pleased. "Okay. Call me if anything hits the fan."

"Go catch up on life."

Everything I had said was true, but I still felt calmer when he had gone. Sean was trying to hide a chuckle, not succeeding well; he was too young for subtlety. I turned back to the screen and saw that the agenda displayed still had last week's date.

I dialed Toni Messner. "Toni, Paige Smith at the *Spectator*," I said. "You said the agenda was going up? Just checking."

"Oh, I'm off my *feet*," she said. "Hilde decided to take today off too. And everyone around here's got an attitude this morning. It's slowing me down."

"Here too," I said. "Can you just e-mail it to me?"

"Not—a—problem," she said, sounding as if she was typing as she spoke. "Nothing much changed. A couple more site plan amendments on the consent agenda, an appropriation for the Domestic Violence Prevention program, and then of course there's a minute of silence at the beginning for poor Hector." She dropped her voice as if someone might be listening. "Are the police getting any-where?"

"Nothing I can put in the paper yet," I said. Yesterday's conversation with Flanagan's spokesman had reeked of coverage control: "persons of interest" had been interviewed, a few eyewitnesses had been called back, no other statements could be made without risk of jeopardizing the investigation. Chief Flanagan would be giving a weekly update for press in the police briefing room starting Monday morning, which translated to "you get news if someone comes and takes my picture." Porous evidence lockers and wino-baiting were not mentioned.

Toni sighed heavily. "Oh, did you ever clear up what Hilde dropped off for you? I can call her at home if you need me to."

"Not necessary," I said. I thought quickly. "But I did mean to call her back—it was a disk I couldn't read. Could you maybe ask around which of the members asked her to send it and find out what it was?" There, that should put them off balance.

I spent the rest of the morning on the phone with the hospital press office (opening of new dialysis facility slated for the end of the month), one of the state delegates (chronicling the history of a bill that had died in committee for the third year), and Mark Lewis, currently vice chairman of the Republican Commit-tee, detailing all the reasons he had found why the county could have set lower tax rates. "Between you and me, Pastorelli and his damn dinosaur aren't doing us a bit of good," he said. "I wish he'd *stop* it. It makes us look like a Punch and Judy show."

I ran out of people to call by lunchtime. Sophie and Sarah had gone out, leav-ing Sean at his station with a can of Jolt and me bleakly contemplating the stack of books beside my blotter. Last night's spill had left only a faint rumple in the top calendar sheet. As I bent to restore the books to the bottom shelf the phone rang; Marlaine's voice came down the line when I picked it up.

I closed my eyes. More bad news, I thought.

"Got a look at them subway tokens," she said. "Boston. Seems New York don't use em any more."

That almost spoke against Flanagan having any involvement; anything that pointed back to him would have disappeared as quickly as the speech text. Unless. "I hope they don't go walking," I said.

"Oh, no fear," she said. "Trust me and Duwayne. Now listen, last night. Was that anything that helped you out? You didn't sound good."

"It was—an employee issue," I said. "Not a nice thing to find out. But easy to understand how the prints got there. She doesn't work here any more."

"Well, good to hear it. I'll be in touch. I'm still stayin peeled for that wino."

"Got something for you on that. I think his name's Hoople."

"*Hoople*?" Marlaine made a noise like Fang killing her fluffy toy. "Oh hell, Hoople, we *all* know Hoople. Crazy fucker with hair like something exploded, always carryin on about black magic heebiejeebies. Useless son of a bitch, scares the commuters. We broom him about twice a week. No, this guy wasn't Hoople, my buddy said this guy they took in was half bald. Stuff they drink, wonder more'a their hair doesn't fall out. No, I'll keep lookin."

She rang off. I looked around at the all-but-empty newsroom, had a thought, and flipped through my Rolodex. "Audit and Oversight. Pastorelli."

"Angelo, it's Paige Smith at the *Spectator*. You busy?"

"Not doin shit till the AIG gets back from lunch."

"We've had some developments." I filled him in, from Marlaine's discovery of the evaporating speech to Mercedes' recordsetting flight from the tomato bin, editing out any details of the fingerprinting other than that it came back to a former *Spectator* employee. E-mail pinged in as I talked; I flicked down it, one eye on the door for returning staff. Two or three times I heard his characteristic reverse whistle. When I got to the Boston subway tokens he said "Son of a bitch. No *wonder* I had to go tell em the whole story over on Wednesday. Wanted to know when I'd been back to Boston."

"Had you?"

"Haven't been home in months," he said. "They're up there and I'm down here and that's how I like it. Last time I was there that little peckerhead cousin of mine tried to sucker-punch me, did I tell you he got no fuckin job and owns a Lexus? Course, who *does* have a fuckin job these days? Friedman got no fuckin job, his wife's the breadwinner. *Bravo* got no fuckin job, must be developers buying those designer outfits, twenty-five K a year from the Board won't do it. And they'd probably both like to see me disappear as much as cousin Dio does. Now, *me*, if I hung out in the gym all day selling steroids, which is what I think he does when he's not beating people up for extra bonuses, I'd keep my hands off someone who worked for the Drug Enforcement Administration, but no, he still thinks he's got to get even over some crap about his mother. Ah, you don't wanna hear the whole story," he said, then launched into it. Pastorelli could be like this. I tuned him half out and began opening e-mails again; almost deleted something large from *mistressbast@globalhemp.com* as spam, then clicked on it to find an unwieldy photograph of a half-familiar scene. It took a moment for me to recognize the table mat, the teacup, the cards spread out so that I had to scroll from side to side as well as up and down. "One of these days," Pastorelli was saying, "I'm just going to have to put the little bastard down *hard,* he probably packs heat, I'll just have to hope I see him coming and get in *one good punch*—" he broke off abruptly. Probably the Assistant Inspector General was back from lunch.

I was gazing at the Knight of Swords at the top of the reading, leaning impossibly forward over the neck of his caparisoned horse, brandishing a sword with the expression of a comic-book superhero roused to wrath. *I think a crazy-brave person is going to help you out...Make sure he knows you need him.* Something clicked into place. "Angelo," I said, "can you still talk?"

"After I get home," he said. "Try me after four."

"You speaking at Public Comment tomorrow?"

"Probably be up till midnight writing it. Lemme let you go, Smitty." He rang off with the same briskness I'd seen in my own employees when I entered the newsroom. When Sarah stepped up behind me five minutes later I was still musing on the cards without quite taking in what they depicted; I started guiltily, and the image that flashed through my head was not any of the storybook illustrations in the Tarot deck, but a black cat, unblinking, tail-tip curved, staring in through a casement window.

✳   ✳   ✳   ✳

The third time my stomach went hollow at the sound of the fax machine kicking in, I called Slate's place.

✳   ✳   ✳   ✳

Pastorelli sounded as if he had just gotten in; there was a tearing sound as he opened mail. "I am *down* with it," he said. "Hell, I'll bring Taxopotomus just for effect. They will *hate* it. And *that* is how we know it's good."

"OK, I'm sending you e-mail now," I said. "I'll see you before the meeting. Phyllis coming?"

"She has a vet appointment for Fang. I called her earlier to make sure she was taping it." Pastorelli keeps videos of Board meetings going back several years; I've borrowed one more than once. The meetings go out live over County cable, which would work for me.

"Tell her I'll personally pay for copies."

"You da man, Smitty. Oh, I have been waiting for this day for years. Can I call you when I have my comment written up?"

"Let me know how late you'll be awake," I said after a short hesitation. "I'm going to be out."

*   *   *   *

"The race, it was my first trip down," said Mercedes as we walked down the canal after a decent, if slightly overpriced, dinner at outside cafe tables, where occasional gusts had made the awning snap like the sail of a ketch on a brisk day. "Before, while mama is alive, Hector always comes up to New York. She is so proud and shows him off, her son who works for the Congressman." She grinned. "She liked to talk as if this Murphy does nothing without his advice. The son, it is a big thing." There was a strained lightness in her tone. "Me, she only asks why I am such an age and not married."

Slate had found her clothes from the shelter's donation store; the jeans fit but the hooded jacket was oversized, making her look waiflike and not at all of an age for anyone to question why she wasn't married. She belonged on the Georgetown side of the river; among the khakis, Banana Republic T-shirts and cyclists walking their bikes through the populous stretch of the towpath, I was the one who felt out of place.

"See, I remember this part of the race," she said, pointing at the verdigris railings of Key Bridge a short distance away. "This was where I got in one of those little *concurso* you get in a long race, with a man runner who matched me. We both try to break away all along the bridge, running like two in harness, then we start to go uphill on other side and I break away from him. He pass me again in last mile. But it was a good race."

Two young women, one looking too chunky for the sport, jogged past us as if on cue. Their shoes uttered a syncopated crunch on the pebbly grit of the towpath.

"I suppose I was sulky," she said. "I am sorry now. When she began *exclamar* about Hector, wanted to show me pictures he has sent, news clippings, I ask why she does not talk that way about my college, my scholarship, business, and will not look. Then I am e-mailing with Hector about what he does, because I am proud of my brother too. I only want her to be proud of me also." She kicked a big pebble into the canal. "Now, both gone." A couple paddled past us in a rental from the boathouse between the bridges, level light glazing the paddles and sketching fractals in their wake. "I was sorry, very sorry she did not live to see the election. But glad she is not here for this."

She looked after the boaters, dropping unselfconsciously into a runner's stretch on the grass verge.

"I had a choice, the weekend of the race or the week of the election. I really did not believe he would win, and the race was where my heart was. So I missed his party. That was why I came down this time."

She squatted on her heels and skimmed a pebble. While she watched the ripples I tried the same forward bend; my back expressed polite disbelief. She straightened a little more quickly than I managed, caught the movement, grinned a little.

"We should start back," she said. "It will get dark." The long thoroughfare of the canal was already reflecting a twilight sky in the Maryland direction, a few threads of luminous cloud throwing scrawls on the glassy surface. A pair of cyclists chimed their way out of the long tunnel of dusk, edging us into single file as we started back.

A short way along the railed sidewalk on the eastern side of the bridge she turned and looked downtown, resting the heels of her palms on the bridge parapet. "I would like some slow film for this," she said, contemplating the lights winking on in the arc of the harbor.

"You sound like Selby."

"Ah, my Knight of the Tomatoes. Your Slate is telling me that he mentors her, takes plenty time, shows her ways to work that her teachers leave out. A good man." I had not been really aware of this. "The support is good too. She tells me her family are all lawyers, business and so on, they are not supporting her wanting to be in any kind of arts, so she has to go to community college and live in this group house with the other women. They are nice girls, all involved with shelter I think."

She did not move from the parapet. The breeze over the water had picked up a little bite.

"My brother now, he always say to me, Mercedes, you be whatever is inside you and do not let anyone stop you or make you ashamed. That was a gift, and I go forward with it. So now many of my friends, women my age, all married, kids, even when that is not what they wanted when we were young, it is what the family expects, while I go to school, start this business, live on my own, he always supported that and many other things." She did not have to repeat: And now he is gone. Her face was turned away from me, the headlights of cars washing by us.

"You are very quiet," she said suddenly. "I talk and talk, and you have suffered with this business too. You take time out of your life for me, and I know it is not your only concern. You looked like something bad was happening last night, you did not seem well."

"I'm—all right," I said, hearing it sound like the completest fiction I had ever uttered. "I had just found out someone...close to me had a criminal record. Lied to me, had been lying for a long time. It was a shock."

"So big shock that the Knight of the Tomatoes washed your head." There was a sudden mischief in her tone. "Okay, I will not ask more. But I think I understand, a little. There was a woman in New York, I thought she was my loyal *amiga*, we shared an apartment a couple of years, and one day I wake up and she is gone, and so is my spare cash and all my gold jewelry. Losing the things is bad but the person you thought you knew, a lot worse." A boat powered by below us, its lights sketching her profile. "But you go on."

"Yes," I said, out of politeness, thinking of the silver heart flashing out into the dawn sky. She pushed back from the parapet.

"We will freeze to this thing if we don't walk," she said. I followed after a moment. I had just been starting to get comfortable there.

✳   ✳   ✳   ✳

I had left my car at a parking garage in a maze of deep canyons, a block or two below the Rosslyn Metro; driving into Georgetown is a mug's game and I knew Mercedes had been cooped up all day. Now my feet were complaining about the shape of my loafers, but I had other reasons to sit down on the last bench before the lot entrance.

"Can't get a connection through the concrete," I said, extracting my cell phone. "I just want to check with a couple of people."

"Nooo, nothing so far, least on the dispatch I've heard," said Phyllis. "I don't think they want to report her *missin*, because she might just be difficult enough to tell someone *why* she wanted to be missin'. No news is good news, 'n other words. You have a nice dinner?"

Pastorelli was in a livelier mood. "Oh yeah, almost done with it," he said. "This is going to rot their socks off. Eight o'clock?"

"Eight, in the lobby."

Mercedes was looking at me with amusement and what might have been admiration. "You are planning something for the *consejo* tomorrow, aren't you?" she said. "Shall I come?"

"I think you'd better stay with Slate."

"I would be pretty safe in a crowd. I could dye my hair tonight! *Mira! Una rubia!*" She yanked on the ponytail swinging over the band of her now unnecessary sun visor. "Slate's roommate has hers all green."

"Give us till nine," I said.

*   *   *   *

Slate lived in Arlington Woods, in one of the boxy old postwar houses that throng the slopes going down to Upper Potters Run. Two roommates sublet the second bedroom and the basement, and a transient sputter of shelter refugees used the couch. All three women were gathered around the television when Mercedes knocked.

"We're having Ben and Jerry's, you want some?" The young woman who answered was stocky but not actually plump, and her hair was not only faintly green but cut *en brosse*. She had a baby face, or perhaps everyone was starting to look more baby-faced to me. Slate looked up from the screen.

"Lucy and Zoom are cool with this," she said. "We've had the drill down for a long time. It's always someone's sister or cousin or college friend visiting if anyone asks. Sit down, we're watching to see if anything comes on newschannel eight about all this."

Zoom seemed to be the one with the green coiffure. She brought out the end of a pint of Cherry Garcia for Mercedes, who sat on the hassock to dig into it.

The coverage at the moment seemed to be about whether augmented bus service would be as efficient as light rail along Liberty Pike, with a stand-up at one of the major stops (near my building, as it happened) and several talking-head interviews. I had been here before, and was glancing around the room at a couple of intriguing theater posters when Mercedes made a noise as if the ice cream had gone the wrong way. Zoom moved to smack her back, but she shook her head, swallowed and said "No! That man they are interviewing! Smitty?"

I turned. Zoom's rather two-by-four figure was blocking the screen. "That is the big man who is there when they talk about getting the disk back, the one who said he knew who to ask, who got you beat up."

By this time I had edged my way to a clear sightline.

Ryan was right to do it himself, I thought. A gap closed. She had never looked at the photos Hector sent home. I felt flash memories of the texture of asphalt, strobe lights, the smell of splashed coffee; saw the tufting of white hair on fleshy knuckles.

"Oh, no," I said heavily. "Much simpler than that. Mercedes, that was your brother's old boss. U. S. Representative in Congress. And former prizefighter. B, r, i. Brian. Murphy."

*   *   *   *

"So this man beats on everyone?" she demanded, through hitching tears, though I could not tell quite what about the situation had made her cry. I had explained about Tuesday night, and the long history of more than embarrassing incidents that Hector had somehow left out of his letters home. "This is my brother's big *bienhechor,* a *boxeador* who punches up reporters and poor crazy men?" I felt cold all over, suddenly wanting only a scalding shower and bed, and also a little piqued to have Mercedes put me in a category with Jim Schulz.

"He's a pretty scary crazy man," I said. "We thought…" I had been about to say *We thought he might have shot Hector* and shut my mouth before my foot could get all the way in. "His whole life seems to be hating the Board, Murphy and everyone in between."

"Then he is not so crazy and I call him *camerado,*" snuffled Mercedes, breaking down again. The other women seemed to know what to do about it. I did not. Nonetheless she pulled herself away from a sort of lopsided group hug to see me out the door with a dry, kind kiss sketched somewhere near my ear, smelling faintly of Ben and Jerry's. She had left the water bottle from her hip pack on my floorboard. I thought of going back in with it and didn't.

When I let myself in the phone was beeping, but it was only an earlier call from Pastorelli, crossing mine. His e-mail was the last in my inbox, with a sizable attachment. aLL sYSTEMS gO, it was subject lined. He never could remember to take off the caps lock. I tossed my shirt in the hamper, turned on the radio, and sat down to read.

CHAPTER ELEVEN
LOCAL COVERAGE

The entrance to the County Building is set at an angle on Courthouse Plaza, and two curved steps, flanked by access ramps with brass handrails, lead up to the heavy glass doors. They face roughly east, so that early on a Spring morning— like this one—the light, once it has climbed the hill from Rosslyn, not only saturates the plaza but flushes the rather drab lobby. A place of brochures and uninspiring display cases, it used to harbor some rather comfortable chairs, but those disappeared a couple of years ago after several seasons of chronic loitering by Scrape and his ilk. This morning it conducted a steady stream of citizens so earnest in their zeal to attend the first Board meeting after a gruesome murder that they had turned up before the doors were unlocked. I reflected that this was perhaps the only way that Hector could have ever packed the boardroom.

"You will love it," said Perry Reardon, catching up with us in the third-floor lobby, which hugs the front of the boardroom but extends in a staggered array of squashy chairs and tables around a railed well that opens straight down to the ground floor. "Schulz has got a *babe*."

"Naaah," said Pastorelli. "Unless she was inflatable."

"Personally, I don't *care* about Jim Schulz's sex life," said Angie, who had had to remove him from the boardroom more than once.

"No, she was seriously *hot,*" said Reardon.

"You think *Bravo* is hot," said Pastorelli.

"She was driving him," said Reardon. "He usually drives that heap van?"

"Must be the booty shorts," said Angie drily.

"It's just the *other* Concerned Fairmont Citizen," said Bob Beach, but Perry was not to be convinced. I considered suggesting he compare notes with Sophie; other than Betty Bravo, there was nothing that enchanted Reardon like a tissue of gossip, however flimsy. It suited me. Something about a shot out of left field had captured my imagination, and I preferred to have people dwelling on anything else in the meantime. I slid away from the conversation. Roughly everyone who was anyone in the county had showed up, to the point I expected an overflow from the boardroom into the lobby, where three closed-circuit screens relay the proceedings over the largest clutches of seating. Beach, using his laptop as a desk, was filling out a speaker slip almost under Reardon's elbow; a larger than normal complement from the Republican Committee was clustered near the windows, including Mark Lewis, a blowzy woman in a pink cashmere twinset straight out of 1955—her name was Petrowicz or Palowicz or something like that, and if she had even been born in nineteen-*seventy*–five I would have been surprised—and several other half-recognizable folk who usually only came out of the woodwork during budget hearings.

And, of course, Elisa. Currently she was in close colloquy with Ron Carroll, the County Manager, next to a small architect's model of Courthouse Plaza that stands glassed in at about chest height near the left-hand door to the boardroom. The glass complicated the sightline between us, which was fine with me.

I caught Mark Lewis' eye. "Any discussion of a candidate so far?"

"We've all just been a little too shocked," he said, looking as if any shock he had recently sustained involved getting out of bed too early. Out-of-cycle elections were his party's best shot at a seat, and he would probably relinquish the chairmanship to run again, but was dancing around it now; it would be awkward to remark too obviously that Hector's murder was the best stroke of political luck he had had since the last election.

There was a general movement toward the pews inside; no one quite wanted to be one of the groundlings making do with the lobby TV. I heard Pastorelli addressing "Brother Beach" in his incongrously light but carrying tenor voice; glancing his way, I saw that he had extracted a small lavender stuffed hippo from his briefcase and was holding it aloft. "Taxopotomus" had been a gift from Hugh Sprague after last year's budget hearings, whose significance I had never quite grasped. Lewis followed my glance, closed his eyes with a grimace, then rolled them up to heaven.

"There's still *plenty* of time, you could have finished putting on *all* your clothes," came a snide voice. It was the pink twinset woman. On this peculiar utterance the press nudged me into the back of the boardroom, where I seized the end of a pew; a few beats later I saw a white-lipped Dvorah Steadman, a spot of red flaring in either cheek, enter just ahead of an apologetic-looking Lewis. No clothes were missing, exactly, but her skirt and top were not quite speaking to one another. I focused very hard on my pocket calendar.

The center chair was empty, not flag-draped as in Mike's cartoon but covered with a plain black cloth, and Pinky took the seat to the left of it, where Toni had already placed the gavel. He made it right under the wire at eight-thirty sharp; I made a note. The before-curtain murmur subsided as he called for a minute of silence in honor of Hector de la Roja; like most such occasions in modern life, it was punctuated by distant traffic noises and, at one point, the distinct burr of a vibrating pager that someone had left on the seat beside him. Paulsen winced, thanked the assembly and opened Public Comment.

This involves pretty much anything you can think of, so that the first speaker humbly implored the Board to note that her neighborhood had been waiting for curbs for about two years, and the second requested that English be publicly designated the official language of Arlington County. As his three minutes ran down I heard Pastorelli stage-whisper to Beach, "Showtime," and edge up into the space near the podium. He had Taxopotomus on his shoulder, like a kitten. Everyone but Bravo was suppressing a smile; you could tell that none of them expected to take his speech seriously but anticipated a much-needed laugh from it. When Toni called his name he strode forward as if into the lists, flourishing a sheaf of paper and an outsize brown envelope.

"If you've got extra materials I'll need a copy of them, Angelo," said Toni reprovingly. "You'll have them, m'am," he replied in a tone that was almost ominous. Betty Bravo fidgeted. When he thumped the podium, it was usually at her.

"Ladies and gentlemen," he began, "for *yeahhs*" [the Boston accent had grown wings and a tail] "I have been chronicling for you the arrogance and the incompetence that riddle this county's government.

"Today, we observed a moment of silence in honor of the late Hector de la Roja. Hector was not my favorite board member"—Several people made restless noises; this was in poor taste. "But he was growing as a leader, and today I come before you with the proof of that. I come before you with proof that Mr. de la Roja had resolved to do what no other board member has done, defy the culture of denial in our police department and forthrightly call for action on the plague of gang activity in this county. I come before you with proof that" (here there was a decided rustle) "Mr. De la Roja had resolved to do what no other Board member has done, and question the cronyism and complacency that has concentrated our low-income housing into the crumbling neighborhoods where *"those"* people live." His voice shivered with an irony that, admittedly, would have been more effective an octave lower. "And I will show you evidence—not for the faint of heart"—he held up the envelope. "That this county's police department" (he turned directly to Carroll, who had hired Flanagan) "is either corrupt from the top down, or incompetent from the inside out."

Betty Bravo had gone white. Paulsen looked bemused—or, rather, his constant look of bemusement had deepened—while a look of terrible intelligence and intensity was developing on Hugh Sprague's GQ-model face. Friedman was going from red to purple; I was indeed, as Dvorah's cards had said, looking at a ruthless woman and an unimaginably angry man. There was also nothing they could do; cutting off a speaker other than to call time was unheard of.

"These remarks that I am about to hand up to the Board Secretary," said Pastorelli, laying the incongruous lavender puppet carefully on the podium in order to wave the sheaf of papers aloft, "were intended to be delivered by Mr. de la Roja on the day of his tragic death. I have confidence that they are genuine, and the individual closest in the world to Mr. de la Roja will attest"—

There was a clatter and shuffle, suddenly, whose direction I could not at first make out. Friedman's head snapped around, so it must be close to the dais. Betty Bravo turned too, and I was focusing on her look of barely contained fury, so that when the shot nearly deafened me it seemed almost as if she had produced the explosion. My first thought after the split second it took to register *gunfire* was that she had actually decided to take out Pastorelli; then I saw Friedman, who had started out of his chair, fall heavily back into it, left hand clamped to his right shoulder, looking no longer enraged but sucker-punched. A second of horrified silence was cut off by a woman's shriek somewhere to my right; out of the corner of my eye I registered a half-risen Elisa de la Roja. Blood began to well through the herringbone suit jacket and between Friedman's fingers.

"Fuck," said Jim Schulz in a voice that seemed absurdly small after Pastorelli's thunder at the podium, stepping out onto the dais from the recess room door. The pistol in his hand was sizable, the one tucked into the waistband of his shorts rather less so, and some third firearm not quite visible enough to identify was slung on his back with a strap of webbing. "That was supposed to be a warning shot. You moved."

He leveled the pistol at Betty Bravo's head; it seemed ridiculously long, with a taper to the barrel that, perhaps because of the proximity to Bravo, made me think of a spiked heel.

"Everyone clear out," he said. "Mess with me and we're gonna see if there really is anything inside her hatrack or not. Behave, and these folks will just go in the backroom with me for a way, long overdue conversation."

*   *   *   *

Pastorelli had already hit the floor behind the podium, rather heavily, and scrambled between the pews, crowding the knees of a woman from the traffic-calming work group. He had a tendency to overdramatize but I could see his point. A last moment of stunned hush was already giving way to a near stampede; I flattened myself against the wall and began dashing down notes as the exodus hovered on the edge of panic. Coats, briefcases, and for some reason, a potted plant remained on the pews as their owners pressed toward the doors at the back of the boardroom. The Navy pilot from Caerleon Park seemed to be keeping his head admirably and was directing the traffic, almost like an usher, in the far aisle. Things were more of a crush near me. The pink twinset woman, looking more offended than frightened, kept trying to turn and get back to something she had left until the opposing momentum bounced her into me. She glared as though I had intentionally invaded her space and huffed through the doors.

Pastorelli made it as far as where I was standing, swiveled back against the wall beside me. He was empty-handed except for his thick reading glasses. Whatever he started to say was drowned out by another shot, this one well over our heads, which shattered the clock in the back—something Schulz hadn't actually intended to do, judging by his expression.

"Keep moving," he snapped. He had gotten the smaller pistol—a "nine," possibly, like the one that had shot Hector; I don't know guns—out of his waistband and looked absurdly like Yosemite Sam as he pointed it left-handed in the general direction of Hugh Sprague, who was staring at him as if to size up whether he could be rushed. The long pistol, which he had just fired, returned to angle at a faint-looking Betty Bravo's left earring. Friedman was buckled down toward the microphone behind his nameplate as if he had something important to say, still clutching his shoulder, the blood now trickling liberally down his hand and onto a scatter of papers in front of him. Above this tableau, the boardroom screen, which usually featured the current speaker, remained focused on a podium empty except for the farcically smirking Taxopotomus.

"Where the hell's Angie?" I heard Ron Carroll say as we emerged into the lobby. He must have been finishing off his morning latte when Schulz fired; at least, a good bit of it laced his sandy beard and slightly convex shirtfront. A few people remained hovering near the furniture, most were retreating in a steady stream down the stairs at the middle of the open well. Halfway between here and there, Elisa de la Roja was clutching Toni Messner's arm in both hands, as if it were an oar, and shaking with sobs; apparently this had been the final shock that shattered her almost supernatural calm.

Pastorelli had his phone out. After a moment he snapped it shut and drew even with me; I was glancing, still dashing notes, up at the other closed-circuit screen where dwarf images of Schulz herding the Board members into the recess room at gunpoint hung over the largest of the tired couches, as if someone had found a way to tune the boardroom TV in to a black-and-white suspense thriller. Hugh Sprague was propping up Friedman.

"They've already had two calls," said Angelo. "Let's get the hell out of here before PD runs over us." I could already hear sirens, and by the time we reached the lobby—still filled with the light of a crisp, clear spring morning—two cruisers had pulled up, nose to tail, onto the crosslaid brick of Courthouse Plaza, leaving a sooty stripe of tire rubber on the side of the flagpoles opposite the steps. A ragged crescent of people lingered just beyond them, next to the new bed of guy-wired cherry trees. Carroll intercepted the larger of the officers; I heard the words "got off two shots" and "hostage situation." The other cop, listening, unholstered his radio.

A few people were still trickling out. Reardon lumbered through the glass doors; probably the first time his feet had ever touched the stairs in that building, I thought. Seeing him reminded me of something. I approached the police; more cruisers were pulling around by the second, the station being only a block away.

"He may have an accomplice," I said. "He was seen arriving with a woman this morning."

"Who're you?" snapped the cop.

"Paige Smith, *Spectator* papers," I said. "Covering the meeting. This is Jim Schulz in there, one of the county activists. He's been calling my paper all week and he's been more irrational each time. He was in a confrontation at a meeting earlier in the week, and his wife may have left him that same night. Something must have snapped."

"Fuckin A something snapped," muttered the other cop under his breath.

"Who was this other person?"

"I don't know. Someone else saw them. Perry!" I called, but Reardon was leaning on a railing, grey and out of breath. "The large gentleman," I said, nodding. "He might be able to show you the vehicle."

"Okay, stay right here," said Larger Cop—I noted his nameplate, Kowicny—and moved to direct one of the new arrivals to Reardon, who looked up as they approached, nodded, and after a short exchange began a slow, huffing progress to the parking lot. Kowicny returned.

"We'll try to ID it," he said. "You've been talking to this guy? What was his issue?"

"A lot of things," I said heavily.

"Yeah, it usually is," said Kowicny. "OK, you stay right where I can find you. We might need you." He moved off to brief the new arrivals.

"How do you like this for boring, Meggie?" I said, looking up at the almost luminous facade of the county building. I wondered if this would make the news in Chicago. I wondered if I any longer cared.

*   *   *   *

By ten a.m. a perimeter of sorts was in place outside the boardroom: from what I was able to pick up, Schulz wanted no one at all in the boardroom itself, and had managed to sound jumpy enough that they let him have it. He had a cell phone, and had allowed each of the three uninjured Board members to speak briefly to Kowicny; Paulsen had reported that Friedman was conscious if pale and didn't appear to be bleeding dangerously.

I was sitting in the back of a cruiser in the courthouse parking lot, pounding on Bob Beach's laptop. For as long as the battery lasted, it had a wireless connection, and I was uploading copy direct to the Spectator website, at least if I knew what I was doing (I thought I did). The police were tolerating me there because of my familiarity with Schulz; Pastorelli, a deflated-looking Reardon, and Carroll were in a small knot a short distance away.

A medic unit had pulled even with the curb nearest the county building and a woman medic was giving Elisa de la Roja attention that seemed more supportive than medical. She had refused to leave the area, and put up a fuss when the increasing swarm of police insisted we get out of gunshot range of the windows. The medics had been called in for Friedman, but so far the most work they had had involved Angie, who had been found stunned and punchy, with an egg-sized knot on her head, slumped behind the lobby counter where on weekdays citizens pick up recycling bags and information leaflets.

"Good sign," said Kowicny tersely. "Not shot. It means he's not all that eager to hurt people. He could be a soft takeout."

I knew he was mainly speaking for my benefit. Two hostage negotiation experts had made it in from home, one in a weird state of half-uniform, the other forthrightly in his yardwork clothes with his PD name badge on his flannel pocket. They would have a lot more to say about the matter.

Kowicny's radio crackled. He raised a hand, signaling, and said into it "We have connection." A small figure on the skyline of the courthouse movie theaters could be seen waving back; they were getting sharpshooters up on the nearby roofs. I hammered another paragraph into the laptop.

Most of the boardroom audience had cleared out, but a loose cluster of the regulars, including Lewis, the Navy pilot, and the offended pink Petrowicz or Palowicz (Josie? Joanie?), had been augmented by several latecomers who had come in to address specific agenda items and gotten parked just in time to be told to move and make way for the house-trailer-sized mobile command post. The air was thick with heavy startup fumes from the rows of cruisers and sheriff's vehicles they were now having to clear out of the way. Pairs had been positioned at either end of Caerleon Boulevard and at the parking lot entrances, boxing the plaza in. With admirable dauntlessness, the proprietor of the Wrap Artist, who opened for breakfast on Board days, had brought out all the ready-prepared food he could carry when he was ordered out of the shop, and was stationed on the far sidewalk. Lewis was munching absently on a wrap.

"Sir, stop there, please," I heard a woman officer say behind me. I glanced over my shoulder and saw Selby.

"That's my photographer," I told Kowicny, who had turned to look. "I called him, if he can stay."

"He'll have to keep back from the team if he's shooting," said Kowicny. "This ain't a fuckin wedding party."

"Got it," I said. I folded Beach's laptop and retreated across one traffic aisle to where Selby stood. I had barely had time to fill him in when the woman cop—*Fraike*, I read on her shirt pocket—was back.

"We'd like you to listen," she said. "He's back on the line. Randall"—this was apparently Kowicny—"says you've been dealing with him."

Somehow Selby ended up with the laptop and I ended up inside the trailer wearing a headset. Schulz's voice was coming over a crackly connection as I settled it against my ears. "–don't want 'help,'" he was saying. "I want my rights and justice for the citizens of this county. I have a specific list of conditions. This will have to go to the governor. There is no one here with sufficient authority. These will require a binding commitment from the governor."

"He's not freaking right now," said Flannel Cop. "Let's just keep him talking."

Better call Richmond, wrote Half-Uniformed Cop on the nearest notepad. *Anyone in Warren's office.* His mouthpiece was apparently live; he had a deeply weathered face and near-white hair in an even quarter-inch cut, what there was of it.

"Meanwhile, I am not comfortable with your men in the building," continued Schulz. "They're too close. I want them moved back. I'm feeling listened to. We have a lot to discuss in here and it's private. Repeat, these bozos need to move back."

"Yeah, and bozo to you," muttered Kowicny, whose headset mike was still swiveled up by his ear.

"It's possible we can do that," said Half Uniform. "I can understand the need for a comfort level. But we're also concerned about Mr. Friedman. You might say that's our comfort level. We want to keep help close to him. How's he doing?"

Schulz's tone took on a ghastly geniality. "How ya doin', Grover?" he called in an aside that the cell connection caught tinnily. I could hear Betty Bravo's tones. "I didn't ask you, Garden Club Lady," he said. "Plus, you're ugly." There was another short silence.

"He says being shot hurts like a son of a bitch but he's got at least another eighteen quarts where that came from," Schulz relayed almost gaily. "What does that do for your comfort level?"

"We'd be a lot more comfortable if we could get him to treatment."

"Well, hell, I know first aid. Ask Pinky here."

A scuffle and Paulsen's voice. "True," he said. "He's got pressure on it." An echo effect signaled Schulz reclaiming the phone.

"What about this, Mr. Schulz," said Half Uniform. "We'll pull back the perimeter on the third floor and give you some genuine privacy if you'll let medics come up and release Mr. Friedman to them. Would that be an acceptable deal?"

A silence. "Well, crap, I am getting a little tired of looking at him. He isn't joining the conversation."

"Come onnn," breathed Flannel.

"Plus, he's the only one I can't keep tied. When I do he starts bleeding again."

"Tied?" I mouthed. Half Uniform echoed me aloud.

"Hell yes, you can't turn your back on any of these bastards if they're not tied," said Schulz. "I always said so."

"Mr. Schulz, are you willing to let Mr. Friedman go?"

"Pull your guys back."

Flannel squeezed his eyes shut and turned a thumb up—more in hope than triumph, but a few exchanges later the medic team was double-timing into the building. The connection snapped out abruptly.

"Anything to offer, Mr. Smith?" said Kowicny.

"He sounds a lot less ready to blow than last time I heard from him."

"Of course. He's in control. For the moment. We need to keep him feeling like he's in control without selling out the farm. What do you think he wants?"

"No clue," I said ruefully, feeling as if I was throwing away my next turn at the headset.

Selby was where I had left him behind the next to last aisle of parked cars, now thinned out. "Hoisted a gurney through the doors a few minutes ago," he said. "Did you talk to him?"

"No, I'm the expert witness."

He looked at me sharply. I could hear the radio in the medic unit crackle.

"*We have the patient…white male…gunshot wound to right shoulder, hemorrhage, in shock but conscious…starting a line…*"

A slight flurry near the impromptu wrap stand heralded the arrival of Mrs. Friedman. I caught sight of her—in a sweat suit as if she had been at the health club, and pale as concrete—just as the squawk signaled that the medics were coming out with Friedman. I stepped toward her, wondering if I was heartless enough to ask even two questions. The medic unit's diesel began to roar and belch. "M'am?" I heard Officer Fraike calling. Turning, I saw Elisa moving, with dignity but rapidly, across the asphalt. "M'am, you'll have to stay back, *m'am*"— She broke into a run as the medics negotiated the gurney down the steps, intercepting them halfway to the rumbling ambulance.

"*Grovie!!!*" she shrieked, then a cascade in Spanish that I couldn't begin to follow. "Shit," breathed Fraike and fingered a fellow officer to pull Elisa back from the ambulance. She crossed the path of Mrs. Friedman, being escorted to the unit by two other officers, with an indescribable glare.

"*Grovie?*" said Selby. We plowed behind the cops all but frog-marching Elisa back toward the courthouse sidewalk, where she collapsed onto a bench, sobbing.

"I don't understand! I did everything, I buried the charms, I burned the candles and did the *moyuba* to Oshun, I called all the *orishas* for him. *Ye-ye kari imbamoro…*" Rocking, she chanted the sentence over again several times, but I was only able to fix the first few syllables in my mind. I was sure Micaela back at the Botanica could have told me what they meant.

Sirens deafened us. No sooner had they receded than others wailed toward us; Fraike had apparently decided that Mrs. de la Roja needed sedating.

"Well, now we know why she didn't give a rat when Hector got shot," came a voice at my elbow. Phyllis Bell stood there, a portable scanner crackling in her saddlebag of a purse, Fang tucked under one arm.

"Just had the idea to turn this on coming back from the vet's," she said. "Been here just long enough to get the picture. I could see Pinky. I could see *Hugh* if he was in the market for women. But *Grover?* What the *hell* would make any woman lose her mind over *Grover...?*"

I looked across the small crowd into the absolutely stunned eyes of Ron Carroll, who appeared to be thinking much the same thing. I debated who to interview, or whether to just take five in the courthouse lobby men's room, but almost as soon as the men's room won out had to jump back on the sidewalk to keep a satellite van from running over my feet. Another one pulled in behind it, and they jockeyed briefly for place. Live coverage had arrived, and that meant Chief Flanagan could not be far behind.

$$*\qquad*\qquad*\qquad*$$

Fraike invited me to use the "head" in the command post. What she meant was that the hostage team had all assembled at last, and wanted to shake me down. I spent the next twenty minutes debriefing on every word Schulz had spoken to me over the course of the week, the scene at the Civic Federation, and even the shouting at Murphy as reported by Ryan. "Get this Tabor fellow in," said the senior negotiator almost abstractedly, a woman well past retirement age whose hair would have been white if it hadn't been dyed blonde.

"Does he have any female associates you could name?" she asked, turning back to me.

"Lots of names," I said. "Until today I would have said they were all fake e-mail addresses. He makes them up and sends out messages from the 'Concerned Fairmont Citizens' group."

"You know this?"

"We've all thought so for years."

She looked at a notepad. "The car Mr. Reardon identified was still in the lot, a Dodge Neon. The plates came back to Enterprise Rent-a-car, who seem to be having a *computer problem* ID'ing the customer—"

"I always use Alamo," muttered Kowicny.

"Unless you have any idea—?"

I didn't, but felt as if I should. "There are people who work on his election campaign," I said. "Check his website."

"*Election???*"

"Ssshhh," said Half Uniform, holding up a hand. "We may have some progress in a mo—ment—Mr. Schulz? Mr. Schulz, this is Bill Weller out at the command post. I talked to you earlier. You'll be glad to know that Mr. Friedman should be okay. You did a good thing letting him out."

Kowicny handed me a headset. Apparently I was still an asset.

"...told you he still had plenty in him," came Schulz's voice. "He won't have to take his blood pressure medicine, that's all."

"You're a funny man, Mr. Schulz."

Silence. Flattery was perhaps not the best tactic.

"Mr. Schulz, I'm on the phone with one of Governor Warren's aides. He's expressed concern that one of our citizens could have gone unheard the way you seem to have, and he's very anxious to know what it is you need. You haven't made that clear to us yet. I can patch him through to you now, and you can explain things to him directly."

"Put him on."

Half Uniform scratched something on his pad, and passed it to the blonde crone, who snorted. She turned it in my direction. *Actually my B in law,* it read. *Psych prof Crim Justice Program GMU.*

"We'll be able to listen in," said Flannel. There were electronic noises as Weller did something with the phones, then a springy, youthful tone that was damn-all like every fresh-faced Congressman's or governor's aide to wear a pin-point oxford.

"Hello? Hello, this is Eric Brandon in Governor Warren's office? Am I speaking to Mr. James Schulz in Arlington?"

"No, he's speaking to *you,*" came the answer. "*You* are going to listen. I know damn well you're all part of the same party machine. You could have avoided this, but no, the machine just kept rolling on. So do I have your attention?"

"You have my complete attention, Mr. Schulz."

"Then let me speak to the governor."

"He's in a meeting. I can transmit anything you say to him, and I have some limited authority to act."

"You have some limited authority to yank your twenty-year-old plank. All right, let's boogie a little. I have three members of the Arlington County Board in here with me. They're not going anywhere for a while. In fact they're not going anywhere at all unless I get the justice I'm entitled to." His voice began to get the familiar edge.

"Second time he's used that word," whispered Blonde.

"So here's what I want. From this day the machine stops. It stops, you got me? If they're going to come out of here in the same shape they went in, every one of these tinpot tyrants will have to surrender office and confess frankly to all of their crimes and conspiracy agains the citizens of this county.

"Second, we will have *free* and *fair* elections in this county to be held *immediately* with no party affiliation of candidates and no party financing. There will be *no* promotion of candidates by holders of higher office."

"I'm writing this down, Mr. Schulz."

"Third, *all dogs* in this county will be confined to their owner's property *at all times*"—his voice was starting to rise now—"except for a dedicated and owner supported dog run on the grounds of the county sewage plant. There will be *no more* terrorization of *inconvenient* citizens of conscience by dogs. Also, they are a public health problem. They generate filth."

"I'm still with you, Mr. Schulz."

"Fourth and last, and *hardly* least, Mr. Eric Still-In-Your-Pampers, I am to be immediately informed of the whereabouts of my wife who is being held under false pretenses and probably with the aid of brainwashing in the county's so-called shelter system. This was done with the express purpose of breaking my resolve. You see what it's done instead. And I am to be immune from all charges in this matter. The idea was to force me to some action where they could put me away. I had to take charge."

"I've got all that, Mr. Schulz. I'll speak to the governor."

"I want documents signed by him. Verbal contract isn't good enough. A fax will be okay."

"That could take a little while."

"Got all the time in the world."

"We'll be back to you, Mr. Schulz."

Blonde Crone—Janet—dropped her headset back around her neck. "Well, he's easy to please," she sighed.

"Dogs, huh," said Weller.

"He believes Pinky Paulsen sends people to harass him with dogs," I said.

"So we either use K-9s or we make a point of not using them."

"Let's give it some time," said Janet. "Did we actually get Richmond?"

"Yep."

"Let's see if they'll buy into faxing up some sort of counter-offer on the right stationery. Let him stew a little and we'll try it on him. Buys time."

"Could use a break," said Weller. "See if that hustler across the way is out of sandwiches yet."

✱   ✱   ✱   ✱

Pastorelli was speaking to a Channel 8 EJ unit outside, with Ron Carroll adding commentary on the running sideshow of Schulz at Board meetings. As the reporter wrapped the standup Pastorelli looked at me, and then at the command bus, longingly.

"Shame he couldn't have fired the wrong gun to begin with and just shot his dick off," he said, looking as if he actually hadn't had this much fun in years. "Flanagan just finished talking to the press. You missed him." The last sentence was heavy with fake pity. "I tried to talk to them about my Public Comment but they cut me off." I couldn't tell whether he felt more wounded in his idealism or in his vanity.

North Fifteenth Street was now thronged with TV vans. One of the roach coaches that usually worked the area had taken over for the Wrap Artist manager, who was sold out but hanging around in apparent hopes of being interviewed too. Phyllis ambled over with a Dasani bottle in one hand and Fang's leash in the other. Fang immediately began demonstrating an excited interest in Pastorelli's trouser cuffs. "She's not going to *pee* on me is she?" he asked.

"She just loves her Uncle Angelo." Angelo didn't look as if he knew quite how he felt about that. I looked out over the parking lot. Nearly out of sight, a festoon of yellow tape and some orange cones suggested the location of the rental car. A fire marshal's vehicle had parked alongside the command post; Phyllis nodded in its direction. "They're scoping out the floor plan. Flanagan wants to try some kind of maneuver. I don't think the team is for it. They getting anywhere in there?"

"Fake calls to the governor's office."

"He buying into it?" said Angelo.

"Maybe."

Fraike materialized at my shoulder. "We'd like you back in there, Mr. Smith," she said. "Warren's office is actually on the line. We may be able to soften him up, your thoughts would help."

I was an expert on a nut. "Go get 'em," said Pastorelli.

"They're fiddling with the wording on an offer to allow him a partial amnesty and put him on the phone with his wife," said Fraike. "Not that anyone's found her yet. Yeah, we *are* checking the shelters but those women don't give up anything. Hedging on the other stuff by saying the General Assembly would have to pass on it."

"Is he considering it?"

"Haven't got it all sewed up yet. They were wording a fax when I came out."

Weller was talking earnestly into his headset. "We're standing by for the transmission now, Mr. Schulz. How are Mr. Paulsen, Mr. Sprague and Ms. Bravo?"

"Well, I had to take Pinky to the can. Must take a lot of coffee to get him running on Saturdays. But everyone's A-OK. We've been discussing what they need to confess to in writing. I'll want a special insert in the *Spectator*. Screw the Journal. They suck."

I raised my eyebrows. It was a testimonial of sorts.

The fax started churning. My stomach felt hollow again; I realized that sound would remind me of only one thing for a long time to come.

"We can have this walked in by an officer," said Weller. "It doesn't cover everything you need but it's a starting point. I think you should look at it."

"No fucking cops," he said. "I don't trust you."

"Well, think it over," said Weller. "This should take a few minutes."

A younger officer stepped in and caught Kowicny's attention off to my left. "Enterprise is still fucked-up," he said. "Now they're saying the plates come back to a rental by some guy at *O'Hare* over a week ago. This is bullshit."

Weller was asking Schulz if he would accept a civilian employee of the police department. I had the headset over one ear only, half listening as Schulz refused again. "I want it to be someone I know. Toni," he said. "You could send in Toni. Toni has never said a rude word to me at board meetings." Actually, it was true; she seemed able to manage him, but then she managed everybody.

"It's a big responsibility asking a civilian to do something like this, Mr. Schulz."

"Is Pastorelli out there?"

"Oh, Christ, no," breathed Kowicny. Some people did think of Angelo as just west of Schulz on the nut scale; probably the dinosaurs.

My mind was reaching for something it couldn't quite catch from the last time I had seen Schulz in the flesh. Pastorelli hoisting him into a folding chair, Murphy shouting "He went for me." Sodium-vapor lamps flushing a parking lot blurry through my old prescription. A woman driving a Neon. Ryan had heard Schulz shouting on the way out of the police station.

"Yeah, we could send in some lunch," Weller was saying. "I've been trying to get someone to bring me some lunch, myself. They work me pretty hard here, you know? If we rustle you up some lunch will you at least look at this offer? And let one of our people bring it in? How about Officer Fraike? She's here with me."

"You think I'm going to roll over just because it's a woman? Women are as two-faced as it gets. Look at Garden Club Lady here."

A faint voice came from some distance away through the cellular crackle. "Ah, shut up," said Schulz, almost genially.

My stomach swooped away as if I had put it on an elevator and pushed all the floors. I knew what I was going to do, though.

∗   ∗   ∗   ∗

"I am not really comfortable with this," said Janet. "You are taking a huge chance. You realize he most likely won't release you."

"I think I can talk to him," I said. "He may not let me go *right* away. But he gave us the hint when he asked this to be in my paper. It'll be like the Unabomber. He needs me." I didn't tell her what had been going through my mind during my few minutes in the command post bathroom, where I'd had to retreat again after making my decision. "And I have a long history of disparaging the Board."

"Yeah, well he's gone light years beyond *disparage*." Janet nodded across the tarmac to where another officer was arriving with a case of soft drinks and some garlicky-smelling boxes from the Pizzarama across Caerleon Boulevard. "We got what you asked for. I guess you have some idea about his tastes."

"He didn't really order so I ordered for him," I shrugged.

I took the awkward flat of provisions and started across the plaza with two officers as escort. One of them handed me a card with a recognizable County number penned on the back. "You've got your cell? That'll get you straight to Weller if you need to."

I nodded. Speaking was not working out for me.

The elevator huffed to a halt on the third floor. "We'll stay in here," said Card Cop. "We have *got your back,* Mr. Smith. As much as we can. I'm sorry I'm not the one taking this in."

With an effort I got my throat to open. "You have guns," I said. "I have ink. What he wants." It wasn't as poetic as *the pen is mightier than the sword,* but it would do. I had something else, too, which would have taken too long to explain to him.

The lobby echoed. Taxopotomus was still grinning inanely on the tiny black-and-white screen. I walked into the boardroom, up past the real Taxopotomus, and around past Toni Messner's station to the recess room door. I had actually never been back here. The floor was a particularly biological color of cultured marble, not improved by splashes and squiggles of Grover Friedman's blood, now dried almost to black. A coppery pong came from the high-backed swivel chair he must have been tied to, extruded from the recess room to sit askew on the dais, the archipelago of stains on it ranging from matte-dry to damp.

"I heard the doors," came Schulz's voice. "Paige Smith? You're alone?"

I got my voice past the chokepoint again. "Alone," I said.

"I'll want to see your hands up."

"Carrying lunch," I said. Breath was coming a little easier, though I felt oddly weightless. So did the pizza.

"OK. Come in". The first thing I could see was Hugh Sprague, who still looked as if he belonged in a rather conservative men's clothing catalogue, except that his jacket was creased (from having his arms tied behind one of the tall-backed swivel chairs) and smudged with Friedman's blood on one cuff. Paulsen sat facing me, at Sprague's right around the corner of the recess room's meeting table, as if they had just settled down to discuss some serious piece of Board business.

Schulz was leveling his pistol at me. Close up, it looked like something you would use to stop wild game, absurdly extravagant for threatening humans— matte-black, angular, functional. "Put it on the table," he said. I did. "You can stay for lunch. Just turn out your pockets."

I fumbled a little as I did. They seemed to satisfy him: keys, wallet, a used hanky, the prescription vial left over from Monday night, eyedrops and gungy comb, my cellphone. He gave me back everything but the phone.

"Stay for lunch," he repeated, waving me to one side with the pistol. "You can eat while I read this shit over. Help Pinky and Hugh chow down. I don't think Garden Club Lady stoops to *pizza*, do you? Play nanny and we won't have to tie you too."

"Oh, I wouldn't bother tying him up anyway," came a voice from my right, opposite where Betty Bravo sat; she was trying to glare but beginning to be too frightened and exhausted to bring it off. "Smitty couldn't be dangerous if he tried, could you?" I turned, a scurfy handkerchief in one hand, a key chain in the other, like the youngest son in the fairytales going into the giant's house with a bean and a ring and a feather, standing, as if Dvorah's tarot reading were a prophecy that would never stop coming true over and over, between the catastrophically angry man at one end of the room and the unexpectedly ruthless woman at the other.

"Hello, Meggie," I said.

CHAPTER TWELVE
RIDING THE TIGER

"Brian must not have hit you as hard as I thought he did," she said. "Good. I thought you were hurt a lot worse." She had changed her hair—cut it, and dyed it a mahogany color that made her face look harsh. She wore a T-shirt and a short jean skirt, the kind of thing she used to leave at my place to change into after work.

"Was that why you used my phone to call 911?" I said.

"Well, we couldn't have used his could we? It would have come back to him." She held Schulz's smaller pistol in her hand, almost casually, as if she were carrying a clutch bag at a cocktail party. I couldn't gauge whether this was because she was very used to it or not used to it at all. "I *told* him you'd probably had the combination changed anyway, but then I couldn't try it with you still there. We waited about an hour for you to come out. But maybe he was OK with that too." She smirked. "He likes to hit."

"They're all bullies," said Schulz. "He's just the King Bully." I could see faint, curdling bruises on both shins where Murphy had dropped him Tuesday night.

"I'm glad you cared enough to call," I said.

"Old time's sake."

"I noticed you took the cash," I said. She shrugged.

"His idea. Said it would just look like the usual that way. I think he was pissed we couldn't get in, just in case you'd printed it out or something."

"I don't know why you even went to that dumb gorilla," said Schulz testily around a slice of pizza.

"He'd always been generous," she said. Her chair, and Bravo's, adjoined a side table at the end of the recess room, nearest the hall leading to the offices. I judged she was there to cover the entrance, and Bravo was there as a human shield. "But he was never more than just business, you know that. And I mean, your *wife,* Jim. She picked up the first time I called on Monday." "Didn't turn out to be a problem, did it?" he muttered with a broody look, wiping pizza-greased fingers on his sock tops.

"And I didn't think he'd go ballistic when I told him about the Chicago thing, I mean, he'd just been booked *himself.* And I only found out it was you the next morning."

"Next time you'll call me first, won't you? Instead of someone who worries what might show up in Smith's paper. *Congressman harbors fugitive ex-Spectator reporter.*"

"*You're* going to be Congressman," she said in tone of conviction that made my nape prickle.

"Work something out, won't we?" he said. "Have to keep up appearances with the wife anyway, once they give her back." There was a faint blackish smear on his cheek and his wire-rims looked smudged, but with his coiffed mane of silvery hair and runner's build—I suddenly discerned his underlying vanity—he looked not unlike a media Congressman. He was facing the door, still, while he wolfed pizza, as if he expected SWAT teams to storm it any minute. From this angle I could see that the firearm slung on his shoulder was a machine pistol of some kind, and as I say, I know very little about guns, but it looked like the kind of thing you would use to shoot your way out of something. It raised possibilities I preferred not to consider.

I looked over at Paulsen and Sprague. "Uh, pizza?" Paulsen grimaced and shook his head. I wouldn't have had much appetite either.

"It'll suck cold," said Schulz. "Paige, did you read this piece of shit?"

"I just brought it in," I said. "I'm here as a newsman."

"Be glad you didn't write this," he said. "It's a goddam joke." He got out the cell and punched up a number which, I assumed, reached the hostage team in the command van.

"That Weller?" he almost shouted down the phone. "Does Warren think I'm an idiot? *Amnesty* isn't the point. *Talking* to that traitor isn't the point. The point is this corruption has to end. I'm not the only one they've persecuted, I'm just the one who had the guts to stand up…" I could tell Weller was letting him rant.

The longer he went on, the more chance they had to think of something else, or just play the hope that he'd run down.

I looked back at Meg. Her expression was, of all things, amused, as if the entire turn of events were a birthday-party entertainment. I had seen that same half smile in the first filtering of morning light, against the pillow while I spilled my heart to her.

"Meggie," I said *sotto voce*, weakening, tilting my head to indicate the expostulating Schulz. "You could have come to me if you were in trouble."

"I know, Smitty," she said. "You're so noble." Her brows lifted and she sketched a little kiss, blew it at me.

"Old time's sake?" I echoed bitterly. "Look, I found out…" What word would consent to be pronounced? "I know you have a record."

"Good newsman," she said. "You shouldn't complain. It got me through journalism school. Honors list, remember?"

"*Look,*" Schulz was hammering into the phone, "we're talking about *years* of systematic suppression through the front of so-called *citizens' groups* who were operating on Paulsen's orders"—His color was rising. He sat bent forward, leaning on the gun arm, which was propped on one knee and still pointing far too accurately in my direction.

"And when we were together, Meg?" I said. "Once you were *working*? Why then?"

"You think your piddly little paper pays enough to buy a girl a little blow now and then?" she said. "What's the matter, Mom teach you to be scared of diseases?" I was acutely aware that Betty Bravo sat close enough to hear us, though she looked too far gone in some land of inner panic to take it in. "I'm not a sloppy ho', Smitty. I learned fast. Occasional, selective, high-dollar. Lobbyists. Congressmen."

"Sitting and"—I hoped the irony in my voice was heavy enough—"hopeful?"

The wide grin of pleasure that I remembered from too many moments. "Jim's personal."

"When did *that* happen? And…" *Why* seemed too small a word for the huge insanity of it.

She cocked her head up as if searching the memory banks. Schulz was talking in lower but rapid and furious tones; I suspected they had patched him in to the "governor's aide," or maybe the real thing.

"One of the Board meetings I covered for you," she said. "Hard to put a date on it, you know? He wanted to make something understood to the press. I, well…I just wondered how he'd react to being *really* understood."

"Yes," I said heavily, "you do that well."

She dipped her head, a diva acknowledging the accolade. "It would have gotten awkward if it weren't for his wife. And that helpful way you insisted on being *discreet*. I think my business side actually kind of fascinated him, I made fun of Brian to him, you know? But I never mentioned you. And *you* don't want to be the one to tell him." She nodded meaningly at Schulz, whose volume was rising again.

"You like dangerous men, don't you, Meggie?"

"What would you suggest?" she answered, leaning back in her chair. "Boring drones whose idea of a hot evening out is the Autograph Theater production of *Little Women?*"

"*No, it is NOT a fucking deal!!!*" shouted Schulz suddenly, making me (and even Meg, a little) jump. "Call me back when you have a serious offer!" He snapped the cellphone shut and with frightening violence pitched it into the far corner of the recess room, then rose and began pacing in a tight circle, still clutching the pistol grip, as if he were an automated toy that had malfunctioned. His lips moved in a soft rapid speech of which not one word was intelligible. I felt clammy, and Hugh Sprague, who was far too close to Schulz's circuit, managed to sidle his chair back on its wheels a little, nearer to Paulsen.

Meg rose and closed the distance between then, put up her hands to Schulz's shoulders. "Bitsy," she said. "Sit down. They're trying to rattle you."

He stared at her as if he couldn't decide who she was, then after a long moment sank into the nearest chair, spreading the palm of his free hand against his temple. It was a regular secretary's chair, facing me almost directly; she set her gun, a little flat ladylike affair, down in his lap as she stepped behind him, and guided his hand down over it. He seemed only half aware of her while she worked the webbing sling down his arm and hung it on the chair back; slid her hands along his shoulders, and began kneading them slowly, making a small farrier's hiss between her lips. After a moment he dropped his head back against her, eyes drifting shut. His breathing slowed.

"You let them stew a little," she said soothingly. "You're in charge now. You've finally called them on it. They never thought someone would do that. Stay. With. It."

Her hands crept down the front of his rumpled Oxford, over his narrow chest. The dusky color was fading from his face; tilted back from me, it had the waxy look of a peevish invalid's. She flicked the top button of the shirt and slid her fingers inside, stroking outward as if to quiet his heartbeat, over and over. It was horribly fascinating, that rhythm. I looked up to her face and her eyes locked with mine, still crinkled with distant amusement. Schulz sighed deeply, and put one hand up to hers.

"You're right, Meggers," he said. His eyes opened, unfocused. "Let's make them wait a little."

"Smitty's here to tell your story, remember."

I pulled myself away from watching Meg and tried to focus him. "That's right," I said. "Help me help you here. Tell me what's been happening. Things you couldn't tell me on the phone?" I suggested.

"Why don't you tell him, Meggers?" he said. Her fingers were combing through his silver-glass hair now. Craziness was, not exactly leaving him, but pulling itself back into a coil inside.

"About Brian?" she said. She reached with her disengaged hand to retrieve the small pistol from his lap. "See, you're glad I went to him after all. Look what you've got on him now. Once the public knows this he'll have to concede half an hour after the polls close."

She spoke past him to me. "It was Friedman, you know, and Mrs. Queen Bee here. *Too much sugar to risk on a schoolboy editor and post-mortem muckraking from a Salvadoran whistleblower.* Brian's words, not mine. They all take care of each other's little problems, but I think he saw that as an opportunity, the *Spectator's* not been really nice to him, have you, Smitty? He just went too far getting rough with me." She withdrew her hand from Schulz's hair with a last lingering stroke. "And with *you*, Bitsy." She tucked the gun into her back waistband, and lifted the sleeve of her T-shirt to show me an eggplant-colored smudge on her upper arm.

"They'd found out what Hector's wife likes to do," she went on, returning to the chair beside me and stretching out her legs and arms as if she had been spending her time in nothing more than a long meeting. "Juju gods and nasty little bundles of herbs and lizard feet? That shop on the Pike is *so* out in the open," she said. "And *he'd* found out which developers and contractors lie down to sleep with Mrs. Queen Bee here." I felt an almost physical wave of fury from Betty Bravo. "Brian totally *let his hair down* knowing that I'm not in your newsroom any more, he was simply *itching* to talk."

"So they thought they had a truce, she stands down and lets him be chairman, he keeps his 'vision' away from their little rackets. They must have been really, really pissed off when their police chief told them about the little maiden speech in Hector's pocket, and they realized he must not be that concerned about his wife's rep-u-ta-tion." She danced along the syllables. Schulz went to retrieve his cell phone.

"Friedman," I said.

"Oh, you figured that out, did you?" said Meg. "Brian told Grover it was the stupidest stunt he'd heard of in a month of Sundays."

"I still think *Brian* was involved in the harassment," said Schulz, accenting the name with heavy contempt. "They'd gotten to my wife. I'm not sure how, but I caught her too many times. Making phone calls and then hanging up. I found a gym bag packed with clothes in her closet once." He peeled open the twelve-pack of soft drinks, pulled out a sweating can and popped it; grimaced as he swallowed.

I thought of stories Slate had told over the breakroom table, as if she were the first person to learn how abused wives edge toward an escape. Schulz was probably telling literal truth.

My cellphone on the long table chortled. I jumped, Schulz glared at it, Paulsen looked hopefully down the table as if the call might somehow signal a rescue. His Beaver Cleaver features were a little shiny, anxiety-sweat, and his sandy hair ruffled for the first time I'd ever seen it.

Schulz reached for the phone. "Yeah?" he said. A silence. "Yes, he's all right. Are you working with me on this, Weller? Are you *really* trying?"

A longer silence. "We're having *lunch*. That was what he came in for, lunch." He took another pull from the can, then anchored it back in the crotch of his cargo shorts like any Bubba trucking down the road with a can of beer. "Next time, send some fuckin' Coke or maybe iced tea. This stuff tastes like antifreeze." A beat. "Yeah, you can talk to him. *One* minute." He handed me the cell phone and glanced down at a triathlon watch, bulky with buttons and functions.

Weller's voice came down the line; the calm was practiced but I heard an edge. "Are you okay, Mr. Smith?"

"I'm fine," I said, feeling Schulz's eyes fixed on me. "We're having lunch."

"Is he treating you well? What about the others?"

"Mr. Paulsen, Mr. Sprague and Ms. Bravo are all in good health," I said. I chose my words carefully; the more definite the answers the happier Schulz would be. I did not want to see him pacing again.

"Does he have a friend with him? Could you ID him or her?"

"Yes," I said. I met Schulz's eyes. "I've been learning some things I absolutely would not have believed if I hadn't worked all my life in the news business. I'm hoping this will be quite a story. In my opinion, Mr. Schulz is going to be completely vindicated." There was a scrape behind me; Meg crossed to the table and took a slice of the pizza, refused the drink Schulz offered her and gurgled a cup of water out of the Deer Park cooler in the far corner.

"Are you free to leave at any point?"

"We haven't discussed that yet."

Schulz rose and snatched the phone back. "Time's up." I heard a tinny distant sound of Weller's voice hailing him before he put it to his ear.

"Yeah, well, I dropped it. I'll see if I can turn it back on." He snapped my phone shut and I hoped he would forget and hand it back to me, but he laid it carefully by the pizza boxes; picked up the empty can, crushing it in long knuckly fingers. He opened another, glanced around the Board members trying to shift their weight. "Sure I can't get you guys anything?" he said.

Sprague and Paulsen shook their heads again—a few empty cups suggested a round of water earlier—but Betty Bravo, in a voice much frayed from her usual Boardroom headmistress tone, said "I'd like a drink."

"Fix her up, Meggers," said Schulz. Meg took another plastic cup from beside the cooler, popped, poured, crossed and held it to Bravo's lips. A trickle hit her expensive-looking lapel.

"Just Fresca, your dry cleaner'll get it out," said Meg as if they were side by side at a buffet. "Smitty, *normal* people don't drink this stuff." She had teased me in the same words, how many times?

"No one ordered, so I picked," I said.

"They tell you I'm crazy?" said Schulz, looking at me owlishly.

"What I hear and what I can judge for myself are two different things," I said carefully.

"I know what gets said. They know I'm the only one who'll dare to break the silence, so it's *crazy* and *Mr. Schulz I'll have to ask you to leave the boardroom* and *Mr. Schulz please settle down.*" The P's were starting to spray a little. "There's nothing to settle down about. That's the glorious twenty-first century for you, Paige Smith, everyone goofy and mellow while the robber barons loot and crush. If you have passion, you're *crazy.* If you care, you're *crazy.*" I thought suddenly of Mercedes. "People in this county with money dripping out their assholes, they don't care what happens to their taxes, they don't care if Herrity and Jones sends Queen Bee a weekly cashbag for looking the other way while they cash in on illegal labor—"

"This is outrageous," said Bravo in an undertone, as if she were out in the boardroom listening to a speaker and not tied to a swivel chair. I saw Hugh Sprague squeeze his eyes shut as if trying to send her a *be quiet* message. Clearly he and Paulsen had decided early on that saying nothing was safest.

"You're an ugly bitch, you know that?" said Schulz as if it had just occurred to him. "I don't know what Reardon sees in you. You don't do a damn thing for me." Bravo's eyes widened. Apparently she had never been told that Reardon considered her, if I remember his exact words, "hotter than salsa picante." (He did tend to think in terms of food.)

"I can produce individuals," Schulz went on as if his aside to Bravo had never occurred, "who have *repeatedly* lost water service after supporting me in the primary against Mr. de le Roja last year. I can guarantee a paper trail from transportation contractors to Mr. Friedman that explains every instance of his indifference to *serious citizen concerns.* I can subpoena call center records that show *no response* to *dozens* of calls about harassment by dogs. Unless Flanagan's had them all doctored." He was walking up and down again with barely repressed urgency, but not in the alarming locoed-beast circle of before. "Mr. Paulsen, you *did* admit to meeting with the DogsNow! group, didn't you? We went over this."

"I made a surprise visit to their first meeting," said Paulsen cautiously. He was leaning forward at an awkward angle; I judged his shoulders were starting to cramp. Sprague, still something of the athlete he had been in college, looked more relaxed. I could see from this angle that his arms were bound to the chair, not so much tightly as thickly, in the kind of shiny yellow clothes line that's in every car trunk in the nation. A sizable coil of it remained half in and half out of a small duffel partway under the table. Plenty left for me, if I stepped wrong.

"And it was just *coincidence* that after that the visits started?" said Schulz, wheeling on him like a melodramatic prosecutor. "Just *suddenly* the barking begins to wake me at three a.m.? You know, if you want to break someone's nerve, deprive them of sleep. You thought it was easy, didn't you?"

Paulsen was saved from answering by Schulz's phone, which seemed to have survived the previous impact.

"I'm doing fine," he said a few seconds after answering. "How are *you* doing, Mr. Weller? Are you getting anywhere with the governor? Did you get across the *picture* that this county needs reform dictated at the *highest level?*" A pause. "Yeah, funny how everyone wants to talk to me now I stood up for myself. Okay, put them on." Another pause. He paled a little, pushed the heel of his hand almost brutally up his cheek into his hairline; I could see now where the smudge had come from. "So they fuckin' got you, did they? When did they come for you? When I was at work? At the Federation? While Murphy was pounding on me? Did you enjoy hearing about that?" Surreally, I realized that Schulz actually held a job.

"Must be Mrs. Schulz," said Meg under her breath. "Poor little thing. Just not up to handling him." She still looked entertained, but flashed a cute scowl at me as she picked up the last bite of the pizza. "You know, you're finally going to force me to drink this." She filled her cup from the can that she'd opened for Betty Bravo. "Garlic. Water won't cut it."

Schulz was orating into the phone again, emphasizing his words every so often with a snap of the pistol hand, which did not make me comfortable. "*I remember* you coming home after me the day I got home early from the conference. You don't? I can tell you where you were. *I remember* you making all the calls…"

"So he's easier to deal with than my taste in plays and soda?" I said.

She wrinkled her nose daintily. "For me," she said. "You saw." She retrieved the little lady-pistol from her waistband, running her thumb across the safety as if it were sensually interesting; I decided she had handled it quite a bit indeed, and had a sudden unwanted vision of Schulz guiding her arms into a shooting stance, their hands together on the grip. "The physical thing, that's kind of a challenge sometimes, the meds, you know? He might be off them, actually…He said once he'd want to do that, if he had me *for keeps.*" Her faint smile hovered between indulgence and condescension. "Kind of sweet, isn't it? But he's mostly what we call a talker anyway. Sometimes I think it's just that I'm not scared of him. Like *she* is." The corner of her mouth turned up. "It's quite a ride."

"And this?" I said, meaning the whole situation. "A ride? Why go along with—" I broke off, nervous at being overheard, but Meg appeared to know exactly how much—or how little—Schulz would take in when he was at this pitch.

"Oh, Smitty, didn't you ever do anything *just to see what would happen?*" she said. "What's to lose? I was already hot when I left Chicago. You sell the wrong thing to the wrong person? Now and then someone wants a few extras with the evening, you get that with some of the, what Jim calls plutocrats." She shrugged. Schulz's tirade at his wife was filling the room. "This kind of bleaches out a little coke rap, you know? I can always say I *was* scared of him. The Stockholm thing. Maybe write a book, I'm a journalist. And there's Brian; I know where *his* sugar comes from. I even know who looked the other way when Ed Flanagan made that crib sheet of Hector's disappear. Didn't you always say I had good reporter's antennas?" She winked at Bravo; there was a slight tomato stain on her lower lip.

Bravo pretended she had not heard this, but with considerable mortification made it known that she needed the ladies' room, in an urgent way. Meg lifted both hands in a gesture that would have said "But of course!" were it not for the pistol in one. "Scuse us, Smitty," she said as she worked at the ropes behind Bravo's chair, holding the small gun against the back of the expensive jacket as Bravo tottered up. "You know girls always go together." She smiled at Bravo with an animated lift of her brows. "We can *gossip.*"

She waved at Schulz, who was flushed and beginning to sound hoarse but leveling off. "Bitsy? Bathroom break." He flapped a hand at her impatiently as she chivvied Bravo into the side corridor. I felt a return of the earlier weightless sensation as I turned to look after them; reached into my pocket for the unlovely hanky and blew my nose sharply. Schulz was still belaboring his wife. "Afraid of me? That's crap, I never laid a hand on you, you just switched sides…" Good. I only needed a few seconds to steady myself.

By the time I turned around, dry-eyed, pocketing the disgusting handkerchief, Weller was back on the phone, or perhaps it was 'Eric.' "None of these bastards will be free to go until they've *owned up* to what they've done," Schulz was saying. "And when they do that Warren will be *embarrassed* into asking them to resign if they're not ashamed to still hold office. Nor will the citizens *stand* for another *mockery* of an election. The hell with impossible, he will find it politically *necessary.*" He ran his hand up the side of his face again, listening.

"Okay, that's fair. Half an hour." He snapped the phone closed, glanced over at me. "What are you looking at?"

"What you said got me thinking. It's time to get to work," I said. "Uh, room for me over there?"

"Walk slow," he said. He was resting the gun in his lap, but muzzle forward, and he swiveled his chair to follow me as I crossed behind Sprague and Paulsen. I held my hands at shoulder level.

"What we need to have is what in the news business we call a page conference," I said. "The special I'm going to put in for you? There are ways that people read the paper, things you learn about getting the news out with punch. Here." On the lower shelves of a bookcase stuffed with binders of neighborhood maps and the County Code, there were lined pads and some rolled ordnance maps; a good size. I unrolled one and spread it blank side up on the table, gestured at a desk set full of office tools at the table's far end. "One of the big point markers and some pencils?"

Schulz got them. I mocked out columns with the half-dry marker—god, I had always done a clumsy looking job of this. "Your statement should be on the front. This'll be where the meat is. You'll just need to hold out a few inches for a sidebar on the right cover to make people want to look inside, OK? A short list of the hot issues." I folded over the map—it was an elevation of Aurora Heights—and drew a rudimentary sidebar box with lines and bullets. "You'll want photos in the middle. I think the public should see these folks being treated like the felons they are. Can I use my cell phone a moment?" As Schulz's eyes hooded, I said "Just the camera part."

My fingers were shaking. I didn't know if I had taken a picture of Pinky or of the Arlington Seal on the wall behind him, but there was some sort of comprehension in Hugh Sprague's intense gaze as I tried to fix him in the viewfinder. There was a movement in the hall door.

"Cheese!" said Meg. "Smitty's such a *nerd,* he always has great gadgets." Bravo's hands were crossed on her chest, apparently on order; scarlet thumbprints of humiliation flamed on her cheeks. As Meg reached for the rope she said "Let me at least take a drink instead of you *pouring* it on me."

"Bottoms up," said Meg. Bravo gulped and then grudgingly sat, lower lip caught in her teeth as Meg worked behind her.

Schulz's cheekbone was propped on his hand. He turned the paper around, then over.

"How long a statement do you plan on?" I said. "Roughly."

He shook his head a little, got up, paced up and down once, thrusting the heavy pistol into his belt, which sagged alarmingly. "Trouble thinking," he said. "I shouldn't have talked to the bitch. That was a setup." He caught my eye as if it was especially important that I understand. "She uses influences on me sometimes. I've seen her make gestures, you know, ones that you can tell are taking your energy? They're trying to use her. She may have found out some way to do it on the phone."

Meg was regarding him with a measuring expression. She had her own cup in hand and held it out to him. "Seconds for me?" she said rather meekly. "It was even worse flat."

He reached toward the hand that held the cup but instead of taking it closed his fingers around her wrist, knuckles mottling as they tightened in a grinding, probing grip that must have hurt. The cup quivered a little but stayed level.

"Smith's on my side now, but what about you, *Margaret*? What were you two talking about in there all that time?"

Her eyes danced. "Favorite tampons," she said. Betty Bravo's face went rigid and Paulsen, rather delightfully, flushed scarlet, which made me feel less conspicuous doing the same.

Schulz eyed Meg with his head a little cocked. She took a step toward him, ignoring the way his grip forced her arm out at an awkward angle. "Smitty'll take good care of this, you'll see," she said. "You can make him your press secretary. The truth is the best campaign, isn't that what you said the other night?"

Instead of answering, he slid the gun back out of his belt. "Is that what I said, *Margaret?*" he asked in a lower, more personal voice, his eyes not leaving her, and lifted the gun thoughtfully to rest the end of the tapered barrel against her cheek;

then after a long moment began moving it across her face in a slow caress—delicately, as if it could feel. "Were you listening to everything I said?" This was so soft, almost tender, that I barely caught it. The small flange of the sight dimpled her skin when it paused. She did not move; he was the one who seemed unsteady.

Paulsen closed his eyes. I could not. The almost dainty muzzle traced a path to her underlip and hesitated there. I thought of the tomato stain.

The silence was so complete that I could hear not only the ticking of the cheap clock by the door but an actual reverberation inside its case. Meg's smile gathered into the ghost of a kiss, as if what rested against her lip were nothing more lethal than a fingertip. I had the lurching feeling that she had been here before.

Slowly he lowered the gun; let her wrist go, and raised the hand to cover his face, pushing up the wire-rims to rub eyes which looked bruised and tired. I heard rather than felt myself release a long breath I had been holding. The dot-dashes of nailmarks were visible on Meg's arm. Her eyes closed once; otherwise I saw no reaction. He nudged her aside, sat.

"You go watch the Garden Club Lady till we're ready for her," he said, adding, almost to himself, "Don't want to hear another *bitch* run her mouth right now." But he did not protest when she stroked the back of her hand up his nape, only tilted his head back against the touch in what seemed an often-rehearsed gesture. The nakedness of the expression that crossed his face made me feel, to my own surprise, queasily ashamed for him.

Something must have still showed in my look when she stepped back. She held my eyes a moment, the little smile playing on her lips again, and took her drink back to sit across from Betty Bravo, women at a luncheon.

"You two—" My voice wavered like a choirboy's and I covered it with a cough. "You two are going to have to help," I said meaningly to Sprague and Paulsen, trying to pull Schulz's attention back in my direction. "It'll just be worse for you in the end if you don't. What you say to me now will be the bones of an interview, really. We'll flesh it out more when the authorities have you in custody." I scratched <u>Paulsen</u> at the top of the pad. "Pinky, before we start, this issue with the dogs has to be cleared up. I need you to name your contacts in the DogsNow! organization for followup."

Paulsen cleared his throat and named, in a grudging tone, a few men and women who had pled the cause of dog parks at Board meetings. I felt like pumping my fist; he had the picture.

I was buying time, but maybe more than that. In my undergraduate days, for my sins, I had to take a psychology course; the instructor picked up on my appetite for a good story and lent me an anthology of case studies that were much better reading than the textbook. (I managed a B in the end.) In the one I remembered, a patient with delusions only slightly more baroque than some of Schulz's—all right, he had a secret identity as a galactic explorer—returned almost indignantly to reality when his therapist, entranced by the tales he spun, began participating in his fictions. I didn't expect to render Schulz sane, but I would settle for making him waver enough to put the gun down.

Sprague and Paulsen warmed to the task, owning up (I learned later) to half the manipulations imputed to them in the first hour inside the recess room and a few more they thought of along the way. Sprague in particular delivered a good performance of reluctant, repentant confession. I filled a dozen or so pages—when making notes for a story, I have the scrawl of an eighth-grader—then sensed Schulz getting restless and returned to the page mockup.

"Now, once your reader has taken all this *in,* Jim—once they've started to get the picture about what's really going on—they'll want to know what they can do. That's your back page. If you want to associate your campaign with this, that's where you ask for volunteers, solicit support...." I was very careful not to say "contributions," remembering his letter during the Board primary campaign, when he had claimed rightness of position would reach the heart of the voter better than lavish funding. "You grab them right when—"

"Shut up a minute," he said. "This is giving me a headache." He stood again, hitched the machine pistol on its webbing over his head; my stomach did a slow flip. I willed him to keep looking in my direction, barely suppressed a blurt of alarm when his phone burred again.

"Yeah," he almost barked. I looked up at him over the tops of my glasses. "What can I say, Bill? The time got away from me. We're working on an article here.—Yeah, yeah, they're right here.—Okay, but tell them to make it quick." He reached across the table and handed the phone to me. "Put Pinky on," he said. He was back to fidgeting with the gun, pointing it more or less in my direction as I held the phone to Paulsen's ear. After a moment Paulsen shuddered so deeply I felt it through the phone.

"I love you too," he said in an unsteady voice. They must have located his wife. A silence. "No, we have someone here helping us. The *Spectator* editor. I'm going to see you soon. Hang in there." He did not look at all sure of this. "Yes. I love you a lot." He bit his lip, turned to me and gestured with his head: "Hugh." I stepped—slowly, Schulz glaring at me—to the end of the table and held the phone for Sprague. The conversation that followed was much the same as Paulsen's.

No one was waiting to talk to me. I raised the phone anyway, said "Paige Smith here. We've been hard at work. This has been a revelation." I looked pointedly at Schulz, who was drumming the fingers of his empty hand.

"There's someone here for Mr. Schulz, if he'll come back on," came Janet's voice.

I handed him the phone. "If it's her again, I'm not talking to her," he said testily and put it to his ear.

"Aaaaangelo! Well, still can't stay away from the County building, can you?"

I chanced a look in Meg's direction. Her chair was still turned mostly away from me, facing Betty Bravo, whose head half slumped toward her shoulder, mouth slightly open, escaping the indignity of the situation for the moment.

"I wasn't paying attention, was I? Had other things on my mind. I'm sure he's still out there."

Schulz paced, a little bounce coming back to him.

"No, I'm not going out to get him. You can come *in* and get him if you want, how about it?" A beat. "No, I mean *you,* not one of Flanagan's thugs. Promise you immunity, cross my heart." A few more beats. "Okay, they can walk you to the perimeter. I'll come out as far as the dais and say hi, would you like that? Wedge the door open behind you so I can see they're staying back. Should have done that with Smith." He folded the phone. "Poor Pastorelli wants his cuddly toy," he said. "Careless. Left him on the podium. He might as well come visit, what's a blind guy going to do?" He stepped toward the door to the dais, peered out. "Putz. Thinks he's the big gadfly. Pastorelli'd blow Grover Friedman for a bus stop a block closer to his condo."

He stepped further out onto the dais. "Mind the store, Meggers," he said. The idea of the world beyond the recess room door was disorienting, as if I had spent the last two hours in an isolation tank. After a short while I heard the outer doors opening.

"That's right," said Schulz. "Just prop it open. Both hands where I can see them. That's fine. You been having a good time, Angelo? Lots of press out there to talk to? You like that."

"Just missing my little buddy," came the faint tenor, barely intelligible through the echoes in the empty boardroom.

"Well, come on up and get him. It's interesting seeing you from this angle. It would have been fun to sit up here."

A few faint footfalls. As quietly as I could, I stood again, catching Sprague's eye and pursing my lips: *silence.*

"There, see? He's been safe as houses all along." The near gaiety of the morning's first hour was returning. "I tell you what, let's hear your tag line from up here. You like saying it, don't you? Are there any questions? Go on, let's hear it."

A pause, then Pastorelli's voice delivering the line that always concluded his testimony. "*Ahhh* there any questions?"

"That's good, but it's missing some punch," said Schulz. "Do it again."

I stepped soundlessly across the rug to Meg's chair. She was upright, hand resting on the gun in her lap, her eyes closed. I lifted the hair at her temple in a fan, dropped it slowly so that it floated strand by strand to her cheek; that had been my favorite way of waking her up, weekend mornings when we had plenty of time. She stirred a little but didn't open her eyes as I slid the gun out from under her hand. Pastorelli had gotten a windup into it this time. "*AHHH* there any questions?" There was a robust echo. Schulz, pistol-encumbered or no, managed to clap.

Half a week's supply of Darvocet, the powder painstakingly decanted from the gel capsules in the restroom of the command bus, had knocked both Bravo and Meg out for the count. I hadn't been able to remember whose glass was whose once they retreated to the bathroom an hour ago, and had to settle for dosing both of them. Between the despised Fresca and the garlic pepperoni, she had chugged all of it without noticing. Schulz just had too tight a relationship with his drinks.

"Say I was chairman, Angelo," he was saying, "what would you say to me on New Year's Day? Would you have a *life* if this county were being run the way it should be?" I ducked to the duffel under the table, rummaged in it as silently as I could. The rope ends I had seen were knife-cut and fresh. There. A common Ginsu knife was in the duffel's bottom, among ammunition clips and a weird, last-minute assortment of first-aid supplies, as if they had cobbled this plan together in the time it takes to pack for an impulsive weekend trip. I turned without rising, grabbed the bonds behind Sprague's back. "Why don't you start now? Go on, go. Take your fuzzy. Go rollerblading or something." Schulz was no Boy Scout. Cutting through two turns of the rope was enough to let Sprague pull the whole rat's nest apart. I was half through the tighter ropes binding Pinky Paulsen when I lost my balance. The noise I made catching myself was negligible but enough to alert Schulz, who snapped around in time to see the last of the rope falling from Sprague's hands.

Rage flooded his face. I felt my heart drop out of me, thinking only *Pinky can't get loose yet* and then heard a sharp, barking sound. Had Schulz shot Hugh that fast? No, his gun arm was only half up. He was turning back toward the boardroom. The bark came again, a volley of the sounds this time. I sawed through the last turn of rope holding Paulsen, made it upright, just as Schulz roared *"Get that damn dog OUT of here!!!"* He held the pistol out in a movie-cop's two-handed stance, swiveling from side to side; I could just see past his narrow back to the dais and beyond.

A flash of pale purple from near the podium, a fusillade of yapping as a white streak closed on it just inside the lobby door. *"I SAID GET RID OF THE FUCK-ING DOG!!!"* I fumbled for the safety on what seemed more like a workshop tool of some kind than a gun, acutely aware that I had never really handled firearms. Schulz squeezed off a shot just in time for Sprague, an Olympic finalist in college, to launch at him, bearing him bodily to the dais with an audible *whuff* as the breath was slammed out of him.

The long gun spun across the floor like a bottle at a party game; Schulz was struggling to get a purchase on the machine pistol, which was wedged into his armpit. Sprague straddled his hips and got a grip on his collar, and Jim Schulz, who had spoken out passionately for gay rights (along with every other minority's he could think of) and solicited campaign appearances at the Arlington Gay and Lesbian Alliance, snarled "Get *off* me, you fucking faggot." "In your *dreams*," said Sprague, and rapped his head sharply against the cultured marble of the dais. He went out like a cheap cellular connection.

"Couldn't you have let me do that part?" said Paulsen disappointedly, chafing his wrists as he limped to the door of the recess room. But Sprague was at one of the microphones on the dais, calling in a joltingly amplified voice to the SWAT officers who were already double-timing in the rear door of the boardroom, "We're OK, he's *down*, the other one's down, DO NOT FIRE."

Fang trotted up the aisle between cargo-trousered legs, Taxopotomus clamped in her jaws, and deposited it at the end of a pew. Angelo Pastorelli rose painfully from the floor, the tail of his jacket hanging oddly, and took the stuffed toy from the little dog; winced again as he straightened.

"Close friggin' thing," he said. "Nuts always want too much gun. Ouch. *Crap.* Do me one favor? Never, I mean ever, let *Whack Job* there know how close he came to shooting me right in the ass."

He dropped gingerly to a pew, holding Taxopotomus. SWAT was already swarming up the dais. I fell heavily into Betty Bravo's chair, and began to shake with what felt like sobs, only they were dry.

CHAPTER THIRTEEN
RESTORATION COMEDY

Selby was photographing the kicked anthill that was Court House Plaza, shifting and changing level like someone on a surfboard as medics, bystanders, and cops milled in a humming multitude through the landscape of unfamiliar vehicles and tape that had sprung up. As I approached he photographed me too, acknowledging me only when I got close enough to hear a normal tone of voice.

"Watch the birdie, boss."

He dropped the camera to dangle on its neckstrap and looked down at me as if I were a rare jazz album that had showed up in some dusty bin.

"They wanted press to stay back on Fifteenth Street, except *Spectator* people," he said. "I abuse every privilege I get."

"Good to see you," I said inadequately.

"I'd kiss you if there weren't already rumors about us," he said without changing expression.

I wasn't steady. I covered it by sitting on the raised base of the flagpoles. I wanted a shower and bed. I wanted to be in the *Spectator* office pouring this into the computer. I wanted Meg's feet. I wanted never to have met her.

"Janet was a hard sell to begin with and Kowicny's having babies," he said. "They were both fucking livid. Pastorelli got off the phone and they both said *no way* are they sending a second civilian up there out of range of the SWAT teams. Flanagan was the one that overruled them. If Kowicny doesn't resign from the force, color me pink and call me ofay."

"It worked," I said. "Was it his idea about Taxopotomus?"

"No, that was Pastorelli. No, both of em. He was next to the command post with that little Johnny-Mop-on-a-leash watching Flanagan do a striptease for the press, you know how he gets. Someone shoved a mike at him and asked his thoughts and he said 'I just wish I had Taxopotomus back.' Got in a couple of sentences about coming here every meeting to battle for the citizens and how he'd always been able to calm Jim down, which we know is crap, but by the time they wrapped him Flanagan thought he'd had a brilliant idea, and you know Pastorelli *ate it up*."

"The dog was the part that worked," I said. "He told me Phyllis got tired and he said he'd walk her. You need to meet Phyllis."

"The dog?"

"No. Mom. Dog's mom." I wasn't tracking. "One of the perimeter officers was supposed to be holding her. Must have loved that. Fang loves her Uncle Angelo." I felt hysteria bubbling, focused on the chaos in front of me. For once I didn't have a pad, paper, the endflap of a book or a menu to scribble on. A medic unit sidled into place beside the curb, farting and rumbling. A paramedic team was still checking over everyone inside, including Angelo, who had been forced to the indignity of dropping his trousers; Schulz's bullet had actually creased his buttocks, if no more deeply than a rug burn. They had let me go after I swore I'd never been tied or tampered with, and that I had a story to get out. "Oh, the *little* paper," one of the medics had said when I showed him my card. Momentarily humiliated, I had rallied when he added "The *Journal* sucks."

A heliograph at my right signaled the opening of one of the glass doors of the County building. A gurney, piloted cautiously by medics with a female officer in attendance, pivoted cumbersomely toward the ramp. I saw the mahogany fan of hair at the top and held my breath a moment, then advanced toward the officer. It was Fraike. "*There* you are," she said irritably, as if she had actually been looking for me and not escorting an arrestee to an ambulance. "I told them we needed to talk to you."

"I won't be going anywhere too soon."

"Good. Don't leave without checking in at the command post. I gotta babysit Jane Doe here."

"Her name," I said, leveling my voice carefully, "is Margaret Ellen Stannard. Date of birth May 17, 1978, unless she was lying to me about that too." I kept my eyes fixed forward, away from where the medics were loading the gurney into the back of the unit. "You'll find she's got a record."

"Thanks," said Fraike. She scratched down the information, caught up with the others and hoisted herself into the back of the unit. The doors accordioned shut.

Selby was looking at me, when I turned back to him, as if there could be no further news in the world now. "I guess maybe this is when we ought to talk about it," he said. "If you feel like it."

I didn't know what I felt like. I was saved from trying to decide by young voices materializing out of the hum. "There he *is!!!!!*" one squealed as if someone had caught sight of a rock star. Selby turned and I followed his movement in time to see Mercedes, flanked by Sean and Slate, who had shouted, breaking into a run past the cherry bed. Mercedes pulled ahead of them, seemed to be intending to break through me as if I were the finish tape at a sprint race, and at the last minute mashed me in surprisingly strong arms.

"Oh, *madre de Dios,* you are safe! *Viva!* You are hero!" She took off into Spanish that I couldn't follow. My glasses were tilted off my face so that the scene took on a non-Euclidean skew, but I could see Selby giving me a resigned grin, half concession and half congratulation.

She stood back, looked at me, and mashed me again.

"She was still sleeping at eight-thirty, so we let her," Slate was saying. "She was so upset last night. But then we turned on the radio about ten-thirty and heard what was happening up here, and I got Sean on the phone and we all came up. We've been talking to this nice big old lady over by the bus stop, just an *Earth Mother.* Did her dog really attack him?"

Mercedes was looking at me with tears standing in dark shining eyes. "Now I think it all makes sense, this man has been going crazy a long time," she said "My poor brother he shoots first, and now this. But you are all safe, the poodle man too, *milagro.*"

Another gurney was being maneuvered carefully through the doors, with no police escort this time. I saw Betty Bravo's face, almost childlike in repose, hair still perfectly coiffed against the pillow.

"That is Ms. Bravo, no?" said Mercedes. "I feel bad what I said now, she did not deserve this. They could not find her husband, he is away. But there was a big fat man who was very distressed. Look, that is him now."

Reardon was approaching the paramedics.

"No, a friend," he was saying. "Perry Reardon. The *Taxpayer Watchdog?* I give her a lot of budget information on a regular basis. I know her husband's still flying in. I think a friend should be there when she wakes up…?"

The medics looked at each other. "Immediate family," one said. "Nothing stopping you waiting at the hospital though. If she's OK, it's up to her."

Perry moved faster than I'd ever seen toward his car in the courthouse lot.

"What was that play we covered at the kid's theater last year, boss?" he said. "The fairy queen wakes up and falls in love?"

"*Midsummer Night's Dream,*" I said. "Maybe Perry's seen it."

I looked for a place to prop myself again, pretending I did not see the high emotion in Mercedes' eyes. "And after all this we never got Hector's speech out in the open," I said. "Will you be staying? I'll cover it if you need to pay a penalty for taking another flight—I mean the *Spectator* will—"

"Uh, Mr. Smith."

It was Sean, who had been bouncing on his heels as if gauging for a broad jump.

"Mr. Smith, I was wanting to tell you."

"Yes?" I noticed his spiked hair was interestingly squashed on the side that had fewer earrings; this seemed to be the punk version of "bed head."

"About that file with Mr. de la Roja's speech."

Apprehension met and wrestled with Sean's obvious delight. He looked like a kid who had made the honor roll and gotten a date for the prom but also let off a stinkbomb in the gym locker room.

"Well, when Slate called me I activated Plan B."

"Plan B??" Now we seemed to be in some sort of roleplaying adventure game.

"Yeah, I—well, you remember I said yesterday these were *not* going to get lost again? I hacked into the County website. I mean I did it then, all I needed to do was launch. So around eleven o'clock this went out to everyone on that e-mail alert list they have." He thrust some folded sheets of paper at me. I opened them out and read:

Arlington County has released a new press release entitled:

BOARD PUBLISHES FINAL REMARKS OF TRAGICALLY SLAIN BOARD CHAIRMAN HECTOR DE LA ROJA

These remarks were intended to be read at last Saturday's meeting. The Board here publishes them in full, with the original attachments, and pledges to honor the vision of Mr. de la Roja as Arlington seeks to transcend this tragedy and take its place as a world-class community...

"Is he not a *maravillo?*" said Mercedes. "I am going to make him teach me to do this." Sean beamed as she squeezed him too, kissing him forthrightly on the beardless cheek.

The hubbub seemed to be calming. Police were escorting a shaken-looking pair, a woman with puffy eyes and a mustached man in jeans and a cotton sweater, to the open space in front of the County building. The man looked slightly familiar. I recognized Hugh's partner just a moment before Hugh did, almost tripping as he lost his usual suavity of movement and half slid down the steps into a locked embrace. Mrs. Paulsen didn't wait for Pinky; she covered the last two yards in what seemed like one leap as he emerged and threw her arms around his chest, sobbing.

"There's the story," I said, focusing now that I had a sheet of paper in my hand. I was scratching words and phrases down on the back of Hector's statement, explaining at the same time how Hugh had body-slammed Schulz, the delicate subtext of our conversation over the "page conference." Mercedes' eyes widened as if she might explode with the continuous supply of amazing news, like a pinata. I looked around for a flat surface, raked my hair in frustration, dropped to the bricks and filled a page, heard Mercedes laughing. She had a very pretty laugh.

"Smitty?"

I looked up. Hugh was standing there, hand in hand with—Bill? Bob? I could never quite remember.

"Coming in there took a lot of guts. Thinking up what you did—I—I've just been telling Clive here—" ClivenotBillorBob broke away from Hugh and pumped my hand, lost for speech.

"Mr. Sprague?"

Mercedes had become slightly muted. Hugh turned.

"Mr. Sprague, we met at the church, Mercedes de la Roja."

Recognition dawned. He looked as if he had been placed on the dais and asked to speak on an unexpected subject. "Were you inside?" he said, taking her extended hand in both of his rather than merely shaking it.

"No, no, I came late—I—it is a lot, we must talk. But it is so emotion, so many things! And a gay hero! There will be much press and Smitty here, I know, but can I interview you before I go for my paper in New York? I mean it is not my paper, it is a queer Latino weekly, *El Zorro*, I write a column called *La Lesbiana Loca...*" She fumbled out a card from her hip pack, wrote Slate's number on the back. "That is where I am staying. It is my real business on the front, *Grafico-Arcoiris.*" Hugh turned it over, looked at the rainbow logo. Clive was back at his side, arm cinched around him as if he might slip away again.

"I'll call," he said. "Or here." He passed her his card, and turned back to me. "I—we'll be in touch, Smitty. Just—thank you."

They walked toward the press gauntlet arm in arm, two lovers reunited in the spring.

"You didn't mention writing for a paper," I said. Selby was looking at me over her shoulder, the expression on his face saying *Oh, well.*

"I do not know your feelings before," she said. "One is careful. But I see you speak of Mr. Sprague and his *esposo* like anyone else. Oh, Smitty, you are a wonderful person."

She squeezed me again, and began crying and hugging Slate and Sean as well.

Schulz had not yet come out. We stayed, the three of them asking more questions than I felt like answering, though I did anyway. Finally an escort of four officers flanked out a last gurney.

His glasses were gone, his head half lolled to the side. He looked small, and ill. "Crazy son of a bitch," said Selby.

I watched the unit as it whined off toward the hospital. When I turned back Pastorelli was emerging from the County building, his head-wind gait punctuated with a faint hitch that he was trying to pretend didn't exist.

"They kept you that long for being shot in the butt?" said Selby, having taken in the story as Slate and Mercedes extracted it from me piecemeal.

"Just being one with the boys," said Pastorelli (though at least two of the medics I had seen transporting Schulz were female). "*Crusader Squirrel* woke up when they were checking his pupils for dilation. *Baaaaad* scene. It took ten mil of Valium to knock him down." He was chirpier than Ed Flanagan at a press conference.

"Must of seen you," said Selby drily.

"I *am* the man," said Pastorelli with mock modesty, reaching inside his jacket to hold aloft a slightly slobbered-on Taxopotomus. "*Astuto!*" giggled Mercedes, taking the little toy and placing it on her shoulder, then making faces at it.

"I give the leash to Sergeant Vandevoort, it says here on the nameplate, he's in all this SWAT gear, you'd think he's invincible but no? A two-pound poodle gets away from him and comes running for me! Because I am the defender of the citizens and even dogs love me! And *Nut Boy* goes postal over a fluff ball and goes into the Weaver stance, and the only thing I can think of is throw my little buddy here, get her out through the doors..." He took Taxopotomus back and patted it as if it truly needed consoling.

"And *then* he shot your ass," Selby reminded him.

"Poor man!" said Mercedes. Pastorelli looked like he was trying to decide whether he had a glamorous wound or not.

Security was relaxing now that the last of the ambulances had left. A small cluster of people, most of those who had stayed after fleeing the boardroom, was moving past the command van; I thought of all the odds and ends left inside, including the potted plant (a dracaena, I had ascertained while the medics were asking if I was sure I was all right), and wondered how long the scene-of-crimes people would make them wait. A couple detached themselves from the crowd as it straggled past us, the woman leaning her head toward the man and pointing at me. It was Mark Lewis and Dvorah, and she was practically hauling him behind her by the time they reached us. Bob Beach was a little way beyond them, his laptop back in its padded case. I made a note to buy him a battery.

"Brother Lewis, Brother Beach," saluted Pastorelli. He bobbled Taxopotomus in a say-hello wave. Lewis half-scowled. Dvorah clopped straight on to stand even with me, beaming, expensively fragrant, scarlet-nailed hand on my arm.

"Smitty," she said, "you are such a *hero.* I can't imagine you just going *in* there. Our brave little newsman with the brave big heart." She flowed up against me in a haze of scent and pressed her cheek against mine, whispering, "And the nice tasty *schmengie."* The brave big heart, if it was, discharged all four chambers at once and I must have pulsed visibly as the warmly flocked tip of her tongue saluted my ear. "Call me," she breathed.

I decided I might, at that.

"Hey, what about me?" said Pastorelli. "Taxopotomus and I did some hero stuff."

"Oh, *you too,"* she said in the exasperated but affectionate tone of a mother dividing attention between siblings, turning on tiptoe to sketch a kiss in the air somewhere near his face, her hands just reaching his shoulders. "We've been hearing all *about* the Taxopotomus. Flanagan was giving a statement." She glanced at Lewis, who was looking surlier by the moment. "I think I'd better go, are you leaving?" She looked mischievously back at me as she followed him toward the parking decks. "Mark drove me up this morning. His Miata's just the *cutest little thing.*"

"I think these are your eyeballs down here, boss," said Selby when they had gotten twenty yards or so away. "By your shoe toes."

"Do you know any Yiddish, Shel?" I said vaguely.

"You're asking a schvartza?"

"You're 'Positive Pundit'?" Mercedes was saying to Beach.

"Have been for two years. I just got on those boards because some people need to know that even all *seropositive* gay men aren't knee-jerk liberals."

"I'm 'Lipstick Latina'," remember the big discussion about hate crimes?"

"Here comes Ryan," Selby said.

Here came not only Ryan but Sophie. They seemed to be actually speaking to each other. He extended a hand, rather formally.

"Ryan, I owe you one," I said. "Just never ask me what it is."

"Owe me one? You gave me the day off yesterday. Looks like you did need me today, too."

"We've been doing eyewitness over on Fifteenth Street," said Sophie.

"You've been doing *tearjerkers.*"

Well, at least they were speaking.

"My notes from earlier are in the command bus," I said. "If I can stop them from holding me prisoner in there until I'm debriefed I'll pull together a little more copy."

"I'll, ah, come by with you," said Pastorelli whose brief exposure to the gadgetry in the command post had only whetted his appetite for police toys.

"Mr. Smith?" called Slate. "We're going back to my place, we just all need to chill a little. Unless you need us?"

"Not till later, Slate."

"Or you could come over later."

I decided I might do that, too.

Mercedes blew a kiss, then moved off with them, still delightedly arguing hammer and tongs with Beach, who appeared to have been invited.

The pink twinset woman passed as we were picking our way through flapping yellow tape over the parking lot curb to the command van, hair wet and flattened to her scalp. She was fuming to her companion, a small drab woman whom I remembered from the Republican table at the County Fair.

"And I kept trying to get a *cop,* and they were *all* too *busy* even after everything was safe and we *knew* it was safe, and that *bitch* just...." she Dopplered out of range.

"I think I see what happened there," said Selby.

"What?"

"When they relayed you were safe I hit the men's room in the Courthouse," he said. "Overdue. I think it was your little friend there in the boots I heard in the ladies' next door shouting '*Fuck you, you Republican cow!*' Then somebody flushed."

I decided never to criticize Dvorah's wardrobe, if the chance arose. "And I thought *you* gave *me* a rough time," I said.

Selby looked at me very seriously for a moment, then smiled as if he were trying not to.

"Shame whoever caught Hector in the heads didn't leave it at that," I added. Thinking: and a shame we can't tell as easily who did it. Because despite what Mercedes said, despite what everyone was going to assume, I knew in my gut that, as had been said at the outset, if crazy, disintegrating Jim Schulz had fired the bullets that killed Hector de la Roja, Pastorelli was a Democrat.

"Come on," I said. "Let's go get out a special edition."

Chapter Fourteen
Arlington Notes

Schulz insisted on representing himself *pro se*, calling himself a political prisoner and hero of the people, but faltered shortly after his opening arguments when his initial examination of a recovered Grover Friedman degenerated into one of his pacing rants and he had to be escorted from the courtroom. Shortly afterward the state reversed its decision on whether he was competent to stand trial at all. At least one forensic psychologist insists that the machine pistol he never fired—a MAC-10 for which there were several magazines in the duffel—suggested he had his heart set on a firefight where he would go out with as much company as possible. I remembered the cop who told me about finding Angie only stunned, commenting that Schulz would be a "soft takeout." I can't decide what to think.

He remains in a kind of legal limbo, from which he routinely sends lengthy screeds to me as the *Spectator* editor, having never, apparently, ceased to believe that I had every intention of bringing his cause into the public eye. I keep all these things, I don't know why. In the last one he plaintively appealed to me to learn what agency, person or persons might be intercepting communications between him and Marguerite [sic] Stannard. The unsealed enclosure which he implored me to transmit veered between the delusional, the accusatory and the uncomfortably intimate; it was signed "Your Bitsy," the "your" underlined three times. I forwarded it without comment.

No physical or eyewitness evidence was ever produced to support charging him in de la Roja's murder, but most people thought he was responsible, all the same. The gun that was reclaimed at the scene was untraceable; obliterated serial numbers, mentioned in a news release later in the month, suggested it had drifted through the black market. Every other firearm catalogued as in Schulz's possession was legally purchased and registered, including the nine-millimeter Smith & Wesson (now I knew) that I had taken from Meg's hand at the end.

Meg's record stood against her, but she attracted the sympathy of a number of women's groups who pitched in for a workmanlike defense, to include my testimony (true, as it happened) that she had always been a competent and talented employee. Nothing about any other relationship we might have had ever surfaced, and somehow I left the stand without recounting any specific remarks she made in the recess room; I found it a fair exchange.

She came off as a victim of bad luck, desperate personal choices, and intimidation by a man far more delusional than she had suspected during their previous association. Photos of her right wrist, mottled with deep blackish-purple fingermarks, were introduced into evidence by the defense, along with pictures of more faded bruises that mapped where she had been gripped by both shoulders and probably shaken. The witness that served her best was Betty Bravo, who likewise mentioned no private conversation with her but enlarged on her "cool-headed" conduct. The only sentence not suspended was a mandatory three-year-minimum for the use of a firearm during an abduction. An appeal is pending.

I let Ryan handle the *Spectator* coverage; took my vacation the week of sentencing, and studiously ignored an edition of *National Enquirer* which floated around the office for a few weeks, folded back to a center page headlined—in 72-point italic Helvetica—*LOVE SLAVE OF A MADMAN*. The photo of Meg entering the Courthouse escorted by two female wardens showed the blonde at the part of her dark hair, a disturbing effect.

U.S. Representative Brian Murphy's name never came up during testimony, but, as the annual sponsor of a women's issues conference, he was a contributor to two of the groups that supported Meg, and lunched with the Commonwealth's Attorney shortly before the surprisingly light charges were filed. He himself managed to fall on his feet when the charges stemming from his confrontation with Schulz were nolle prossed (I congratulated him with heavy irony on the editorial page when that happened; there was a spot on my right side that still felt sore when it rained.) At last report his campaign was still going swimmingly, and the Republican District Committee had not found a candidate.

Schulz's wife filed for divorce, and moved out of the townhouse in Fairmont. Sophie told me she'd gotten a dog. Mrs. Friedman didn't file for divorce, but got a dog too, and a reasonably attractive male jogging partner.

Hugh Sprague dumbfounded everyone by launching a primary campaign against Murphy for the Congressional nomination, late in May. Forty-eight hours later, he withdrew it, commenting only that he had reconsidered.

Betty Bravo made a public announcement of thanks for the shoals of flowers that continued to flood into her office for a week after the siege, and was featured in *Washington Woman* (Perry Reardon was seen reading the issue). She reassured the county that no effort was being spared to follow up on the issues that Hector de la Roja had uncovered and hoped to pursue during his term as chairman. After that she had little more to say about it, though "Spider" Walters took a position with a national housing advocacy nonprofit, and Grover Friedman had the unenviable job of assembling the task force that eventually issued the "Preliminary Report on Housing Affordability." Most people in the County, of course, had no idea this report existed.

Friedman is running for state Senate and seems to be gathering momentum, so perhaps Elisa knew what she was doing after all. At one of his campaign appearances, where I had wrapped up an interview with him, he stopped me as I began to turn away and asked if the renovation initiatives south of Liberty Pike were affecting the *Spectator's* lease. Since no sign of the renovation initiatives has materialized so far, I told him "Not that I know of." He looked rather grave, and said that he hoped it would stay that way. "We'd all hate to see the *Spectator* run into problems," he said. "I know it matters quite a bit to me what's in it every week."

I understood what he was telling me. For a few days afer Sean's bogus news release hit everyone's inbox, as I had predicted, phones rang from here to Fairfax; before my next week's edition the damage control machinery had already glided into gear, the county behaving as if corruption in the development sector was just the thing it had been thinking of all the time. At about the same time, the County Manager let it be known that because of a few previous embarrassing incidents involving child porn, the County had sieved the contents of every hard drive in its government offices. If nothing else, all those ampersands on my Web pages threw them off the scent.

I took Phyllis' advice and told Sean I looked forward to hiring him when he finishes school, if some more exciting employer doesn't snap him up.

Flanagan made no public response to requests that he cooperate with the Fairfax County Gang Suppression Unit, but surprised us all later in the summer with the news that he had taken a job with the Department of Homeland Security in Colorado. An old journalism school friend in Denver e-mailed drily to me last week that at several successive public appearances, while maintaining a lively rapport with the press, he had failed to show any sign of understanding exactly what his office was supposed to do.

I had decided not to confront him, after an aside spoken as Schulz's trial was brewing made the point that digital pictures were inadmissible as legal evidence. What I didn't know was that Phyllis Bell had a quiet, private conversation with him, naming no names but emphasizing that several people were aware of breaks in the chain of custody of evidence on the de la Roja case, and that he owed the citizens of the County redoubled security, and perhaps forensic re-evaluation, on what remained.

She invited us to dinner—me, Selby, Pastorelli, and her friend Marlaine—as June was nudging into a hot Washington July, a couple of weeks before Flanagan's surprise Denver announcement. The dining room was still clogged with file boxes when Selby and I arrived, but Marlaine led us out back to a picnic table beside which a grill was smoking and popping. We beguiled an hour worrying kebabs free of their skewers and fumbling the components into our laps; Fang was appeased with ham.

"What they should a done, was Superglue it," Marlaine said, causing Selby to raise an eyebrow and me to wonder if I'd heard right. Phyllis saw our expressions.

"Fuming process," she said. "Brings up latent prints on things like cardboard and paper."

"Like the *Out of Order* sign from the front lobby where one of our smarter boys noticed the can wasn't out of order," said Marlaine. "But seems Mr. Ed has, um, decided on his own that it was all Schulz all along, on account Schulz is who's in custody. Oh, Ed's still telling everyone how his keen instincts *sent your familiar face into the boardroom to connect with what was left of Schulz's sanity.*"

"To nearly connect a .44 slug with my *ass,*" winced Pastorelli, who had endured the solemn public presentation of a seat cushion "for his permanent place in the boardroom" by Hugh Sprague on his birthday a week or so before. I am not sure how Sprague became aware of the date but I suspected Phyllis.

"So something *was* left of his sanity," said Selby out of the twilight.

"Anyway, Flanagan likes that and that's how he wants it left. He actually pulled one detective off the investigation after you went in, Phyl. But Duwayne was on shift last week. So I paid him a visit and I took me a field trip."

I waited.

"Nephew down at Quantico," she said. "Doin' what I wish I was still young enough to do and goin' to the Academy. Has the family streak. Loved the idea of seeing if we could steal a march on Mr. Ed. We had a little huffing party, I guess you could say. Now I'm tryin' to decide who to tell that we rang the cherries, and how."

She reached in her bag, a floppy tote with a pattern of dancing frogs.

"Matches up to the Boston subway tokens, at least all the arrest locations. Makes me think how Mr. Ed Flanagan made a point of tellin everyone at roll call he's sure *you* dropped them things on the way out of the can. You got any, um, ideas about this, Mr. Pastorelli?"

I suddenly felt a chill that was not from the evening breeze. She had sounded less like Marlaine than like Officer Givens when she said that.

She handed two sheets of printer paper to Pastorelli. He flipped his bulky reading glasses out of his shirt pocket, then dug in his trousers for a keychain and thumbed on a little LED light; took his feet down from the drink cooler where he'd had them propped and stamped them on the concrete. The reverse whistle was the only thing he uttered for several seconds.

"Son of a bitch," he said.

Pastorelli dropped back in his chair. I had never seen him lost for words.

"Son of a bitch," he muttered. "Son of a bitch."

We were silent, until Phyllis said tentatively, "Yes...?"

He reached across to her with the printouts and the light, saying "Just call me the man who dodges bullets." He rubbed his hand over his cop-crop in a gesture that reminded me momentarily of Schulz. "*That* one wasn't aimed at my ass, either."

Phyllis passed the sheets to Selby, who passed them to me. I was glad to note that I had gotten so I could look at a rap sheet without my stomach knotting.

A thuggish face, like a walk-on from *The Sopranos,* looked out at me from the grainy photo. *Dionigi Del Ricci,* read the name. *Aliases, Dino di Rosso, Danny Russell.* A middle-sized list of assault charges, mingled with one Disturbing the Peace and one Sale of Controlled Substance, followed the photo.

"You like that?" said Pastorelli. "It's not like I don't call home, and they still never tell me anyone's coming to visit."

"You gonna explain?" said Marlaine out of what was now complete darkness, deepened rather than lifted by a neighbor's floodlight in the far yard.

"My little peckerhead cousin Dio," said Pastorelli, "the one who can't shut up about my disrespecting his mother." I remembered the long story Pastorelli had launched into on the phone, about inheritances and legal weaseling and real estate transactions—family bickering that I'd tuned out in favor of more urgent matters.

"Are we saying," said Selby, "that this *model citizen* was gunning for *you* in the bathroom and shot de la Roja instead?"

Pastorelli spread his hands. "Dio's *stupid.*" He was silent a moment. "Not *that* stupid I guess. He figured out where to hide at the last minute, and when they did bring him in later, they let him go again. Maybe it was just moron's luck."

"Bring him in?" said Marlaine. "When would that of been?"

"The little wino they pulled out of the parking lot? The one who wasn't Hoople?" I had told him that side of the story, winos being a favorite animadversion of Pastorelli's.

"Yeah, the little bald guy."

Pastorelli passed the sheets and light back to her. The photo had shown a receding hairline, and the physical details had read 5'6".

"He *hates* that," said Pastorelli. "Vain son of a bitch. The wino act was pretty good, too, but he must have hated *that* only a little less than he hates me."

"You're saying he knew where you'd be and…. how would he?"

"I always send my press clippings home," said Pastorelli, sounding remarkably like Flanagan. "And back when I used to babysit the little pinhead, he made fun of Cousin Angelo for spending time in the head. Six people in the family, where are you going to get any privacy?"

"And that sign," I said, "meant there was only one working restroom on that floor. Lots of people don't know it's there, if they're not the regular crowd."

"So to speak," said Selby.

"Jesus and Mary, I even *told* em last time I was there that I knew the Secret of the Boardroom Head and crapped in the same exalted bowl as Pinky Paulsen."

"Wasn't that when your brother told you to get a life?" said Phyllis.

"He would have loved doing me right there at the County Building," said Pastorelli, "and hell, the whole *Board* would have been under suspicion. Half the Democrats in the *County* would have been under suspicion." He did not succeed in disguising that he still sounded shaken.

"But it all hangs together," he said. "The bum clothes, all you have to do is walk through the Plaza on a weekday afternoon to see they got a wino problem. Stairs to the parking lot are right there around the corner, anyone found him, he's a wino managed to wander in and spend the night in the crapper. Probably left street clothes somewhere, say under the pedestrian bridge where they all stash their shopping carts."

"If it really was him they brought in he took it pretty far," said Marlaine. "Randall said he 'bout stunk em out of the station."

"Ah, that's from where he was hiding," said Pastorelli. "I'm thinking he didn't get away clean, *if* you know what I mean."

"He got out pretty damn fast," said Phyllis.

"Lost a few minutes," said Pastorelli. "He'd have been in that back stall. I'm thinking he heard me say hello to Hector—who was in there looking like stage fright on crack. Now we know why. He was still in there when I left. Pinhead would expect Hector to be the one going out and me to be the one he was left alone with. And I've always said that when he came for me I'd have to just be fast and put him down hard; I got size on him and he knows it. Or he might have lost his cool when he heard Hector start to go out, didn't want to blow his chance, just jumped out and fired."

"Well, damn," said Phyllis.

"How come you didn't smell him him in there?" objected Marlaine.

"Like I said, that's from where he was hiding," said Pastorelli. "Peckerhead heard Brother Rearend coming back there, hell, the floor shakes when he walks, and Angie coming from the other direction. There was only one place to go."

"Oh...God...." said Selby, who had heard my description of the scene several times. "The *janitor's cart...*"

"That big industrial wastebin with who knows what in it, all the plastic bags of crap from the bathrooms and the Board offices," said Pastorelli. "Like it says there, he's a little guy." An incongruously high-pitched laugh, sounded on an inhale, like his whistles, came out of the gloom. "And five seconds later, Brother Rearend's *breakfast....*"

"It was a big bin," I agreed, "and there were some boxes too, I think they were restocking the towel holders and there were some four-gallon cases of hand soap..."

"Yep. Enough stuff it didn't seem too heavy when they rolled it out of the way."

"Rolled it?"

"Well," said Pastorelli, "you're *Flanagan's* PD, right? You *fuck things up* as a way of doing business, right? Angie told me how she thought they did a crap job of preserving the scene, but she was thinking of losing prints on the door, when they shoved that cart onto the landing to get the stink out of there..."

"And out he went," said Phyllis. "You want some more iced tea?"

"Not me, thanks," said Selby, who was clearly still reifying the experience of hunkering down in a wastebin and being barfed on.

"We gonna do something with this?" said Marlaine. "Must be some way to light a fire under the Homicide people without getting Duwayne and me in it..."

"This is family shit," said Pastorelli in a closed way that I hadn't expected of him. "Give me a few weeks to find some things out."

The following Friday he copied me on an e-mail to Phyllis that said: *Uncle Beppo told me, and I quote, 'Guys who get their personal lives mixed up with their profession have a way of going missing. Sad, but it happens in our line of work.' Tell Marlaine not to waste the department's money.*

De la Roja's murder is still officially unsolved.

Mercedes bought a commemorative tree for him, one that stands in the little garden area at the top of the courthouse lot, popular with winos but also with county workers who have stopped by the Wrap Artist for lunch. Several people have remarked on how quickly it shot up. I had suggested to Dvorah that she pay it a visit.

Late in May, I took the green candles from the Botanica out of their paper sack, where they had been lying on my coffee table gathering dust the entire time, decided it was either toss them out or use them, and burned them three nights running, the way Micaela had told me. I said to myself it just freshened the air in the condo; I still don't clean as often as I should. Sarah Wellborn landed a handsome account a week later, though, and circulation bumped up, but I assume that was a result of the hostage case. I've considered going back in the store anyway, but don't know quite what I'd want to try next.

Pinky Paulsen is still gaveling the meetings to order on time. I get there to record the fact, but not as early as I used to. I sleep a lot more soundly these days.

NOTES AND QUOTES [FOR THOSE WHO CARE]

Smitty, a man of letters and the theater, recollects in his cups the wounded fury of Catullus, a Roman poet of Caesar's time, on realizing that his mistress 'Lesbia' (probably a woman of noble family named Clodia Pulchra) was not exclusively his but had, to put it mildly, an experimental approach to men. Apostrophizing his friend Caelius, Catullus lamented

Caelius, our Lesbia, that Lesbia
Whom Catullus loved more than himself and all he owns
Now works the back alleys and doorways, gulping
All that's offered by the generous sons of Remus.

Selby, not a Latin scholar of any degree, is puzzled by a name which did not have such definite implications in Catullus' time.

The remaining quotation is from Shakespeare's *Troilus and Cressida* [Act V Scene 2], probably the archetypal drama of romantic love cynically betrayed. Smitty grabs almost random lines from Troilus' speech. But he is pretty far gone by then.

The system of Board Chairmanship rotation is somewhat potted from Arlington County's normal operation which goes by seniority instead of seat, another indication that I made this all up. The usual system does manage to get the chairman out front in most election years, though.

The Santeria spells depicted herein are also potted. There are people who will set out this kind of thing complete in print for any interested reader to imitate, but the author is not one of them. Even the sketchy details here given vary from what is actually supposed to work. As Micaela said, the *orishas* are very particular, and the author took her quite seriously on that head. Things this should be left to professionals and not tried at home.

Watch for *Murder out of the Loop,* the second community-politics mystery from Jane Barcroft, featuring reluctant detective Paige Smith.

CHAPTER 1
SKYBOXING

Paige Smith, October 2, 2004

I didn't start out trying to catch the woman double-timing up the Rosslyn escalator, but after the first dozen steps it became a reason to keep moving. She was not a woman that you would want to catch for conventional reasons, athletic without grace and moving in a way that suggested knocking down anything in her path, but I was certain I had seen her somewhere before and it nagged me that I couldn't recall where. I was not going to get to ask her, though. I began to think she did this every day to wake up, while for most of the past ten years I have rolled out of bed and into my clothes and hoped the coffee at the newsroom was fairly fresh. By the time I got to the top of the escalator she was lost from sight, my lungs felt scalded, and my legs were wobbly. It was a sensation I had had a number of times recently, and I was not getting fonder of it.

Someone had had the bright idea that a flag team of Arlingtonian public figures should run the first 5K of Ron Zeff's newly fledged Arlington Marathon, to show support and generate publicity. I believe it was me. I believe it was in my weekly editorial commentary in the Arlington *Spectator,* where I usually manage not to make quite such a reckless fool of myself.

The County Manager and a good number of local personalities had embraced the notion. There was no earthly way I could weasel out of it. I had had to buy an actual pair of running shorts, which felt like wearing a cross between lingerie and a plastic grocery sack, and endure the appalled disparagement by Ron's flag team coach, Terry Tripp, of a perfectly adequate (I thought) pair of sneakers. I had had to run something mysteriously called "splits" on the Yorktown track. I had discovered what it was like to get out of bed and hobble to the bathroom like an octogenarian.

I had a little over a week of this left until the race, and was trying to pretend to myself that I was not really fascinated to see visible muscle surfacing on each calf and to find I could trot up the stairs in my building when the elevators were slow. The Metro escalator defeated me, though.

I surfaced into a slightly brisk October morning. Rosslyn is not the ghost town that it used to be on Saturdays, but most of the foot traffic at this hour—just shy of ten a.m.—was headed in the same direction I was, the pedestrian concourse landscaped onto what was supposed to be a bridge until the builders belatedly discovered someone had made an architectural mistake of cosmic dimensions: its two halves simply failed to meet cleanly in the middle. It's still called the Loop Bridge, though the legend on the side facing the city reads *Freedom Park,* and you can admire a lot of the Washington memorials from a pleasing elevation. Looking straight down onto the steep asphalt slope of Wilson Boulevard, the elevation is not quite so pleasing, but then I have never been fond of heights.

This morning's event was not athletic—counter-athletic, perhaps. After a pitched battle in the press (my Letters page had groaned under it), a period of dormancy, some rumors, and an occasional sputter, the Governor's Bring Baseball to Virginia Committee had mounted one last campaign to situate a ballpark in Arlington—exactly, Ron Zeff had maintained to me, along the sightline to D.C. from the Loop Bridge. A group called Vote No Ballpark, which I had likewise assumed more or less dissolved, had risen from the dead, dredged its circle-slash VOTE NO t-shirts from the bottoms of drawers, and started congregating along commuter routes with matching signs. Wherever they appeared, you could count on ballpark supporters to materialize with placards reading *PLAY BALL!!* The hostility hanging in the air between these two groups was as dense and toxic as bus exhaust. The biggest news, in my opinion, was that someone hadn't thrown a punch yet.

This morning's rally was supposed to belong to the Vote No group, but I could already see a smattering of *PLAY BALL* signs and shirts in the increasing streams of people coursing up the slope of the Loop Bridge, past artified chunks of the Berlin Wall and the Journalist's Memorial. This always chokes me up a little bit—a rainbow-glazed spiral of transparent plates emblazoned with the names of scores of journalists killed in the line of duty.

I report on transcendently soporific local government meetings, and the scariest thing I usually encounter in pursuit of a story is the traffic on Caerleon Boulevard. Once, and only once, my life became less dull. None of the shots fired on that occasion had been aimed at me or passed closer than several yards away; what I had lost during Arlington's "boardroom hostage incident"—as the papers, my own included, tersely called it—was harder to quantify than life or limb. Some sort of innocence, I suppose, if a man past forty can be said to retain any such thing. I had spent the half year since appreciating the dramatic pacing of committee meetings and awards dinners. I hoped that no one would ever ask me to talk about what had actually happened.

I stepped outside the flow of demonstrators, some carrying signs, who were trooping up the brick cobbles to the grass terraces that occupy the section of Loop Bridge directly over the street. I always read a few of the names on the iridescent glass of the memorial, out of a sense of obligation. It also gave the stitch in my side a chance to pass off completely.

The crowd was the usual mixture I remembered from earlier Vote No rallies—a core of retired Arlingtonians with time on their hands and a mulish resistance to change; Federal workers who maintained their commutes would become nightmares if a ballpark arose by the last Metro stop before the river; and do-gooders righteously inflamed at the BBVC's proposal to buy out the Harbor Vista housing cooperative, whose riverside location they saw as an irresistible lure to the contested team. Several carried signs reading "Old Team: Ottawa Sockeyes = New Team: Arlington Tycoons." A small hard core of the county's anti-tax Republicans made strange bedfellows with this mostly liberal contingent, distributing leaflets about bond funding and opportunity cost in small print that made the average citizen's head reel.

I spotted Ashonza Tebo up ahead. Since the ballpark issue had gone dormant, she had used the high profile gained as Vote No's spokesperson to launch an independent campaign for County Board, making it a three-way race with incumbent Betty Bravo—who could probably stay home until Election Day and still win—and Ralph Keller, a transplanted New Jerseyite who bombed my letters page with weekly critiques of County policy until I felt like charging him for campaign advertising.

Keller was unabashedly pro-ballpark, and some of the PLAY BALL contingent were carrying his signs. I expected him to turn up, and was not looking forward to it. He was a large, slightly intimidating person with the slabby build of the construction worker he claimed to have once been. In person the effect was a little overwhelming, but it went against him in debates, where he seemed like an Archie Bunker sparring with the diminutive (and vapid) Betty Bravo and the even more diminutive (and far from vapid) Ashonza. I suppose if you are a black woman in the deep South who comes up about to the shoulder of a short man, you develop the scrappy personality of a mongoose. I pitied the man cornered in a dark alley by Ashonza.

"Morning, Smitty," came a no-nonsense voice at my elbow. It was Mandy Fraike, new sergeant's stripes on her police uniform, departmental tackle bulking her waist. She had been ubiquitous during the boardroom siege, and always gave the impression of being simultaneously concerned for my welfare and annoyed with me. I suspected she seemed a little annoyed with everyone; some people are just like that.

Her radio was crackling with crosstalk about the effect of the rally on Wilson Boulevard traffic—so far, minimal. "I thought we were through with all this," she said. "Why can't people stay home and watch the Skins?" Amanda has blonde hair that some women would kill for, and cuts it short and blunt in the way of women who don't want to think about their hair. She isn't especially large, but looks bigger than she is; I think it's the way she stands.

"They always lose?" I suggested.

"I still put money in the department pool," she said. "You getting along OK?" Of all the people involved with the boardroom incident, she was the one who seemed to suspect I knew more about it than I had ever told, but she never asked. We had crossed paths at one public event and another over the course of the summer, and if unsmiling, she always greeted me, causing Shel Selby, my best shutterbug, to say "Keep her sweet, boss, I'd bet on her against Godzilla *and* Rodan."

A cluster of husky young males in *PLAY BALL* shirts passed us. "These are the guys I can do without," she said. "Bad enough we have to go down to Mr. Knight's every weekend and break up a fight or bust someone for DIP. I was hoping they didn't come out in the daytime."

"Good luck with them," I said distractedly. I had just spotted Ron Zeff, the author of my woes but also a major mover in Vote No, as he seemed to be in every other citizen enterprise in the County, carrying a large banner and an armful of signs. Ron is about my height, which is not much, but carries no more excess fat than an andiron.

He was hard to catch up with. The crowd was getting thick, to the point that I had to edge my way through Vote No partisans, noting recognizable faces I wanted to talk to later. Ashonza was near the podium with Lenny Gore, a beefy ex-Marine who for some reason had grown what was left of his hair into the kind of ponytail that used to get guys beaten up by Marines. I knew him for a gentle person who took zero grief from anyone, a refreshingly rare combination. Mark Lewis, a onetime Republican Board member and return hopeful, who had lost for a second time the preceding May, was standing a short distance away, looking more than ever as if, like the habitues of Mr. Knight's, he did not belong out in the daytime. I remembered his first campaign when his trademark open collar and casual stance made him seem relaxed and personable; now he looked slept-in and exhausted. He and Ashonza, once a celebrated political odd couple, now seemed to be merely at odds.

Zeff was instructing two reasonably attractive and reasonably young women in some maneuver involving Scotch tape and a banner much too heavy to be taped, which he was trying to drape over the PVC pipe that formed the railings of the bridge here over the street. "Maybe we can use a shoe lace," he was saying. It didn't look like a shoelace was likely to work either. "Hello, Smitty, how's training?"

"Okay," I said. The younger woman fumbled her end of the banner again, coming dangerously close to dropping it into traffic.

"Terry is, well, a trip, isn't she?"

Terry Tripp was as lean as Zeff, blonde, perhaps forty. High-energy was a restrained way of describing her. She brought a black Labrador with the same gravity-defying disposition to most of the Tuesday coaching sessions, and spoke so quickly that I imagined the rest of us must seem like a stop-action film to her. I said something to the effect.

"Fun watching her when she does inhale, though, isn't it?" he winked.

The idea had not occurred to me while casting her in the role of galley overseer complete with cat o'nine tails. I supposed Zeff, who ran a faster mile than she did, could afford such thoughts.

"I wanted a few remarks from you," I said. "You've promoted nearly every cause that had to do with sports in Arlington for the past twenty years. This is the first time anyone can remember you on the opposing side; I'd just like some comments about your reasons while we're waiting for this to start."

The banner seemed to have finally defeated the young woman, who was wearing a ONE EARTH T-shirt with Vote No stickers front and back. Zeff stepped in to hold her corner.

"Well, there's one reason over there," he said, nodding at the slightly puffy young men that had dismayed Sgt. Fraike. "I've spent twenty years trying to pry a few dollars out of the county to fund track clubs and bike races. These people want millions in revenue bonds for a place where young people like that will do nothing but drink beer." The breeze flapped the banner, rocking Zeff on his sneakered feet. His legs—he had on the same kind of track shorts I couldn't wait to change out of after training—looked like an anatomical marble. I raised my camera (Selby was on vacation till tomorrow) and snapped a profile of his gnomelike face, which even looking out over the skyline seemed on the verge of a sly leer.

The view, I noticed, did not sweep in the Harbor Vista co-ops that BBVC proposed to raze and replace with a sports park, and from this angle even more was hidden by a weird hemispheric structure that filled most of the space beyond the grass terraces.

"I was sure you could see them from here," said Zeff. it was like him not to have come up to check; Zeff's civic ubiquity went hand in hand with a tendency to fudge facts and ask for allowances. With fingers in so many pies, he had developed a reputation for last-minute planning and uncertain follow-through. I photographed what you could see, which was the Gannett building and the beginnings of the Mall in the distance. When I turned back Zeff had nipped up on the foot-deep concrete curbing of the bridge, sneakered feet inches from the drop, to get a sounder grip on the VOTE NO banner hanging over the inadequate-looking PVC rail for the enlightenment of drivers underneath.

"If you look into the funding proposals," he was saying, "and compare them to the bond amounts the state plans to float for school phys-ed and community gyms, it's pathetic. *Half a tier* of this corporate welfare white elephant could build twenty more miles of bike trails in this county. Don't believe me, 'Shonza has the figures somewhere." I wondered how many people could get away with calling her "'Shonza."

"Sir? I'll have to ask you to get down from there."

It was Fraike, looking a little harried. This was a large assembly for one cop. Zeff, instead of getting down, explained "I'm just making this sign visible," as if that made his vertiginous perch on the lip of the bridge safer.

"This isn't safe, sir. I'm going to ask you again to get down."

Reluctantly, Zeff stepped away from the railing, trying to continue his explanation about visibility to traffic.

"Thank you, sir," Fraike cut him off. She pulled out her radio and said into it "We could use another warm body up here, Rollo."

I followed her sightline and saw what she meant. We were ten minutes to rally time, and about a quarter of the attendees so far present had Keller signs or PLAY BALL shirts. Bill Miller, a spooky hard-right character who had once squared off with Zeff in a TV debate over flag desecration, was way too close in Lewis' face for comfort. Miller had the unblinking and unsmiling gaze of someone with a fund of silent hostility and Lewis was looking more peevish by the minute, speaking rapidly—I couldn't hear him in the increasing hubbub—while a couple of the sports-bar types aimed a camcorder at the exchange from a short distance away. An athletic-looking black man in a *Vote No* T-shirt over shirt and slacks was eyeing the camcorder youth unsmilingly.

"Shit," muttered Fraike, and "10-34," into her radio. "This doesn't look good." She advanced on the camcorder operator. I decided I would prefer moving in the other direction, and left Zeff awkwardly nursing his banner.

I bagged a few more useful quotes from a retired GM-15 and a housing advocate wearing a T-shirt printed with the campaign photo of the late Board chairman Hector de la Roja, in whose name a group had formed to pressure for moderate-priced housing in the Metro corridor. The microphone skreeked. Fraike's presence seemed to have the suppressed the confrontation, and a backup officer was now standing opposite her in rear of the assembly. The Mr. Knight's types, sullen but subdued, were planting PLAY BALL signs in the grass at the approach from Freedom Park.

"Ladies and gentlemen," said Ashonza. "I thank you for giving us your Saturday morning. I'm Ashonza Tebo, co-*found*er of Vote No Ballpark"—a scattered few calls of "Play ball!" from the huskies, one of whom was spoken to by Fraike's partner. "We are here today with some of the latest news and a message for the governor of this state. We are here to tell him that we can*not* be *buffaloed* by sweet talk about bringin *business* to this community when what he is really askin is a free playground for *rich men* to play kids games at the taxpayer expense while other *rich men* sit in the skyboxes."

"Liberals just hate the American pastime," said a voice at my elbow. Miller had mooched up to me.

"You're here in support of the ballpark, I take it, Mr. Miller?" I said diplomatically.

"*Jemima* there had me fooled until I realized she was just another *liberal,*" he said as if the word were synonymous with *felon* or *pedophile.* "All this talk about taxes is a smokescreen. These are people trying to destroy the wholesome America I believe in. They want men to marry men and women to marry women, they think a fetus is tooth decay with a heartbeat, they want anyone to be free to burn the flag and they don't want our young people to enjoy the wholesome sport of baseball." I glanced over at one of the Mr. Knight's types, who was angrily moving a sign so that Vote No supporters couldn't block it from view. He did not look wholesome.

"I would like to introduce to you Mr. Robert Beach, a retired economic analyst for the United States Government—" a muted ripple of applause from near the podium. Beach, a wizened leprechaun in his fifties, was one of the county's most persistent conservative fiscal critics. "He is here to tell you the difference between *truth* and *smokescreens* in this ballpark debate, and lay out the hard facts my *opponents* in this controversy—as well as my opponents for *public office*—want you to ignore."

"This ain't a campaign rally!" hooted one of the young louts near the podium. Ashonza bent to the mike.

"My op-*po*-nent is right over there," she said, tilting her head toward the back of the crowd. "If anyone feels this is a campaign appearance, I will even grant him a few minutes to address you when our scheduled speakers are finished. Right now I'd like you to welcome Mr. Beach." Beach, little taller than Ashonza herself, stepped up to the podium with a thick notebook. Latecomers were still nudging their way in from the Memorial end of the Loop. I knew Beach would make his figures entertaining, and I also knew he'd get his full text to me, if it wasn't already in my e-mail. I dropped into a hunker on the uppermost grass terrace; at one time I'd have been less likely to do that, but that was before I had committed myself to exhausting my thigh muscles every other morning week after week. I dashed down a few more impressions of the crowd. Beach finished and Lenny Gore took the podium, removing the mike from its stand to pace back and forth with the easy grace of a TV evangelist. Even some of the pro-ballpark people seemed to find him likable.

"Now they will tell you," he said, "that this is not money out of the taxpayer's cash flow. What we're not hearing discussed is the amount of money that will have to be found because these funds are tied up, and the projects we'll be asked to fund elsewhere because a viable housing resource in the community has been eradicated in favor of a hole in the landscape that eats money—"

"Some Marine, he looks like a goddam old hippie," came Miller's voice from somewhere behind me.

"Now we've been told that the Harbor Vista has problems, there are code enforcement problems, the building is aging, this is all true. Let's compare the numbers. If the cooperative management of this building can find about three million in matching grant money, it will not only be up to code, it will be renovated, fire safe and functional for the next twenty years. Now I'm not a big fan of government bailouts. But if the state underwrites this ballpark, you and I and the rest of the citizens of Virginia—*as far away as Blacksburg*—will be holding a *three hundred million dollar mortgage* on it with *no security*—"

"*So how about getting your fat asses out from in front of our signs!*" came a challenge from beyond the podium. Apparently a few ballpark opponents had taken the simple step of body-blocking the PLAY BALL signs from the press cameras present. I looked past Gore and saw Angelo Pastorelli, one of Beach's regular boardroom cronies, facing off with a pugnacious youth in a baseball cap. Pastorelli looked amused. That was a bad sign. Angelo has been wanting to get in a fistfight since I knew him, and he's big enough, with a Neapolitan bricklayer back there in the woodpile somewhere, that he'd probably win it; he just wants someone else to start it. He looked close to getting his wish. Gore paused and glanced meaningly at Ashonza. The microphone screeched again.

Sergeant Fraike made it over just in time to stop the camcorder from rolling again. It didn't stop the jock confronting Pastorelli from getting closer in his face. I gathered that, told to retreat from the PLAY BALL sign, Angelo had broken wind loudly instead. That was like him. As if to heighten the effect, a particularly mephitic truck passed under the Loop Bridge, ejecting bad-carburetion fumes and huffing into overdrive gear loudly enough to briefly drown out the shouting match beyond the podium.

A chubby couple in *Vote No* T-shirts added their voices to the fracas. The other cop, who looked like he had quite a few years on the force, had his radio up. I began to edge toward the confrontation.

"Shall I go on?" said Gore to Ashonza off mike. Ashonza took the microphone back.

"At this *time*," she said in a raised voice, "I'd like to introduce our next speaker and the friend of every community undertaking in Arlington. This is a man who can tell you what sports and sports money can mean in a community, a man who has been *tireless* in seeking ways to keep this county active—not warming seats in a three-hundred-million-dollar tax boondoggle. I'd like you to welcome Ron Zeff."

It seemed like a good move; everyone knew Zeff and everyone appeared to like him, even his political opponents. But he was nowhere to be found. Zeff-like, he had disappeared from his station, leaving the uncooperative banner at the foot of the half-globe as if he had been trying to drape it there, probably whisking off to coach a junior high track event or coordinate something for his race the following Sunday. He'd done it before. Ashonza, for the first time in my experience, looked hesitant. What happened next saved her so deftly from losing her rhythm in public that only her expression told me it had not been scripted.

A movement at the back of the crowd—a few yards from where I had been sitting—resolved into the looming figure of the district's Perpetual Congressman, Brian Murphy, another veteran and sometime pugilist, who even rising sixty looked capable of decking any three of the truculent post-adolescents now simmering down on the opposite side of the podium. Murphy had gone on record numerous times in support of the ballpark.

I had other issues with Murphy. Aside from trouncing him routinely on my editorial page—he was a fish in a barrel, whose private life and politics seemed to be eternally mingling in ways that left both open to question—my feelings about him had been deeply personal since earlier that Spring, when an all too credible source had identified him as the attacker who boondocked me in the *Spectator* parking lot after hours one night. I would never be able to prove it, but the closed look on his face every time I saw him in public told me all I needed to know.

Within moments he was on the podium, taking the microphone from Ashonza. He dwarfed her even more than Gore did, his almost luminous white hair and Irish complexion making them look like representatives of two different species.

"Ladies and gentlemen, constituents of the Eighth District," he began. "I'll be brief. I've been listening to this ballpark debate since its inception.

"Initially this seemed like a praiseworthy idea. The Washington area has been without a team since the 1970s. Virginia has never had one.

"However. My job is to listen to what my constituents want. And what I hear and see, day after day, overwhelmingly, is that the population of the Eighth District *does not want this ball park.*"

Shouts of dismay from the Keller and *PLAY BALL* supporters. The back-bench type with the camcorder, now only a few yards from me, was playing it over Murphy at the podium.

"Hence, as your representative in Congress and with whatever leverage my position in this state and district affords me, let me go on record as *opposing* this project and committed to persuading the Governor to rethink it."

The Vote No crowd exploded in cheers. "Backstabber!" yelled a less pleased Young Republican type with a Keller sign. The cheering went on until I almost missed what was happening under my nose: jubilant, Pastorelli gave "the figs" to the ball-cap heavy, mouthing "Oh WELL!" Ball Cap threw a punch, and Pastorelli ducked fast enough to avoid a black eye but not fast enough to keep his bottle-bottom glasses from being knocked off. Fraike had been standing three yards behind Ball Cap. Her hand came down on his shoulder just as he wound up for a follow-through.

None of the remaining speakers were able to hold the crowd's attention too much after that. A half hour later, both sides were dispersing, Murphy was exchanging thanks with Lenny Gore, and Lewis was looking sulky some distance from where Ashonza took turns with Keller answering questions for a local cable reporter. I was piggybacking on this interview when I heard sirens in the distance, up the hill towards Ballston. Nothing uncommon, but under the sound I picked up a burst of chatter from the nearby belt radios. I glanced at Fraike. She was eyeing one of Ball Cap's friends, who was holding a Keller sign in one hand and a PLAY BALL placard in the other in hopes of getting on the edge of the cable journalist's shot. Her partner approached and put his head close to hers.

Lenny Gore and Pastorelli were about to hoist the portable podium, perhaps the most daunting piece of rally furniture. Fraike intervened. I saw Gore nod toward a long snake of outdoor cable where the podium was still connected to some inside power source at the end of the bridge. Fraike rose to the microphone. This was new.

"Excuse me," she said. Feedback hummed and threatened another shriek. Gore did something to a control. "Excuse me. Sergeant Amanda Fraike, Arlington County Police Department. I would like to ask at this time that everyone still here remain on the bridge until we have had a chance to speak to you." Another siren echoed the pitch of the queasy microphone, one of the electronic howlers from the fire station at the top of the hill. "We are going to need to interview anyone remaining who was present on the bridge during the rally. Please remain on the bridge." The next siren was heading towards us, not away, and I reflected that I had never seen how truly annoyed Mandy Fraike could be.

Most of the people questioned by her and her fellow officers had to leave the scene with no clear idea why they had been detained. Out of whatever curmudgeonly affection she had for me, she anticipated the police department news release before letting me go.

"Regular Saturday trap checking County stickers up by the Caerleon Park Metro," she said. "One of those things where two guys from Nicaragua get a pickup truck that'll barely go and a few old mowers and paint a sign on the side, Jose's Lawn Service? These two guys didn't know what County taxes were, the truck was held together with the Bondo and the slats on the sides of the flatbed looked ready to fall off my buddy says. So he has a look over it and checks what they got in back. Two rusted-out lawn mowers. About fifty sacks of manure. And your friend Mr. Zeff. Funny way to hitch a ride."

I looked at her, hoping I didn't understand.

"The *late* Mr. Zeff I should say. I told him to get down off the side of the damn bridge."

But her face told me she didn't think it was as simple as that at all.